EDITORIAL REVIEW




Dragoria: The Lost Dragon Realm
Book Four


*DRAGON'S ROYAL*


"Evil sorcerers who have driven dragons into hiding, whispers of a princess returning after vanishing the night her family was slaughtered, loyal dwarves willing to risk everything for love, a daring theater troupe determined to dismantle the corrupt Sacred Flame coterie and restore the Slosiaran kingdom to its former glory—Dragon's Royal has it all." Amanda K., Line Editor, Red Adept Editing

"Emelyne's entire life changes the day a member of the Sacred Flame coterie appears in her adoptive dwarven village, and the outcome is one she never imagined in her wildest dreams. Samara and her dragon familiar have been on the run from the coterie since she discovered they were enslaving and torturing dragons, and Emelyne's and Samara's paths cross as Samara and her dwarven friends search the land for the lost princess of the realm. Fans of *The Lost Dragon Realm* series will love the next installment as Emelyne and her adoptive parents help rebuild Paddosha Palace Village in spite of the coterie's attacks, and Samara and Ulrieg begin to gather dragons to return them to Dragoria." Caroline P., Proofreader, Red Adept Editing

# DRAGON'S ROYAL

## PART TWO

### DRAGORIA: THE LOST DRAGON REALM
#### BOOK THREE

## KATRINA COPE

COSY BURROW BOOKS

DRAGORIA: THE LOST DRAGON
REALM BOOKS

## Part One

Dragon Moon

Dragon Heart

Dragon Breeze

## Part Two

Dragon's Royal

Royal Alliance

Royal Resistance

*Deni ~ A beautiful soul who constantly proves distance
isn't a barrier to caring.
Thank you.*

# BLURB

**Secrets of hope shouted from the valleys echo to the mountaintops of immorality.**

Emelyne is a human raised in a dwarven village. In her world, nothing about that is abnormal. Yet whenever one of the people with brilliant-colored hair is near, her dwarven parents insist she hides. She doesn't understand why until one of them kills her childhood friend in cold blood. After bonding with a dragon and meeting some unusual characters, she discovers truths about her past. In light of this, she sets out on a journey to rebuild a village and rise against the coterie, fueled by a desire to avenge her friend.

Samara's new life away from the Sacred Flame coterie has opened her eyes to a different world. Traveling with a group of actors, she searches for the lost royal—her best hope to stand against the coterie's rule, rebuild the kingdom, and serve as a stepping stone to free Paxton. The dangers of the past are not behind her.

# CHAPTER ONE

Orange was the color of evil, or so it seemed in the Perpetual Vale. Dwarves scattered from the tall elven sorcerer's path. His brown cloak, cascading from his shoulders, waved its disapproval of the inferior breed native to the area. A golden snub-nosed monkey scampered by his side, baring its long white fangs as it hissed its disfavor to the beings not much taller than it. Long creases lined the young-looking sorcerer's face as he glared at the scurrying dwarves. His age was impossible to tell from his elven heritage. His eyes, as hard as blue crystals, bore into each being, charging them as guilty before they uttered a word.

Towering not far behind him stomped four over-sized beings, their skin green-gray as if they had been born ill. Their faces, each centered around a large button nose, were distorted in a constant grimace. Their big beady eyes darkened with concern as they concentrated on fulfilling the sorcerer's every command. Small loincloths were the only clothing that separated them from being naked.

Breath tight and body swaying from the effort of taking large steps, Gibobo Brightbelt scurried across the dirt road of the local village, her pale face almost white in the light. Prying a tuft of brunette hair from across her face exposed her hairy underarms in her short-sleeved tunic until she gave up trying to hook the strands into her tight bun. "Come, Emelyne. We have to go." She tugged the young woman's hand, her eyes wild with worry.

Emelyne hurried behind the only mother she knew, skipping over a couple of rocks. Her human heritage caused her to tower over her dwarven adoptive mother and the rest of the village of Mirwohr. "What's wrong?" She didn't know why her ma seemed panicky. It wasn't her typical demeanor. Emelyne quickened her footsteps, cursing the long dress she wasn't used to wearing as it tangled around her ankles. "What about our supplies?"

"They'll have to wait. We shouldn't be close to any members of the Sacred Flame coterie." Gibobo clasped Emelyne's hand.

Creases lined Emelyne's forehead. "The Sacred Flame what?"

Gibobo glanced from side to side and rubbed at the light fuzz on her chin. "There's a big gatherin' of powerful sorcerers that run these lands. It's called the Sacred Flame coterie. Luck's been on our side. They haven't visited our village for many years. The members have brilliantly colored hair and familiars. This elf is one of their top sorcerers." She prattled rapidly in the rough dwarven tongue, consistently dropping the "h" and "th" at the beginning of words along with the "g" at the end. "Word is the sorcerer is lookin' for one of its members who defied their rules." She tutted. "Shattered anvil, that past member has some guts. The sorcerer may not be lookin' for us, but it's dangerous to be around them."

The sorcerer clapped his hands, sucking all the attention to him in a vortex. He raised his chin, glancing down his nose at the dwarves as if he had just eaten a sour grape. His eyes displayed a maleficent sneer. "For those who do not know me, I am Kellam, a senior sorcerer of the Sacred Flame coterie. If you wish to cross the border, I will decide if you can go."

Hissing over her shoulder at Emelyne, Gibobo's eyes held warning. "Crouch down to our level."

Several nearby dwarves cast curious glances at

them before turning their attention back to the sorcerer. Racked with uncertainty, Emelyne crouched until she had to shift to the side to see past the wild hair of the female dwarf in front of her. The golden monkey prowled before the sorcerer, puffing out its white chest and baring its fangs at the dwarven audience.

Kellam clasped his hands behind his back. "A past member of our coterie has defiled our laws and escaped our punishment, and they are accompanied by a dwarf. If you have seen anyone with brilliant-pink-colored hair—or shades of it—accompanied by a dwarf, you must report this to me at once. If you see them after I have gone, you must travel to the border and inform me immediately. If you don't, you will bring upon yourself, your family, and possibly your village a great punishment incomprehensible to your kind." He curled his lip. "Do you understand?"

A united mutter passed between the dwarves fixated on the sorcerer.

"Good. Now, have any of you seen these individuals or know where they are?" He raised an eyebrow, scanning the crowd for confirmation.

"Get down!" Gibobo hissed sharply.

Emelyne hadn't realized she had straightened a head higher than her surrounding comrades, and she squatted quickly. The sorcerer's eyes landed on her, and her body stiffened.

Both the sorcerer's eyebrows arched. She was too late.

"Dragon fire! He's seen me," she whispered.

"Don't say that here. Especially with members of the coterie near," Gibobo whispered sharply in her thick dwarven accent.

Emelyne frowned. She wanted to ask why but got the sense it wasn't a good time to ask. She squirmed, not knowing where to look.

Kellam continued, "We will continue to search this village, and anyone found harboring these beings will be punished." He waved a command at the ogres with his fingers, and the tall beings stomped away from the crowd, their limbs muscular and large.

Gibobo grabbed Emelyne's arm and yanked her in the opposite direction. "Come on. We've gotta get outa here."

Emelyne glanced back at the sorcerer to find him watching them. A chill ran down her spine as he stepped toward them and pointed in their direction. She spun to face the opposite direction, hearing his voice over the din of the crowd.

"You there. Wait! Human!" He sounded like he spat the last word, as if dispelling a bitter herb.

Her heart skipped a beat, but Gibobo dragged her forward and around the corner of a building, her pace quickening into a jog. Emelyne stretched her steps to keep up, surprised her dwarven mother could maintain a pace that made her thighs burn.

"Quick! This way!" Gibobo darted behind another building in the opposite direction.

"Human, I demand you stop." Raised an octave, the sorcerer's voice boomed over the dissipating crowd.

Emelyne was mystified at how the sorcerer could call at the top of his lungs yet still make the word sound distasteful. But stopping wasn't an option, especially with Gibobo pulling her along.

Gibobo pulled her away from the last of the buildings and headed for the village cave. "Hurry!"

"Won't runnin' jus' make him madder?" Emelyne asked. "It's not like we've done anythin' wrong, and we haven't seen the people he's lookin' for."

"The look in his eye when he calls ya human is enough to make ya blood chill. And from what I can see, ya the only human in this village. I'm not takin' the risk."

Emelyne quickened her pace, jumping when something hit the side of the rock entrance as she passed it. Glancing over her shoulder, she spotted the sorcerer, arm extended like he had just cast a spell, the golden monkey scampering alongside his feet just out of reach of the billowing brown cloak.

"I said stop!" he bellowed. His orange hair glowed in the sunlight, amplifying his anger at being disobeyed.

She was jerked quickly inside the cave entrance, breaking her line of sight to the fast-approaching sorcerer. "Come on! Once we get inside the cave tunnels, he'll have a hard time followin' us. We just have to stay out of sight of that monkey." Gibobo's strength was admirable for her size, undoubtably a perk from working as a blacksmith alongside her husband for many years.

The second they stepped inside the cave, they were engulfed in darkness. It took a while for her eyes to adjust to the lusterless light of the sconces, which often slowed her human eyes, but her mother dragged her toward the tunnels as though her dwarven eyes had kicked in instantly.

Gibobo's path wasn't straight, as if she had drunk one of the brews from the local ale house. She led Emelyne several steps to the left before heading to the right. By then, Emelyne's eyes had adjusted slightly to the dull light. Her mother zigzagged uncoordinatedly instead of making a direct line to the tunnel.

"Are ya all right?" She squeezed her ma's hand.

Gibobo frowned over her shoulder. "What do ya mean?"

Another blast hit the rocks not far from where Emelyne had been moments before, and she held her free hand over her heart. "Ya walkin' all over the place."

"That's so the sorcerer has a smaller chance of hittin' us because we changed our direction at the last second." She glanced at the shards of rocks that hit the ground from the blast. "At least then it's the rocks an' not you."

The cave walls closed in around them, dark and ominous, as they darted through the tunnels. After almost hitting her head on the ceiling, Emelyne crouched, paying more attention to the occasional jutting rocks from above. The pathways were made for smaller dwarfish beings, not her taller human form. She was glad for her years of practice growing up in another dwarven village and cave.

The monkey's squawking chased them down the tunnel, indicating the sorcerer was not far behind. Over her shoulder, she a glimpsed a flickering light creeping closer, and in the center of the light cast against the wall was the monkey's shadow.

# CHAPTER TWO

Led by Gibobo, Emelyne struggled to keep up as her body fit tighter through the tunnels. Her stomach swirled with worry that the walls were closing in too much for her to keep up the pace. She tripped on her skirt despite working to lift it out of the way with a spare hand. The scurrying and scraping of claws chased them farther, the source just out of sight from the long tunnel, until the ceiling rose and broke into six different channels. Gibobo quickly darted to the left, and with the added height of the tunnel, Emelyne could increase her pace. Their path quickly took them around a large corner obscuring the view of where they'd come from. Placing their soft-soled shoes as quietly as possible, they hurried, hoping that the diversion would be enough to lose the sorcerer and his monkey. The occasional rock clattered in the distance behind them.

Maintaining their speed, they traveled for quite some time before the echo of the monkey's scurrying died to a whisper, eventually silencing. Still, Gibobo only slowed a little, leading Emelyne for another hour before reaching the familiarity of the cave of Bhalwahrum.

They passed familiar dimly lit rooms for families and common rooms until her mother led them out of the mountainside.

"I don't think the sorcerer will come through the caves now, but I suggest ya stay away, out in the external village until we're sure. Actually, why don't ya go meet up with Thiznabo an' practice with ya sword?"

Emelyne cast a curious look at her mother. "All right. I thought Pa might need a hand."

"That's true. But I jus' prefer ya to be away from the main village for a while, at least until we know we're clear of that nasty sorcerer." Mussed after scurrying through the small spaces, Gibobo straightened her clothes on her shoulders, broad-built from many years of helping her blacksmith husband. "I'll go help him an' keep an eye out for the sorcerer. Ya do the same."

"I will," Emelyne said as they parted ways.

Most of the working day had already passed, which meant her friend might be at the alehouse. She wandered down the short dirt street to the only inn in town. Several dwarves from the village who started their work earlier in the day had already made their way in for a knock-off drink after a hard day's work. She pushed open the double doors and spotted her friend sitting at the bar, a large cup of ale nearly as big as her head resting in front of her. Double raised blond braids lined each side of her head and trailed down her back, emphasizing her large hooked nose and the prominent forehead typical of dwarves.

When her eyes connected with Emelyne's, she flashed a broad smile and slapped the stool beside her with a stubby hand. "Come, sit. 'Bout time ya pa let ya off early to join me for a drink." She signaled the bartender to get Emelyne an ale.

Emelyne shook her head. "No. Thanks." She sat next to Thiznabo and eyed the slightly reduced level of her ale. "Actually, I was wonderin' if ya would do some trainin' with me. But I guess that depends on how much drink ya already had."

A twinkle flashed in her friend's hazel eyes. "Ah. I see how it is. Ya come to me after I've been trainin' all day hoping I'm worn out so ya can beat me." She swilled her ale until only a third was left. "I would need at least another four before ya could beat me."

Emelyne chuckled and rolled her eyes. "I guess there's some truth to that. But to be honest, that's the way it should be, considerin' all the hours ya spend training. I do pretty good seein' as I only train when we both have time."

Thiznabo's bushy eyebrows rose. "It's been a while. We'll see how ya go next time." She downed the remaining amber liquid and slammed her pewter cup on the bench, wiping her mouth with her short sleeve. "To be honest, me arms are numb, and I'd rather not. I'll have to put ya to shame another day… after I've had me six ales first. Besides, ya not dressed appropriately for a sword fight." She eyed Emelyne's dress before smiling cheekily and indicating to the bartender again to bring them both an ale. "Have a drink with me instead."

Emelyne's heart warmed. After a stressful day, spending time with her friend was nice, even if it wouldn't wear off the stress like a vigorous training session would. Thiznabo and Emelyne had grown up together, though Emelyne had outgrown her many years ago. "I'll have a drink. Ya lucky that me pa makes swords for ya to practice with."

The coven didn't like the dwarves practicing with

weapons of war, but sometimes it was allowed when the local blacksmith was sanctioned to make them. In the village of Bhalwahrum, Emelyne's adoptive father was hired to make the odd weapons required by the coterie. Because of that, they needed someone nearby to test out their designs.

Thiznabo snorted. "I think it's more ya pa is lucky he has someone as talented as me to try them out an' help him make better ones."

Emelyne shook her head at the playful argument as the bartender placed the ale on the bench before her. She sipped its bitter, earthy flavor, immediately enjoying the warmth that flooded her.

"So, how did ya score an afternoon off? Ya pa usually works ya to the bone." Thiznabo took another long drink of her ale.

"That's only 'cause he's got so much to work on. An' I don't mind helping." Emelyne shrugged. "Actually, me ma and me went to get supplies this mornin' at Mirwohr, but a sorcerer from the Sacred Flame coterie showed up, an' Ma was worried about him spottin' me, seein' as I was the only human in the village. Turns out she was right, an' the sorcerer tried to follow us."

Thiznabo let out a whistle. "That's bad news, that is. Did ya lose him?"

"We think so. But Ma wants me to keep an eye

out jus' in case. It was her idea to find ya so we can get out of the village an' do some practice with the swords."

"We'll definitely practice another time. We can still get outa here. In fact, it's probably best we did. It's most likely the first place an outsider would visit when they come to the village. But"—she held up a finger—"I ain't leavin' 'ere without some ale." She called to the bartender. "Nomud! Can ya pour us two canteens of ale?"

The gruff bartender reached under the bar and pulled out two leather drinking canisters. "Only for you. As long as ya brin' the canteens back by tomorrow, or else I'll have to charge ya for them."

Thiznabo smiled broadly, trying to plaster on sweetness. "You know I will." She placed the coin for the ale on the bench top.

Nomud poured the amber liquid into the canteens and handed them to the younger females, sliding the coin into the money pouch hanging from his waist.

The two females left the tavern soon after and headed straight for the thicket of trees after a quick glance to make sure the path was clear of the sorcerer.

When they reached the trees, Thiznabo elbowed

Emelyne. "Maybe ya should think about goin' to a human village where ya can meet a human man."

Emelyne balked. "Where did that come from?"

"It's not that I want to lose ya, but ya stick out like a sore thumb in a dwarven village. An' ya running out of time to settle down with a family." She slapped Emelyne playfully on her back.

"I'm the same age as you." Emelyne's pitch grew higher.

"True. But ya human, an' I'm a dwarf. Unfortunately, ya don't have as long as I do to settle down."

"Pfft. Ya startin' to sound like me parents. I have a long time yet, even if I ain't gonna live as long as ya." Emelyne took a sip from her canteen.

"That's a shame. I was lookin' forward to seein' how ugly ya little human babies would turn out." Thiznabo grinned.

"Ya have plenty of time for that." Shaking her head, Emelyne shoved her playfully, knocking the dwarf sideways, and they both laughed.

"Is that all ya can give me? I thought ya'd be stronger than that, bein' a blacksmith an' all," Thiznabo quipped.

"Right!"

Emelyne went to chase her friend, and Thiznabo danced from side to side. Her years of sword fighting practice made her agile on her feet, and she narrowly missed the human's grasp. Both women laughed as they continued their rough play, sometimes wrestling each other to the ground—something they had done since they were little girls.

The play fighting ended with them both panting on the ground, tangled in Emelyne's long dress skirt with giant smiles spreading across their faces.

Thiznabo shuffled up into a sitting position against a tree, grabbed her canteen from where she had dropped it, and untied the top before taking a swig. "I changed me mind. Ya haven't got the finesse of a human female. Ya act like a dwarf. Maybe ya won't find a human who likes that."

"Who says it has to be a human?"

The dwarf whistled. "True, but ya askin' for trouble, ya are."

Shrugging, Emelyne sat up and took a sip from her canteen, the liquid dampening her parched throat. "And, of course, I act like a dwarven female. I grew up here, didn't I? Besides, I wouldn't know how a human female acts. I've never spent time with one. An' getting married is the last thing on me mind."

She sighed deeply. All the stress of the morning had been worn away by their play fight. Thiznabo was probably right that human females didn't wrestle, but she didn't care. She thought it was fun. She took another sip and nudged Thiznabo with her fist. "I think Pa wants ya to come and test out some of his new weapons when ya have time."

"Sure. I'll come by tomorrow." She grinned. "Doesn't he trust ya sword-fightin' skills?"

Emelyne rolled her eyes. "Whatever!"

The scent of burning coal and hot steel filled Emelyne's every breath. She pried sweat-drenched wisps of hair off her face and hooked them behind her ear before slamming the hammer onto glowing metal, shaping it into the desired piece. Her long brunette braid slipped over her shoulder to the front of her leather apron, and she flicked away a spark caught in her braid. Taking a small break from her training, Thiznabo sat in the corner of the forge, munching on a freshly baked muffin for breakfast, watching Emelyne and Lozzeak hard at work.

Lozzeak straightened his back. "Oy! Whatcha doin' over there, princess?"

Emelyne cringed at the endearing term her guardians occasionally called her. It was true she was a female, but she knew after growing up in a family of dwarves she lacked the delicacy of a human princess. Lozzeak and Gibobo had taken her under their wing and shown her nothing but love after her human parents were killed. Being the only human in a village of dwarves, she stood out. Letting it slide, she grinned at the male two-thirds her size. His burly red hair, beard, and mustache made it impossible to see his lower face.

"Why, I'm workin' twice as hard as you are, old one. Me pile of spokes is twice as high as yours." She nodded toward his pile about the same height as hers.

He huffed a laugh. "Ay! I doubt that." He shook his head, the tail of his braided beard swiping softly across his chest. "Tell ya what. Let's have a race to see who can make more quality spokes before lunch." He cast a glance at their company. "Thiznabo can be the judge an' make sure ya don't cheat."

Thiznabo rose to her feet, stuffing the last piece of muffin into her mouth. "Other than when she's sword fighting with me, I ain't seen Emelyne cheat yet, but I'm happy to spectate."

Emelyne rolled her eyes before she gazed out of the rustic wooden shack attached to the side of the rocky mountain, taking in the bright morning light shining through the window. Several dwarves rushed past, hustling through their daily chores, and she assessed that it was midmorning. "All right. Challenge accepted. Let's finish the ones we're workin' on an' begin countin' when we start together on the next one."

Lozzeak nodded, and they set to work on finishing the current spike.

After a quick glance over her tools and equipment, Emelyne stoked her furnace and stood by the pile of long metal pieces, waiting for her dwarven father to finish. A clank reached her ears, sounding like a metal object being placed aside. Seeing Lozzeak's hands empty and his tools down, she braced herself, waiting for their race to begin. A cheeky smile split Lozzeak's thick beard hair and mustache, and he positioned his hand over the long pieces of metal, his eyes connecting with Emelyne's before landing on Thiznabo.

The dwarven female nodded, face serious. "Ready. Go!"

Emelyne grabbed a long piece of metal and shoved the end into the furnace. When it glowed a brilliant orange and red, she hammered the ends into the shape required for carriage spokes. Compared to the other items she made, the spindles were straightforward without needing much work. She made several before glancing up at Lozzeak to check on his progress. Sweat beaded on his forehead. He was a couple of spokes ahead of her. She placed the ends of several more metal bars into the furnace and increased her pace. Though in dwarven years, her guardian father was still young, despite having lived one hundred six summers, he'd had a lifetime more practice than she'd had a chance to live.

Her leather apron squeaked as she leaned over, grabbed another piece of steel, and set to work. The hammer banging echoed through the small hut, bouncing off the stone mountain face. Emelyne noticed a commotion several houses down the street and glanced up, trying to piece together the sudden flurry of activity. Several of her dwarven friends darted to the side, suddenly acting busy and engrossed in their duties. Light layers of dust floated up from the dirt street, billowing over the cottage roofs used mostly as places of trade with the humans. She squinted, trying to work out why everyone was acting strangely.

Thiznabo spotted Emelyne's distraction and made her way to the window to peer out. A few moments later, a tall male, handsome for a human, with brilliant-blue hair, strolled down the main street toward the mountain. His gait was confident, shoulders pulled back, and a fox trotted a few paces behind him. He approached a couple of dwarves near him and reached out. They dodged his contact, bowing as they backed away.

Emelyne frowned, meeting Thiznabo's worried eyes. The behavior was strange for the dwarves. They weren't typically afraid of touch and certainly had nothing against humans. Often, they would be the first to offer a hug or friendly slap on the shoulder, yet none of them allowed the stranger to connect with them. She glanced back at Lozzeak. Positioned deeper in the cottage, he didn't seem to notice and had increased his lead. She pushed aside her thoughts and set to work to catch up with him, leaving Thiznabo to keep watch. The cottage's side door burst open.

Swaying quickly toward her, Gibobo's pale complexion turned wan, and her eyes filled with fear. Strands of brunette hair stuck to the beads of sweat dampening her forehead, and she wiped them away. "Get outa here!" She shooed Emelyne with her hands. "Give me your apron, an' I'll cover ya work."

"What's goin' on?" Emelyne looped her apron over her head and handed it over.

The hem fell to the ground on Gibobo's smaller frame, and she tucked some of the length under her thicker waist, tying the laces together at the back. "This ain't a drill. That human out there with brilliant-blue hair is from the Sacred Flame coterie. He's one of the reasons we've been practicing ya escape. Ya can't be found here. That'll only raise suspicion."

Thiznabo twisted to observe Gibobo, her expression filling with concern before turning back to keep an eye on the fast-approaching sorcerer.

"But I'm only a human livin' in a dwarven village. Surely that's allowed," Emelyne protested, watching the strange visitor.

The coterie members rarely visited her village unless they were looking for a weapon or another dwarven slave.

Grabbing Emelyne's hand, Gibobo gently twisted it to expose the strange birthmark between her thumb and forefinger. "Rumors are spreading that the heir to the throne isn't dead, as once believed. It's making the coterie nervous. If they see this mark, they'll kill you. It looks too much like the royal mark."

Emelyne pulled her sleeve down to cover it. "It's jus' an injury I got when I was little."

"It'd be enough for the coterie to end ya life." She reached up to caress Emelyne's cheek. "I'll do anythin' to stop that." Gibobo glanced through the window and down the street before grabbing the tongs and setting to work. "Now, off you run. Go all the way through the caves until you reach the Merciless Sanctuary. If the sorcerer's smart, he might demand to search the caves, but Monut an' his group will protect ya."

Thiznabo called back into the cottage, her voice halting Lozzeak's hammering, "He's too close. I'll go out an' distract him long enough for ya to get away." Before anyone could object, she pushed open the door and pressed out onto the street, stopping directly in front of the sorcerer and blocking his path to the forge. "I'm sorry, but the blacksmith is closed."

Lozzeak silently slid the bar across the door, blocking any access from the street, before he edged his head closer to the window just enough to see out and remain out of sight.

Emelyne couldn't push down her curiosity and crept to peek out the corner of the window at the sorcerer, kneeling next to Lozzeak and Gibobo.

The sorcerer's handsome face hardened, and the muscles rippled along his jawline. "No place should be closed to a Sacred Flame coterie sorcerer."

"Understood, but I'm afraid it ain't open right now to anyone." Thiznabo shrugged.

Blue eyes hard slits, the man reached for the female dwarf. "If I didn't know better, I would think that you're hiding something by refusing entry to a superior sorcerer."

Thiznabo shifted to avoid the sorcerer's touch

before standing firmly in his path, blocking his access to the blacksmith. "Nope. Nothin' to hide here. Jus' simply giving the blacksmiths time to do their important work."

"I command you to move." The sorcerer lifted his chin as if he weren't already much taller than the female dwarf before him.

The dwarf's shoulders stiffened. Emelyne knew she would take offense at being commanded by an insolent being.

The defiance didn't go unnoticed by the sorcerer. His eyes darkened like thunderclouds invading the sky. "Move!"

"Emelyne. Ya should go!" Gibobo tugged at her tunic, pulling Emelyne's attention back inside. "Thiznabo is doin' this for ya, an' I don't think she's gonna be successful. This sorcerer looks rather determined, not to mention conceited."

Nodding, Emelyne glanced toward the back door leading to the cave inside the mountain. Scrambling up from her knees, she went for the only exit that didn't require her to pass the sorcerer, but a wet-sounding thwack pulled her attention back outside. She turned, catching sight of her best friend slumping to the ground, a dagger protruding from her chest directly over the heart.

# CHAPTER FOUR

Long tree roots wound up Samara's legs, rooting her to the ground before wrapping around her torso and strapping her arms by her sides. She stood in the small plain centered around the glowing orb from the coterie building's catacombs and surrounded by a thick forest. The orb pulsed, and small explosions fractured the ward's barrier, releasing slivers of power into a sorceress who stood off to the side, her arms spread wide, her chest thrust forward as the power seeped into it. Her long beige leaf-patterned dress draped to the ground, the folds of her skirt swaying as she moved. The woman's golden headdress glimmered against the orb's orange light.

Samara flinched, trying to pull away from the evil feeling washing through her from the sphere, but the roots held her firm. A muffled, panicked voice reached her ears, and she forced herself to gaze into the orb. Something stirred within the glowing form, something that almost looked… human. She squinted, working hard to decipher the image before her. Suddenly, the shrouded object within the glowing ball lunged toward her, and she jerked back. The image of Paxton's plain and usually kind face was distorted with pain, his mouth open in a silent cry as his arms thrust forward, palm out. The roots tightened their grip around her torso. She couldn't go anywhere. She shouldn't want to go anywhere. Paxton needed saving.

Her heart thundered in her chest, and her breathing grew labored. Not only was the air squashed from her lungs, but stifling guilt racked her body. She didn't want to leave Paxton trapped inside the orb but didn't know how to get him out. She wanted to pull him into her arms to comfort him and reassure him that she would find a way, but it wasn't possible. She wasn't strong enough to break the ward around the glowing mass of powerful magic. And if she could, she was afraid she would release all the evil magic at the same time.

If he wasn't destroyed by the magic, he would likely turn dark, and it filled her with despair. Sweat pooled on her face. She thrashed, trying to break the roots' hold, her wrists chafing from the effort. Something made her glance back at Paxton, and she caught his eyes—open and glowing… red. They looked darker and more sinister than Ulrieg's had even in his worst moods. She gasped, yanking hard against her root restraints, only to find she was being lifted closer to the orb, her face in line with Paxton's. Her heart thundered against her rib cage, and sweat trickled down her temples as she saw Paxton's mouth move. He called her name over and over, the sound muffled by the barrier, before she was slammed against the orb.

*Samara! Samara!*

Her eyes flung open only to find a pillow resting over her face. She pushed it aside to find daylight and Ulrieg's red eyes glaring down at her.

"What's going on?" she asked.

*It seemed like you were having a nightmare, or a daymare, seeing as it's daytime.*

She nodded and glowered at the pillow. "Then why was that over my face?"

*I dropped it while I was whacking you with it, and that's when you woke up.* Ulrieg grinned.

"Nice." Samara pushed the pillow farther away and eyed him skeptically. "It was positioned like you were trying to smother me."

*Trust me. If I were trying to do that, it would have worked.* He tilted his head. *As if I could hurt you.*

Samara wiped the sweat off her brow and glanced around the tiny inn room. They had been offered a room for their short stay as long as they performed for the village that night. "Have you heard any word of a royal?"

Ulrieg shook his head. *Not around here and not during your short nap, but we'll keep our ears open.*

"What about my family or Paxton's?"

A deep sadness settled in Ulrieg's red eyes. *Sorry. No word yet.*

Samara struggled to push away yet another painful wave of emotions. "What about an increase of dragons in the Slosiaran kingdom? Maybe some from Dragoria have come out to see if any dragons are left to save."

Ulrieg shook his head. *No. Nor has anyone mentioned finding Dragoria. Honestly, how long do you think you slept? It's only been a few weeks since we found Dragoria. I think it'll take some time for dragons and people to find the hole you made into the realm. It's probably best that the word doesn't spread quickly, so we can show the entrance to beings we trust.*

Samara nodded. "Indeed. I guess I'm just anxious to get more magic beings together quickly to go against the coterie and whatever magic is inside that orb. I would have liked to explore Dragoria to see how many dragons are left if we didn't have to get back to Forgrac and the traveling team. Besides, we don't know if the dragons are friendly after being trapped in their world for so long."

*I hope they'll still treat the general population well. They didn't trap the dragons in there.*

"We'll have to deal with that problem another day. We need to find the princess and try to unify Slosiaran. Hopefully, we'll also find some magic wielders who can help set Paxton free. So far, we haven't found anybody with magical knowledge that would have any clue how to rescue him from the orb without releasing the evil force it contains."

Ulrieg released a breath and gazed at the ground. *I know. I also long to rescue him. He deserves so much better.*

Samara kicked her feet over the edge of the bed, slipped into her shoes, then ran a hand down her dress to flatten the creases. She still hadn't gotten used to wearing dresses more often than her leather fighting gear. Forgrac suggested it would be a better choice of clothing as it was more relatable for the villages they visited. He suggested the fighting leathers made her seem more hostile and less approachable, making her bad for business. Her thoughts turned to the dwarf. "At least we got

Forgrac back to see his missus and his children. It's a shame he didn't see them grow up."

*That is a shame, but at least Vassuda didn't remarry and now wants to travel with him.*

A rap sounded on the door, and Ulrieg turned invisible as Samara approached it. By the time her hand landed on the handle, the knock sounded again.

"It's me, Samara, love. Jus' in case ya wonderin'."

Samara smiled, instantly lowering the height of her gaze as she opened the door. Wearing a long off-white dress tied around the waist by a leather braid and a dark-blue woolen shawl wrapped around her shoulders, a female dwarf swept the few straying auburn ringlets from her bun to the side covering some of the jawline fuzz.

Vassuda flashed her a smile, the one that had instantly caused Samara to like her when they met. "Are ya ready? We must get ready for our performance tonight."

Ulrieg's hot breath washed over the back of Samara's neck. *Do you really think this play will encourage people to come forward with information about the royal? Or will it just bring trouble for our group? After all, it's drawing attention you don't need now that you're running from the coterie.*

Vassuda straightened her back to her full height

and rubbed her cheek. "Unfortunately, it's a risk we have to take if we're ever goin' to find the royal. Findin' her is the only way forward that I can see, not only for Slosiaran but also for buildin' an ally for Dragoria. It's no use showing anyone the opening you and Samara made if the dragons don't have support to rise against the Sacred Flame coterie and their loyal followers."

*What about the dragon elves? Shouldn't we be concentrating on finding them first?* Ulrieg asked.

"They are definitely a priority, but our only way to get to them is through Wraeyanor or Dragoria. Wraeyanor is more populated with people loyal to the coterie or too scared to go against them because a higher population of magic wielders from the coterie resides there. Forgrac says that Dragoria would no longer have roads. After hundreds of years with only dragons to occupy it, it would be overgrown without a single path. Taking the carriages through there would be impossible. The only way through would be on foot. So for now, we must continue searching for the missing royal with tonight's performance." She turned her attention to Samara. "If you are ready, the audience is waiting."

Samara's stomach turned as her nerves writhed. She nodded, unable to speak at the thought. She didn't know how she would get the words out. She had acted a few times before in front of Forgrac's old village, Oceanfell, and as nerve-racking as that had been, tonight's performance would be worse. She sighed noisily. "You seem so relaxed. Aren't you nervous?"

Vassuda grasped Samara's hands and squeezed them. "I know the subject of the long-lost royal is risky, but there's no better way to get the word out quickly."

Samara's shoulders slumped. "What if coterie supporters are around?"

Vassuda tugged at the ends of Samara's hair. "For one, ya hair is still brilliant pink even if it has faded from the coteries preference, an' the roots are dark. So it might confuse the coterie supporters."

*She has a point*, Ulrieg grunted.

The female dwarf smiled in his general direction, though Ulrieg remained invisible. "An' for another, we don't stay in one place long. It'll be hard for them to find us again if they want to lead the coterie members to our location."

Samara glanced at the ceiling and gave another loud sigh. "I hope you're right."

"You'd be surprised jus' how powerful the message of a play can be in times like this. It could be a powerful way to find the beings we need to reclaim our lands."

"And dangerous too."

"That's one of the reasons I joined ya. If Forgrac is detained again, at least I should be detained with him. Goodness knows I don't want to live so long apart from him anymore." Vassuda rubbed Samara's arm. "I don't want that for any of us, but I'm willin' to risk it if me kids and their children can live in a betta world. An' it's the only way I know to drum up some help to get ya friend out of the dreaded orb. I wasn't around when that thing was loose, but it's been passed down through our generations just how horrid that sorcerer was—darker and more destructive than Callista an' the coterie is now."

Shivers ran down Samara's back. "Which is why I can't let it out when I release Paxton."

"Aye! That's for sure. An' we don't want ya friend trapped in there forever." Vassuda indicated for Samara to squat to her level, and she fixed Samara's brunette wig to cover her brilliant-pink hair, before placing a diadem across her forehead before turning her chin. She smiled. "Beautiful!"

Samara's cheeks flushed. The last couple of months had left a hole in her heart, and she knew dark circles of worry had formed under her eyes. She missed Paxton terribly, and every day she thought about him stuck inside that orb. She hoped she could find a way to get him out before the evil magic corrupted his kind heart. For the time being, they had to travel from village to village searching for the hidden princess while rallying followers to support her. Once found, the princess would need the help, especially if she had any chance to reclaim her kingdom from under the rule of the coterie.

Vassuda coaxed Samara into a stand. "Come. We have an audience waiting. Hopefully, they'll fill our coffers with gold at the end."

Samara glanced briefly into the mirror and shivered as she took in the diadem decorating her forehead. It bore an uncanny resemblance to the one Callista had worn ever since they met.

# CHAPTER FIVE

Darkness filled the night sky as Forgrac Copperfeet sauntered onto the large stone platform at the top of three steps. Hooded in a dark-brown cloak, he held a large torch high, bathing his face in a shadow.

From the side of the platform, hidden out of sight, Samara watched, nerves filling her belly as she gazed at the crowd of humans sitting at the bottom of the steps. Others stood behind them. All eyes turned to the dwarf on the makeshift stage. An eerie sensation filled Samara, as though someone was watching her, someone different from the audience. It felt like a malicious intent beamed directly at her. She entwined her fingers, squeezing her hands hard, trying to release her nervous energy into them. Behind a few standing audience members, a cloaked figure peered between two heads, their face shrouded in darkness. Samara stiffened as the figure seemed to meet her eyes then retreat, the face illuminating under the light of a nearby cottage sconce. Icy tingles ran down her spine as she caught a glimpse of white hair, and she could have sworn the face belonged to Mist.

The anxiety over performing suddenly vanished, and worry of being discovered by the coterie overtook her. The people in front blocked her line of sight to the cloaked figure, and Samara searched, trying to get a better look at the mysterious person and confirm or deny that it was Mist. She saw no sign of them anywhere. Squinting, she checked every dark patch and watched for anyone suddenly darting to the front to attack them. Though, she couldn't find them, and no one raced to the front. She questioned whether she had seen a face that possibly looked like Mist's. She knew that if it was Mist, the sorceress wouldn't waste time before attacking them and returning them to the coterie building, back to captivity and torture. Yet as the time grew nearer to start, no one approached, and Samara couldn't find the mysterious person again. She attempted to ease her nagging worry and concentrate on the play and her part in it.

The audience fell into silence as Forgrac

prepared to speak. He shifted the torch lower, illuminating his face, somber and serene. "Long ago, in the land of Slosiaran, a royal family reigned."

Though Samara had seen Forgrac act several times over the last couple of months, she was still amazed at the way he fell into character, losing his dwarven slang and speaking with a clear, entertaining voice. It was like he was another person altogether.

"And under their rule, the different races lived as equals. Each used their strengths and bartered them to cover their weaknesses. Because of this, food and supplies were plenty."

Forgrac waved his arm toward a table laden with food, and the invisible Ulrieg ignited the torch overhead, illuminating the goods. A loud gasp filled the air as the crowd marveled at the impossible light.

Forgrac pushed out his chest. "The royal family traveled far and wide, into the different kingdoms of Wraeyanor, Dragoria, and even as far as Clialarion, the land of the elves. They worked in harmony with all the kingdoms to bring a balance of peace and trust. Much joy and laughter filled the air under the reign of the royals."

Sitting at the table laden with food, Skorrig, one of her dwarven travelling companions dressed in emerald robes tied at the waist with a gold rope, sat at the abundant table, his dwarven upper body just high enough to see his chest. His normally unruly hair was pulled back into a low ponytail, his burly beard combed and braided down the middle, and a gold crown sat on his head. He ate some grapes, and his large hooked nose disappeared into the goblet as he took a sip.

Next to him sat the female dwarf, Dorabrona, dressed in a golden-edged emerald dress fitted at the bodice and draping in generous waves to the floor. Her long brunette hair had been combed and slicked into a circular display and fitted against her scalp. She clinked her ceramic cup with Skorrig's, joy radiating from their faces.

"Here's to another successful trade with the dwarves, blessed with elven magic. The diadem they have crafted for Bianca is exquisite—the crystals aid any dragon elves hiding in the realms."

Skorrig, acting as the king, grinned broadly, mischief shining in his eyes. "Indeed. It's wonderful! A weapon that could be used against the coterie sorcerers if the opportunity arises." He took a swig of his wine. "We just need to keep it from the coterie members. Any crystal witches could use it to enhance their power."

Dorabrona, the queen, twirled a loose strand of hair, her expression wary. "I hear the head sorceress of the Sacred Flame coterie is a crystal witch. We must tell Bianca not to wear it publicly, or it could be dangerous." The queen nibbled at a carving of lamb.

"That we must. Hopefully, our actions bring unity to the kingdoms, despite the Sacred Flame coterie's rule that brings discord between us. If we unite, there is hope for our kingdoms to rise again and hopefully find Dragoria." He stabbed his knife into a large piece of meat in front of him then took a sip of wine. "The stars know we need something to work in our favor to rid us of this oppression."

Dorabrona placed a hand on his arm. "So much responsibility on your shoulders. Don't fret. We will stick together. I know more people despise the coterie's rule and wish for the old ways. We must be patient."

Quickly, Samara's eyes scanned the audience. She hadn't caught sight of the cloaked figure again. Perhaps it was one of the members watching them with the hood removed, and the white hair she thought she saw was simply the light shining extra brightly on those few blond strands, making it seem paler than it was. It was impossible to tell if anyone was a supporter of the coterie. Almost every part of the play seemed incredibly daring, as if tempting fate. It would only take one zealous follower of the

Sacred Flame to report them to a coterie member, and being discovered would bring their lives on the run instantly to an end. They would be captured and likely put to death. She tugged at her dress, trying to work out some nerves.

Drawing a ramshorn to his lips, Forgrac blasted a note. "But behold! Their quiet battle against the coterie was lost before it began."

The stage was ambushed by a dwarf dressed in a long cape similar to a senior sorcerer's, followed by a few male dwarves dressed in loincloths, their skin painted green-gray, and a couple of females dressed as centaurs with bows armed and ready.

Forgrac cried loudly, "A senior sorcerer led an army of ogres and centaurs into the palace, slaughtering the king and queen."

Forgrac's hands waved dramatically as the imposters slashed their swords and other weapons, killing the faux king and queen. The acting royals fell forward, and the attacking ogres knocked over and destroyed items on the table. A cloth hanging above the acting king and queen burst suddenly into flame, another one of Ulrieg's invisible contributions, the blaze enhancing the terror of the scene.

The crowd looked shocked. Children covered their faces, peering through their fingers as they watched the terror of their kingdom's history and the scattering attackers. By the time the flames of the overhead fabric died down, the fight was over, with the king and queen unmoving and slumped awkwardly over items of furniture. The stage fell into darkness.

Silence roared, echoing through the darkness as the crowd stilled.

Forgrac's voice cut through like a blade. "Though the royal adults had fallen, little did the coterie member or his minions know that lying deep in the palace catacombs, the princess bathed in a hidden pool."

Samara's heart thundered as the king and queen sneaked away in the dark. It was her turn. Her stomach twisted into knots as she silently strode through the dark to the makeshift pond on the opposite side of the stage from the recent destruction. Diadem firmly placed on her head, she squatted behind the rock, edging forward until everything above her shoulders was visible to the audience.

The invisible Ulrieg lit the torches on either side of the pond, illuminating Samara as she fell into character and pretended to wade through the water. Hidden on the side, one of the crew created trickling sounds by running a hand through a bucket filled with water.

Forgrac continued, "The young princess waded,

naive to the devastation above and the company nearby."

A small dragon prop skimmed across the pool's surface, heading for Samara, who played the part of Princess Bianca. It swam and splashed around her, seeming to study her, before darting sharply toward her.

Samara pretended to startle, yanking her hand toward her. "Ouch!"

The little dragon swam in the other direction as she studied the bite mark between her thumb and finger.

"What was that for?"

"Surprised and annoyed more than hurt, the princess didn't know that the dragon had sensed something in her, and the bite was a mark of approval that would be carried down for generations," Forgrac continued.

The little dragon splashed in the water, playfully diving then resurfacing. Vassuda and Dorabrona, dressed as two dwarven servants, ran into the underground, circling the pond.

"Princess Bianca, there you are." Vassuda held her hand over her heart and scurried to the edge of the pond. "Come, get out. The palace has been invaded."

"What?" As the princess, Samara jumped, splashing to the edge and climbing out of the pond.

Her knees shook slightly from stage fright, but she used it to her advantage and pretended it was from the fright of the news. She took a deep breath, calming her nerves. Thankfully, she didn't have a large role. "When did this happen, Dirana?"

Dirana helped her out of the pond. "Right now!" She eyed the princess down to her toes. "Ya soaked. I ain't got a change of clothes for ya, but you'll dry off quickly."

"Haven't ya got her out of here yet?" Dorabrona brushed past Vassuda, rushing toward Samara.

"I jus' got here, Medola," Dirana said. "Did ya manage to bring the princess a change of clothes?"

"Nay. I was too busy running for me life an' trying to find her." Medola grabbed Samara's hand and yanked her in the opposite direction. "Hurry. I don't think it'll take them long to find the passage down here."

They ran off the stage, which fell into darkness when Ulrieg dampened the torches. The stage was cleared in the dark before Forgrac stood in the center, one torch burning and casting him in light.

"The palace servants led the princess away to the only place they knew was safe—the presence of a dragon. The mighty Ommucru, Lord of Fire." The light over Forgrac dimmed as Samara ran back on stage, led by the two dwarven servants. A light illuminated a large dragon's shadow.

"Come. Follow me. I will protect the princess and her descendants for the future of Slosiaran."

Forgrac continued narrating as Samara acted out his words. "Confident that the dragon would keep his word, the dwarven servants left Princess Bianca under the mighty dragon's care. Ommucru oversaw Princess Bianca's safety, making sure she was looked after by loyal families. Several years later, the princess married and had a boy."

Samara picked up a small bundle hidden from the audience and cradled it in her arms, eyeing it with love. Using her free hand, she pretended to look at his hands. "He carries the mark that looks like my dragon bite."

"From that time forward, each descendant carried the mark as a form of birthmark," Forgrac said, "Automatically indicating them as a member of the human royal family. The Sacred Flame coterie members heard word about this mark and how the princess escaped the invasion of her family. From then on, they hunted the family and searched for any human with the dragon's mark."

Each time Forgrac paused, he added emphasis to his words, sending an eerie chill through Samara's veins despite hearing the words many times before.

If it still did this to her, she could only imagine the effect it must have on people hearing the words for the first time. She rocked, cradling the imaginary baby as Forgrac went on.

"Many were killed, forcing the descendants to live in the shadows, hidden in small villages until rumors of the royal descendants faded. The public came to believe that the royal lineage was eradicated." Forgrac paused, giving the audience time to take in the story and feed off their emotions. "But recently, rumors of a living royal descendant have circulated. After many years of believing the bloodline had been diminished, there remains hope that the royal lineage still exists."

Gasps echoed through the audience, and people cast sideways glances at the hands around them, looking for the distinct birthmark.

"The rumors said that when the last of the royals were killed by the coterie members seventeen summers ago, she had given birth to a baby so recently that the Sacred Flame coterie hadn't heard of it. No one knows what happened to the baby, but the villagers searched the house where the hidden royals were slaughtered and couldn't find it. It is believed that the parents hid the baby when they found out they were in danger and a friend snuck the baby away. Despite no one finding the baby, word has reached the coterie, and again, they have sent their sorcerers to find the royal."

Vassuda, with brightly colored hair and dressed in a large brown cloak, wandered onto the stage, and Samara hugged her makeshift baby bundle to her chest and hid, diving in and out of different hiding spots on the stage before handing her baby to one of the friendly dwarves.

Allowing panic to fill her voice, she said, "Here, take my baby and hide it. Hide it in a place it can grow up, away from the suspecting eyes of the coterie."

The dwarf snuggled the baby and nodded. "I promise to protect it with my life." They ran off the stage.

Forgrac took over. "Despite the rumors, no one knows the name of the dwarf who rescued the baby, and to this day, the coterie still searches for more information about her and where she took the human royal."

Samara hid in the shadows, but soon after, Vassuda, acting as the coterie member, found her and killed her with magic. As the princess, Samara contorted her body, falling to the ground, unmoving, and the coterie member walked proudly away.

The crowd booed. Vassuda pretended to hurl magic at them.

Forgrac commanded attention as his voice boomed over the din. "To protect your human royal, please shelter them from the coterie members. They are the only hope for the royal family of Slosiaran to raise an army against the coterie, and take back the kingdom. If you see them, they may not know who they are. They may not seem like much, but with the right encouragement and support, they could be the first step to reclaim our lands."

Invisible, Ulrieg extinguished the torches, and the stage fell into darkness. The crowd roared with applause, and Ulrieg ignited the center torch, illuminating Forgrac again as he bowed. Framed by the remaining actors, Samara stood next to him, still wearing her black wig and headdress. Vassuda, Forgrac's wife, curtsied on his other side. All signs of the mysterious cloaked person were gone, yet Samara couldn't shake her unease.

# CHAPTER SIX

Gibobo's hand clamped over Emelyne's mouth, stifling her scream. Eyes wide, Emelyne kept them locked on her fallen friend. She couldn't believe Thiznabo lay lifeless on the ground several feet from the blacksmith shop.

The sorcerer tugged at the bottom of his tunic, proudly rolling his shoulders back. He locked eyes with his fox familiar as it sniffed at the dwarf's body. A strange, satisfied sneer spread across its furry snout.

Grabbing Emelyne, Gibobo and Lozzeak shoved her toward the back of the blacksmith shop, opened the door to the cave, and propelled her through, shutting the door behind her.

Emelyne gathered enough sense to bar the door behind her, locking the sorcerer out of the cave, at least from that entrance. Her parents would be unable to open it from the smithy's side to let him through, no matter how much he demanded it. She gathered her breath and pulled her thoughts together as she absentmindedly wiped away the river of tears that flowed down her face. Grief racked her body. She didn't want to leave, especially with Thiznabo lying lifeless in the middle of the street. It didn't seem right to leave her best friend. Only the danger of a coterie member finding Emelyne pushed her forward through the main cave of their village and into the tunnels.

They had practiced it many times, but it seemed so wrong to run when the others faced danger. She didn't understand how the sorcerer could think she was anyone worth killing just because she was a human living among dwarves. But she wasn't about to argue with her mother. It wouldn't do her any good. From an early age, she had learned that Gibobo's smallness deceptively hid a spirit that made up for it.

Weaving her way through the tunnels, she passed many caves made into rooms off to the sides. Sconces burning on the walls provided dim light. Mothers labored over children while their husbands probably worked, digging for more metal in the mine. The dwarves were known for living and working in the mountains. Though many had found or been forced into occupations elsewhere, the dwarves were renowned for their mining and metalwork.

Sucking in the dank, musty air to ease the grief burdening her lungs, Emelyne followed the tunnels and crossed the bridge towering over the large drop to the mines. Normally, she wouldn't pass through that area, but because of her mother's fears, they had traveled the route many times to practice for a situation like this. The distant clunking of picks against the stone echoed from the bottom of the mine, the sound seeming to push her forward and quicken her pace. Her nerves fired, and uneasiness mixed with misery followed her through the dimly lit tunnels. She ducked as the ceiling lowered. As far as she was aware, no other humans passed through the area, so there was no reason to raise the tunnel ceilings.

Crouching, she quickened her pace, careful not to hit her head. It was a long walk, and even her young body of seventeen summers ached from the awkward position. The farther she went, the lower the ceiling grew, to the point where even dwarves would need to crouch.

The sound of picks against stone grew distant until a glimmer of light eventually cut through the darkness. She scuffled hurriedly, having to move to all fours before charging toward the light. As she burst out of the tunnel, a wave of hot air washed over her, instantly drying the river of tears down her cheeks. Beads of sweat formed on her face and neck. She jerked her hands off the stone surface. The heat was almost as intense as furnace fire.

Her gaze lifted, and she was confronted by a large creature with a vast array of pointed teeth displayed menacingly in a snarl. She balked, studying the creature's horned snout and finishing with large spikes protruding just above its intense gaze. Flinching, Emelyne stumbled back a few paces, tripping on a stone as the enormous creature stomped toward her, spreading its mighty wings.

# CHAPTER SEVEN

"Monut! Ya startled me!" Emelyne chastised, climbing to her feet and dusting her backside and knees.

*You made so much noise, I thought a crowd was charging through the tunnel. I was preparing to attack.* The dragon furled his wings and backed away a few feet, the sun glistening off his gray scales.

"I can see that!" Emelyne squawked. "A little unnecessary, seein' there's only enough room for one person to exit the hole at a time. Don't ya think?"

*True. But you already seemed on edge by how you were acting. What's going on?* He lowered his snout and peered into the tunnel, looking for danger.

"I am on edge! Some man with brilliant-blue hair and a fox is walkin' around the village. Ma said he's from some coterie." She wiped at the tears threatening to flood her face again. "Ma told me to come here to avoid him. Me best friend, Thiznabo, went outside to delay him from enterin' the smithy while I got away, an' he killed her." She sniffed, her chin quivering. "Jus' 'cause she stood in his way."

*I see. That's dreadful. The members of the Sacred Flame coterie aren't to be taken lightly. Your mother was right to tell you to leave. They have little regard for the life of others.* Monut straightened his neck and ushered her away from the tunnel with his long gray membranous wing. *Come. Let's get away from here.*

Trying to compose herself and save her tears, Emelyne allowed him to usher her away, doggedly following him into the scorching heat that filled the open space of the Merciless Sanctuary. A vast landscape of rocks and arid dirt spread before them. As soon as Monut's shadow moved, she was at the mercy of the sun's blazing rays.

"How is it so hot out here?"

Monut peered back at her, lifting his long tail, careful not to swipe her as he turned. *That's why we call it the Merciless Sanctuary. No one wants to come here because it's so hot and arid. It's the perfect place for dragons to hide. Many years ago, coterie members came here to check it for dragons and enemies. After a quick visit and traveling not far from the opening of the desolate plain, they left and haven't returned. I guess they ruled it uninhabitable because of the lack of plants and animal life.*

"But the dwarves of Bhalwahrum village know that ya here."

*Only a few have traveled to this side. Your ma and pa are a couple of them. They came running out here for somewhere to hide when you were just a baby. I scared them too.* His belly bounced as he chuckled. *It took a while to convince them that I was friendly. For some reason, my winning smile didn't work for them.* He pulled back his lips and flashed his many teeth at her.

Emelyne pulled back and cringed. "Well, if that's ya smile, I can only imagine they found it rather frightenin'."

Monut tilted his head. *It took a while, but they came around. After trust was established, they knew I'd help look after you. After all, I'm the descendant of the great dragon Ommucru, who protected Princess Bianca when her dwarf servants rescued her from the palace after it was overthrown.* He straightened his back and raised his head high.

Emelyne scrutinized him. "And so humbled by it, I can tell."

*One doesn't need to be humble when one is born into greatness. You...*

She waved a hand at him. "Oh, please. Don't tell me I should worship the ground ya walk on 'cause of some act ya ancestor did."

The dragon pulled his head back. *I would never! I was referring to you.*

"That's an odd statement. I don't know my parents, an' I was raised by dwarves. Though I love them, they are clearly not from great ancestors."

Monut cast her a curious sidelong glance. *And wonderful parents your ma and pa have been. Hopefully, their efforts will be rewarded. But back to the stranger, the residents of Bhalwahrum have a great distrust for the members of the Sacred Flame coterie. So they won't want them snooping around and will do their best to keep them out of the mountain.*

"If they don't end up like Thiznabo." Grief pulsed through Emelyne's body just thinking about her friend, and she wanted to keel over in pain. "Why are they such horrible beings? The one I saw in the village was human. So, why would they want to hunt me?"

The dragon turned and led her farther along the desolate side of the mountain. *They are also elves and half bloods. But it's what they can do and what they stand for that is the problem.*

Emelyne realized she had fallen behind and

hurried to walk beside his front legs, sweat trickling down the sides of her face.

*And to make it worse, they force dwarves to become their slaves and ogres and centaurs to do their fighting.*

"How do they manage to make such large, powerful creatures fight for them?"

*By using their magic against them if they don't. They can easily cause much pain for beings of all sizes.*

"Are they really that powerful?" She gazed up at the mountainside that towered over them, and the sun beat against the rock facing them and trapped the heat. It was hard to believe that the other side of the mountain was lush and green, with shrubs growing out of the rock cracks.

*Powerful enough to defeat all other creatures, including the dragons. Which is why I must hide you and not simply stand between you and a coterie member.*

"I still don't understand why it's so important to hide me. Is it wrong to be the only human in a dwarven village?"

*Not particularly. But there are reasons that your ma and pa are hiding you. I think it's their job to tell you.*

Emelyne sighed. "You're all acting like I'm a child. Does everyone forget I've been trainin' to fight with the sword? I'll just make sure I have one in my hand every time I hear one of the coterie members are in the village. Then I can't end up like Thiznabo."

Monut pushed forward, slightly increasing his pace. *And from what I hear, you're very good against the dwarves. But people your own size—or worse, men—are harder to go against. And even with all the training in the world, fighting a coterie member equipped with only a sword is madness. Even Thiznabo wouldn't have had a chance.*

Emelyne hurried her footsteps again. It was difficult to keep up with his large dragon strides. She was glad for the fitness level she needed to work in the shop and the training she had undertaken to test the handcrafted swords. When she caught up to him, she sighed, frustrated to be informed she was weak. "Then I'll jus' have to get some practice against a human male."

*That would be good practice for you, but it's still not enough to go against a coterie member.*

She gazed over her shoulder, barely seeing the entrance into the mountain behind them. "Why are we goin' this way? It's so far from the entrance."

*It's farther from the entrance to the sanctuary, and others can help me protect you.*

"Assuming the coterie member even finds his way through the mountain."

*Yes, that is true. But you can never be too careful. If the sorcerer is with anyone, they could try to enter the Merciless Sanctuary from the gap between the mountains.*

*I don't think they would know of the passage through the mountain, but it's best to be cautious.*

When they reached a rock face jutting out from the mountainside, Monut led her around it. The heat of the sun grew with each step away from the looming peak. Sweat streamed down Emelyne's face, and she wiped it away with her sleeve. Rivulets ran down her back, soaking her clothes as the dragon led them back toward the other side of the rock face.

Monut shifted to the side, exposing a large group of dragons of all different sizes and colors, ranging from just under Monut's enormous bulk to Emelyne's waist height, all gathered inside a roofless cavern. Emelyne paused, catching her breath. She had known Monut lived in the Merciless Sanctuary with a couple of dragons, but she had no idea it was so many. She did a quick head count. Twenty dragons hid behind the rock face, backed by a large cave.

A dragon snorted, and Emelyne stepped back.

Monut peered back at her. *Come stand by me. It's all right. They won't hurt you.*

"Are you sure? They look rather intimidatin', an' a snort sounds rather aggressive to me." Timidly, Emelyne stepped to Monut's side, her sight fixed on the dragons.

*The dragons have lost trust in many beings, whether*

*humans, elves, or dwarves. We have been hunted for centuries. That is why we hide in this desert and only fly at night.* Monut turned to his companions. *This is Emelyne. Remember, you are to protect her. She won't hurt you.*

The dragon that had snorted moved forward. Her large form was between Monut's size and that of a dragon who reached Emelyne's waist. Her scales glistened in the sun, revealing tepid brown and beige stripes. *Ah, Emelyne. We have heard a lot about you from Monut. Welcome. I'm Cyrra.*

Emelyne frowned. "How did you know my name?"

Monut cleared his throat and glowered at Cyrra.

Cyrra cast him a nervous glance and nodded before focusing back on Emelyne. *There is much we know about you and your dwarf village.* The dragon spread her plain medium-brown membranous wings, exposing their vastness and temporally blocking Emelyne's view of the other dragons. Each rib of the wing was finished with a claw the length of Emelyne's hand.

"That's not disconcertin' at all." Emelyne frowned.

Cyrra's eyes widened. *You mean you don't know why...?*

A warning grumble rose from Monut's throat.

The female dragon furled her wings and cowered under Monut's glare before continuing. *We know about you and your village because we like the dwarves in Bhalwahrum, well, the ones that know about us. They have always been generous, providing us with cattle and farm animals to eat when we can't go far to catch our own.*

Emelyne glanced briefly over the twenty dragons. "That's a ton of mouths to feed. I wondered where some of the farm animals disappeared to. There ain't no sign of them."

Cyrra cackled. *Surprise. We were the reason they never returned.*

"That makes sense. Though, why do ya need to hide? Ya look like fierce creatures that could protect yourselves."

A dark-gray-and-white-striped smaller male dragon sat next to Cyrra. *We are few compared to the power of the Sacred Flame coterie sorcerers and their spies. The members hunt our kind. Many dragons have gone missing after the members of the Sacred Flame coterie were spotted in an area. They are keen to obliterate us from existence.*

"If that's the case, they must fear what you can do when you're together."

*Or what our kind can do in large numbers alongside dragon elves,* he said.

Emelyne pursed her lips. "Don't ya have anywhere safe to go?"

The smaller dragon shook his head. *No. Here's about as safe as it gets. All dragons are in hiding. The coterie hid our realm from us many years ago and somehow removed its location from everyone's memories. No one has found it. It simply vanished, making it impossible to find from all kingdoms.*

Cyrra tilted her head and nudged Emelyne lightly with her wing tip. *We're just waiting for Slosiaran's human royal to come out of hiding and rise to take over their kingdom.*

"Who could this royal be?" Emelyne asked.

Breath gushed out of Cyrra's mouth, turning a raspberry into a cackle as she cast a strange look at Emelyne.

Monut poked the excitable dragon with a talon and gave her a stern look before answering the question for her. *The royal heir is an enormous secret that very few know. The informed are sworn to secrecy to protect the heir from the Sacred Flame coterie. Your ma and pa are well educated in where to find the heir and will defend them with their lives. It is believed that only one remains.*

All feeling fell from Emelyne's face. "Are they safe with the wizard in the village?"

*As long as all humans are out of sight, I don't see why*

*not. They think so little of dwarves that they wouldn't think a dwarf knows about the royal family.*

The dragon's voice was deep and assured, easing the worry Emelyne held for her parents and the others in the village. Sweat pooled between her shoulder blades and along her forehead, and she swiped her sleeve across her face.

Monut raised his furled wing and shaded her from the sun. *Does this help?*

The temperature seemed to drop several degrees, so she nodded. "Though a fresh breeze wouldn't go astray." She gazed back at the dragons, realizing all eyes were on her. It was strange but less worrying than when she had first arrived. "What do you usually do during the day?"

*Sleep, mostly.* Cyrra chuckled. *It's safer. Then, we can use the cover of darkness to hunt close to the sanctuary. We have good night vision and take every opportunity to fly between the clouds.* She looked up dreamily. *That's the best feeling—the wind beneath our wings.*

Emelyne couldn't help but feel sorry for the dragons having to be trapped in the hot wasteland to stay safe. "Well, let's hope the royal is found and can help protect ya from the coterie members."

Cyrra clapped her wings against the ground. *That would be wonderful.*

Monut's deep voice cut off Cyrra's excitement. *That would be a good start, especially for this realm. But the royal will need to build a strong army with magic wielders if they are to have any chance of going against the coterie.*

"Well, they can count me in as a fighter. I'll have to try to get it out of me ma and pa who they are. At least then I can put my sword skills to good use other than testing out a sword's strength." Emelyne sat cross-legged beside Monut, making sure she remained under his shadow.

The dragons started to settle, except for a baby dragon who approached her with wide eyes.

"Aren't ya a cutie!" Emelyne extended her arms toward the little dragon, and he dashed into them, so she wrapped them around him.

"If I had known there were so many of ya here, I would've helped feed ya—especially with a li'l one here. I thought only Monut stayed here."

*Knowledge of the dragons' presence here is not passed on easily—for our safety. But you can visit us any time you like, even when there isn't reason for you to hide.* Monut angled his wing to the ground, securing Emelyne under it until the sun set.

# CHAPTER EIGHT

Monut's body shifted beside her as he furled his wing, exposing Emelyne to the stars shining above. The Merciless Sanctuary's arid air had cooled considerably since the sun had retreated, making way for the waning moon. Standing, Emelyne stretched her legs and arched her back as she gazed at the twinkling sky. It had been an enjoyable and educational time talking to the dragons all afternoon, but she was ready to go home and make sure Thiznabo's body had been treated with care, giving herself time to mourn. A wave of guilt mixed with grief washed over her. She had spent a relaxing afternoon with the dragons when her friend had died trying to protect her.

She rubbed at her face. "Surely, the man has gone by now."

Monut shrugged. *It's impossible to know. Best to wait until your parents come looking for you. He may demand to stay at the village overnight. As much as the dwarves wouldn't want to allow it, they wouldn't have a choice.*

Cyrra huffed. *Yeah, we won't even go hunting until we know he has gone. It's too risky.*

The stripy dragon groaned and sauntered up to Cyrra's side. *And trust me, we're hungry!*

"Isn't there another place ya could hunt? What's over the other side of the sanctuary?" Emelyne pointed in the direction opposite the village and across the vast, desolate plain.

Deep worry lines creased Monut's forehead as he followed her finger. *We're unsure if the people on that side are for or against the coterie. It's safer to be seen only by the few people of your village or hunt nearby and try not to be seen by others.* He cocked his head to one side, a curious expression on his face. *Quiet!*

Emelyne and the other dragons fell silent, none moving a muscle as each set of eyes slowly surveyed the area, searching for whatever had caught the larger dragon's attention. No matter how hard she tried, Emelyne couldn't hear anything but the drag- ons' breathing and could hardly see anything more than a few feet away in the darkness. Suddenly, the dragons around her stirred, eyes turning to her.

"What is it?" She squinted, trying to see past them.

Cyrra tilted her head, disbelief shining in her eyes. *You mean you can't hear that?*

Monut groaned. *Cyrra, the humans don't have hearing like ours.*

Cyrra tucked her wings in tight. *Well, that's an incredible flaw, if I've ever seen one. Trumped only by their lack of ability to fly.*

Emelyne frowned.

Monut framed her shoulders with his wing. *Listen carefully. You should hear it soon.*

Emelyne did as instructed, straining her ears for any sound outside the thunder of dragons.

"Emelyne!" A soft voice reached her from the distance.

It sounded like the direction she had come from. She stared up at Monut. "Is that Ma?"

The large gray dragon nodded.

Cyrra clapped the tips of her wings together. *Goodie. She can finally hear it.*

Monut ignored her. *We should greet her so she can find you. That will save her from walking all this distance.*

Cyrra bounded around them. *I'm coming too.*

Monut sighed. *All right.* He led them back toward the entrance of the mountain.

Away from the heat of the dragons, Emelyne noticed the significant change in temperature. Crisp, cool air brushed against her skin, and she shivered. Rubbing her upper arms with her hands, she quickened her pace and edged closer to Monut, hoping to catch some of his warmth. The movement helped, and her ma's voice grew louder as she called into the darkness, searching for Emelyne.

*She's here. I can see where you are. We'll have her to you soon. Stay put,* Monut spoke, his voice filling their minds.

Gibobo's calling ceased, and Emelyne ran the short distance when she realized she was falling behind again.

Monut sniffed before blowing air quickly from his nose. *I smell burned meat. I hope that's for you because I'm not eating that.* He looked down at Emelyne.

"Ma never burns meat. She cooks it to perfection," Emelyne rebutted.

*Hmph! If that's what you call it. I don't know why you lot need to mistreat it so. It tastes much better raw.* The large dragon shook his head.

Emelyne screwed up her nose. "Each to their own."

"Emelyne!" Gibobo's voice reached her through the darkness.

The young woman picked up her pace again, jogging ahead of Monut until she spotted a couple of short figures several yards away. "Ma?"

"Yes, it's me and ya pa." she called back joyously.

Emelyne had almost reached them when their figures were framed by a dark dragon outline from behind. Monut remained beside her, and she turned to search for Cyrra, unable to find her. The dragon behind her ma and pa lowered its head.

*Whatcha got?* Cyrra's face caught in the moon's dim light lodged between the two dwarves.

Gibobo jumped, dropping the items in her hands and holding a palm to her heart. Then, she turned and spotted Cyrra. She whacked her playfully on the snout. "Oh, ya cheeky dragon. Ya gotta stop sneakin' up on me like that."

Cyrra grinned and nudged the dwarf with the side of her head. *When you stop giving me such a good reaction, then I might lose interest.*

Shaking her head, Gibobo retrieved the bag from the ground. "I'm so glad I packaged this before bringin' it." She turned back to Emelyne. "I figured ya must be hungry, so I brought ya some food."

Emelyne reached for the offered leather bag. "Thanks, Ma. But I coulda waited until I came back to the village."

Lozzeak placed a hand on her upper arm. "We're afraid ya gotta stay here overnight at least."

"What?" Emelyne frowned. "Why?"

"That guy from the coterie is bad news." Lozzeak said.

"That's obvious after what he did to Thiznabo." Tears welled in Emelyne's eyes again, and she wiped at them.

Gibobo threw her arms around Emelyne's waist, squeezing tightly, and Emelyne stroked the back of her head.

"We know, love. He did a terrible, terrible thing to ya friend. She was so loyal to ya an' didn't deserve her fate."

Gibobo rubbed her arm, trying to comfort Emelyne before she continued. "He says his name is Kaine, an' his fox has been stickin' its nose into unwelcome places, tryin' to sniff out the missing human royal. We ain't gonna risk havin' ya anywhere near it in case they try to do somethin' to ya."

An unexpected snort escaped Emelyne. "I ain't no princess." She thought she spotted sadness in Gibobo's eyes but wrote it off as lingering emotion about Thiznabo.

"But 'cause ya human livin' in a dwarven village, they might not take any chances." Lozzeak shook his head. "This Kaine has the power to charm the truth out of people he touches. So far, everyone in the village has managed to keep out of his grasp, an' they don't need him gettin' ideas that they know where the royal is."

"Then ya both should stay here as well. The dragons told me that ya actually know where the royal is. That means it's dangerous for ya too." Emelyne clasped his hand.

They both shook their heads.

"That would only draw more suspicion if he notices we're gone. An' he's gonna notice. He's asked for some throwing knives to be made for him while he's here. He's heard 'bout the special metal we use." Gibobo leaned closer to Emelyne, cupping her hand partially over her mouth. "He's not to know that our metal is so special 'cause it's dragon blessed."

Emelyne's shoulders caved. "I guess I'll jus' wait here until ya tell me I can come home."

Cyrra groaned. *Did you bring any food for us? We're starving!*

Lozzeak chuckled. "We ain't strong enough to drag several sheep over here, not to mention the attention it'd bring. But ya should be able to hunt the fields in the far north. The male is stayin' in the village inn with a window to the south. Ya should be far enough out of sight, with the added benefit of him not seein' in ya direction. But still, try not to be seen by his fox. I hear these familiars can tell their bonded what they see, getting many people in trouble."

Monut lowered his head to their level. *Thank you. We will remain out of sight, and I will personally oversee Emelyne.*

Emelyne embraced her ma and pa in unison with a shoulder hug. "Ya two take care an' keep away from the coterie member. I can't have him findin' out that ya know where to find the missin' royal."

Gibobo squeezed Emelyne's forearm. "That'd be a little hard since we have to make his knives. But we'll do our best to not draw attention, an' we've had plenty of practice over the last seventeen summers to keep our mouths shut. Now, off ya go, love. We betta be gettin' back."

The two dragons and Emelyne watched as Gibobo and Lozzeak disappeared into the darkness before heading in the opposite direction, toward the dragons. Emelyne scrunched the bag's opening in her hand and held it close to her chest. The rich smell of roasted lamb called to her tastebuds, and her stomach growled. Still, she wanted to wait until they had returned to the other dragons. She could take her time while they went hunting in the north.

They rounded the corner into the large crevice of

the rocky mountainside. All sets of dragon eyes turned to them.

*You're back!* The stripy dragon said. *What happened?*

Wiggling onto a small boulder flat enough to sit on, Emelyne placed her bag on the surface behind her. "The coterie member is stayin' the night, so Ma an' Pa think it's best if I stay here."

*And is that food for us?* A dragon, the spitting image of the baby dragon only much larger, inched closer, inhaling deeply. *It's burnt, but that'll be a start to dampen the hunger.*

Monut maneuvered in front, blocking their access to Emelyne. *We're to go hunting in the north. We should be safe there. But we need to do our best to stay out of sight and keep away from any foxes. Make sure they don't see you. One of them could be the coterie member's familiar.*

*Maybe we can make the fox our meal,* Cyrra chirped.

Monut released a deep growl and rolled his shoulders. *As enticing as that sounds, it's probably best if we simply avoid it. I imagine a missing familiar would cause a disruption and may lead to more coterie members coming here.*

Disappointed, Cyrra tossed her head to the side. *Oh, you always take away our fun.*

*Only for our and Emelyne's safety.* Monut snorted. *I think it's best to break up into groups and hunt in different locations. And try to avoid eating only the farmers' herds. Twenty dragons taking all their animals won't go down well. It will be noticed, raising suspicion.*

The baby lay at her side as the mom shifted closer to Monut and Emelyne, her brown eyes connecting with Emelyne's. *Can I leave the little one here with you? I don't want to take him out if there's a risk of being discovered.*

Emelyne ruffled the baby's scales, careful to avoid the many horns ridging his back. "Of course, ya can. But I don't know if I'll be a great dragon babysitter. It's not like I can stop him from flyin' off." The baby disappeared from under her hand, and she searched, attempting to find where he had gone. "Where is the little guy?"

Monut and the mother searched the area until rustling behind Emelyne caused her to jump to her feet on top of the small boulder. Glancing behind her in the dim light, she caught sight of the little dragon scratching at something in the dirt. Looking closer, she saw what was left of her bag, torn and spread across the ground, all contents gone.

The baby dragon sat and belched.

# CHAPTER NINE

"**W**ell. There goes me dinner." Emelyne's stomach growled louder as she eyed the destroyed bag.

Guilt filled the mother dragon's brown eyes. *I'm so sorry.*

Emelyne sighed. "It's fine. I was lookin' forward to it, but the little guy is probably hungrier than me. After all, he's growin'."

*I'll share what I catch with you,* the mother dragon promised.

Crossing her arms over her chest, Emelyne shook her head. "Any extra ya bring back should go to ya young one. Go on. I'll stay back and watch him. I'll be fine."

The mother pushed into the air, her wings

billowing breeze down upon Emelyne, Monut, and the baby.

Emelyne strained her neck to watch the dragons take flight. She could see the excitement Cyrra had described earlier on their faces and in their body language. Dragons were born to fly, not hide in desolate landscapes. If the missing royal could help them, she hoped they'd be discovered soon. Her stomach groaned loudly, and she held her hands over it.

Monut lowered his head close to her. *You are very hungry.*

Scratching the little dragon behind the ear, she nodded. "I am. I was up before the sun an' only had a light breakfast before workin' in the smithy. But I'll survive."

*Do you have any of what you call coins?*

Emelyne dug through a couple of pockets on her pants, encouraged by a faint clinking that greeted her movement. "I have a few. Why?"

*As soon as one of the dragons returns to look after the baby, I'll take you to a human village nearby. They have a tavern where you can buy a meal. I'll hunt within hearing distance and keep an eye on you.*

"A human village? I ain't been to a human village before." Emelyne tugged at her sleeve as nerves roiled in her abdomen.

Monut hummed. *I am aware. I think you're old enough to learn how to communicate with humans other than selling them blacksmithing items.* He lowered his head and met her eyes. *But don't give away any information about you or where you're from.*

"Honestly!" Emelyne threw back her head. "What's so bad with tellin' people where I live?"

*Nothing is wrong with where you live. It's just for you and your ma and pa's safety. Anything unusual should be kept hidden in case it attracts the wrong kind of attention.*

"Fine. I'll do me best. I could use a good meal." She clutched at her still-protesting stomach.

She sat on the small, flat boulder, and the baby dragon nuzzled up to her until the mother dragon landed, sprawling a bear in front of him. The little dragon waddled quickly toward the fresh food.

*Are you ready to go?* Monut lowered his gaze at her.

She eyed him. "How am I supposed to get there?"

*Climb on.* He lowered his body to the ground.

"What?" Her eyes boggled. "What am I gonna grab on to?"

He lowered a wing. *Climb up, sit just in front of my wings, and wrap your arms around my neck.*

"Seriously?" Emelyne forced her mouth closed.

*That's how the dragon riders used to do it. It's better if you have a saddle, but I promise to fly slowly and won't let you fall.*

Feeling as though her soul had left her body, Emelyne tenderly climbed up the arm of the wing using all fours, careful to avoid the membranes. Monut's scales were tough and almost crusty, making it nearly impossible for any weapon to pierce them. Reaching his neck, she slipped a leg on each side and wrapped her arms around his neck. She swallowed, unsure if she would like the experience.

*Are you ready?*

She sucked in a breath. "Yes. I think."

*You'll be fine.* Amusement shone in the dragon's voice. He climbed to his feet, bent his knees, and sprang upward.

A cool breeze brushed against Emelyne's face as her braids flew over her shoulders. The dragon rose up and up until he reached the top of the mountain and she could see the dim lights glowing in the distance.

He looked to the south. *That's the human village over there.* Then he nodded to a dimly burning light in the distant north. *We'll be going over there. I can hunt in the forest on the other side of it within hearing range. Hang on!* He quickly dove in the northern direction, and her dwarven village vanished.

Emelyne tightened her grip, adrenaline coursing through her veins. Her head swayed with the waves caused by the sudden change of direction, heightened by the thought of being so high in the air. She smiled as exhilaration filled her, slowly pushing away the apprehension about the height. She tried to focus on their next stop. "Will ya be safe huntin' there?"

*I believe so. Not many people go into those woods at night because of the large bears. I'll just have to land in the forest so the village won't see me. You should be safe there as well. Your ma and pa said nice humans live there. But you still need to be careful,* he warned. *They could have some untrustworthy visitors.*

Emelyne dug her fingernails into the dragon's tough scales, doing her best to hang on as he neared the ground, gliding over dark patches of land. It seemed like no time had passed before he was heading to a small clearing in the forest.

With a slight thud, Monut landed and lowered his stomach to the dirt. *You can climb down now.*

Knees shaky and her legs unstable, she worked through the elation of riding a dragon's back. She could feel Monut's eyes watching her, and though she tried, she couldn't calm her movements.

*Your limbs are acting weird. Did you not enjoy that?*

Reaching the ground, she used the dragon's wing

to stabilize herself as she gazed into his curious eye. She chortled. "Did I ever! It's jus' the side effect of doin' somethin' super excitin' an' unusual. I ain't never thought I'd be ridin' a dragon." She nodded and admired his form. "It's a bit scary. It'd be betta with somethin' to hang on to, but I definitely enjoyed it."

Amusement filling his eyes, Monut nudged her lightly with his snout. *Come on. I'll walk you to the edge of the forest. Make sure you stay between my front legs. That way, I can protect you from anything dangerous.*

Emelyne walked to his front, each step growing steadier and gazed up at him. "Normally, I wouldn't need protectin'. But I don't have any weapons with me."

*Those are brave words for someone who hasn't traveleled out of their own village much. You might be right. However, you never know until you physically experience it.* Monut took several steps forward, and Emelyne hurried to her place at his front. She was surprised by how quietly the dragon walked on the forest floor. His footfalls made less sound than hers.

Soon, a dim light shone ahead, piercing through the trees.

*I'll remain here.* Monut lowered his head to her

level. *Follow the light. That's the tavern ahead. I'll watch over you until you're inside, then I'll go hunting.*

"Thanks, Monut." She stroked his nose. "Ya stay out of trouble, ya hear?"

The dragon spread his lips, exposing his vast array of teeth. *I think I can manage that if you can do the same. Call me if anyone bothers you.*

"I'll be fine. After all, I'm goin' to a human village, not part of the coterie. Surely, I'll fit right in."

A low rumble vibrated in his throat. *Don't let down your guard. You never know.*

She rested her forehead on his snout. "I don't know why ya follow Ma and Pa's requests, but it's nice to know that you'll look after me no matter what. Thank you."

*Ensuring you're safe for your ma and pa and my heritage is an honor.*

Emelyne frowned, the meaning of his words unclear, but her thoughts were interrupted by her stomach giving another large growl. She chuckled. "I gotta go find some food." She turned and trekked through the dark forest, following the dim light of the tavern.

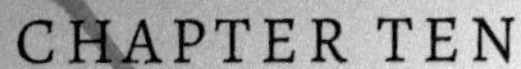

# CHAPTER TEN

Raucous laughter, followed by an overwhelming smell of stale ale, greeted Emelyne as she pushed open the tavern door. She passed a few tables surrounded by burly men and giggling women with low-cut necklines. Seeing so many humans at once was more disconcerting than she had expected. Everyone seemed so tall, with many being larger than she. They seemed giant compared to the village of dwarves. Straightening her shoulders, she pressed past them and was rewarded with the aromatic smell of roasted rabbit and freshly baked bread. Her stomach's protest grew louder. She had to eat.

Pushing through to the bar, a light sheen formed on her brow. The body heat combined with the fire burning in the hearth starkly contrasted with the cold, desolate climate of the Merciless Sanctuary. She looked around the room, noticing many people looking at her. She wondered if it was because they hadn't seen her before. Glancing down, she realized she was still wearing her black-smithing pants and tunic, a far cry from the other women in the tavern, who wore long flowing dresses. She couldn't do anything about her clothes, and she was happy when she spotted others who looked like they had come straight from the field. She concluded that the reason they must be staring had to be because she was a new face. She pressed forward, the smell of food drawing her in.

A man behind the bar with flecks of gray streaking his shoulder-length brunette hair, his face set with a few creases, threw a towel over his shoulder. "What can I get you?"

"A plate of whatever it is that I can smell cookin'. That would be splendid." Emelyne slid onto one of the rounded stools at the counter.

The man grunted, spun around, grabbed a plate, and disappeared through a door behind the large kegs lining the back wall. A moment later, he returned, the plate piled with roasted meat, turnips, and a chunk of fresh bread, and he plonked it in front of her.

Emelyne held out a few coins, and he pocketed them, returning with a mug of ale.

"Thanks." Emelyne grabbed a piece of meat and tore into it.

Noting she hadn't brought her own knife, the man handed her a semi-sharp one. "Here. This will help you break it up."

He watched her as she grabbed it, stuck it into her food, and tore the meat into smaller pieces.

"You're not from around here, are you?"

Emelyne filled her mouth with a large chunk of bread, too busy quieting her stomach's protests to answer.

"I haven't seen you around here before. Plus, you're not dressed the same as females are usually dressed. Not to mention that you have a dwarven accent." His eyebrow rose.

She gulped the partially chewed lump of bread and washed it down with a splash of ale. "I'm jus' visitin'." She took another swig of ale. "Is that all right?"

"Of course it is. I'm just curious. It comes with the trade." He topped up her ale, though it was mostly full. "I'm always happy to have new patrons."

Emelyne couldn't see any maliciousness or harm in the man's questioning and decided to answer him with a half-truth. "I've been spendin' a fair bit of time with the dwarves, learnin' the blacksmith trade. I guess I've picked up their accent while I've been at it." Her lips closed around another chunk of roasted rabbit, the meat melting in her mouth. She groaned, understanding why the tavern was so popular.

The barkeep looked pleased with her reaction, though his curiosity wouldn't quell. "That's a strange profession for a young lady. Wouldn't you prefer to do something more fitting?"

She frowned, shoveling more food into her mouth. "Like what?"

The stool next to her scraped along the floor, and a big man with a rough ginger beard and wild hair a couple of inches long sat beside her. His green eyes roved over her. "I think she'd make a nice addition to this tavern with one of those fitted waists and low-cut dresses. Her jaw is a little too muscular, but I think she should scrub up nicely." He fiddled with the end of one of her braids.

Skin crawling as though covered in cockroaches, Emelyne shifted slightly to the opposite side of her stool, swiping her braid out of his large hand. "There's nothing wrong with what I do. In fact, I quite like it." She reached for her ale.

"That's an interesting mark you have on your hand." The large man leaned closer.

Realizing that her sleeve had slid to her wrist,

exposing the crescent-shaped birthmark between her thumb and forefinger, she tugged it down and took a swig of her drink. "It's jus' one of them random scars ya get, but can't remember how. I think it's from when I was first learnin' black-smithin'. It's easy to injure yourself if ya don't know what ya doin'."

The large man leaned back, one eyebrow raised. "So, you're saying that you've had it for as long as you can remember. Did you have it as a child?"

She huffed a laugh. "I started blacksmithin' as a kid. So, of course."

He scratched his beard and glanced at another man in the tavern before turning back to her. "So, where do you live?"

"I don't see how that's any of your business." She bit another chunk of the roast, her stomach suddenly churning uncomfortably.

"Maybe I want to hire you for some work. See if you're any good at it." His voice indicated he had no such interest as he swirled his ale, slopping some over the side of his tankard.

The bartender cleaned up the spill with the towel from his shoulder. "Why don't you leave her alone so she can eat? I don't need you scaring off new customers."

The large man fixed him with a look. "Would you

rather my friend and I rough up your rooms later when we're staying in your inn?"

The bartender looked taken aback. "There's no need for that."

The man with the orange hair straightened. "I know a group that would pay handsomely to find out where this young lady is staying." He turned to Emelyne. "You said you've been learning from the dwarves. Which village is that? I wager you live there too."

Emelyne frowned and filled her mouth with food. That must have been what Monut was talking about. It was time to finish her meal and get out of there.

The bartender slapped his cloth on the bar top between Emelyne and the man, working hard at a spot that wasn't there. "You're being ridiculous. There is no reason you need know where this young woman lives. She is just a common human who works with dwarves and has picked up their accent. She didn't say she lives there."

The large man stood and thumped his fist on the countertop. "No, but she clearly spends a lot of time there, so it's worth a look. And if she won't tell me, you will."

The barman stepped back. "That's ridiculous! I don't know where she works. There are at least eighteen dwarven villages near here. It's the first time I've seen this young lady." He shook his head. "I can't tell you anything."

The auburn-haired man leaned over the counter. "You must know the names of them all."

Turning his head slightly to the side, the barman lifted his cloth to the side of his mouth, covering it from the large man's view. He mouthed, *Run,* to Emelyne.

Unsure what was happening or why the barman was doing his best to stand up for her, Emelyne bit off as much as she could of the roasted rabbit and stuffed the remaining bread in a pocket. Nodding to the barman, she slipped off her stool and made for the door.

"I expect the names of the dwarven villages to be written down and handed to me before I leave tomorrow." The ginger downed the rest of Emelyne's ale and slammed her tankard on the bench.

Solid footsteps thundered after Emelyne as she hurried, rushing out the door and around the back of the tavern, heading toward the forest. "Monut!"

The tavern door slammed again behind her, followed by two male voices—one of them definitely the large man's deep voice.

She didn't dare yell Monut's name again. Instead,

she broke into a run, longing for the safety of the trees. She wasn't there yet.

"There she is!" the large man shouted behind her.

Her neck prickled, and she ran faster, hissing, "Monut!" She hoped his dragon ears were strong enough to hear her. Reaching the forest, she darted between the trees, trying to lose the men.

"Hurry! We should grab her anyway, in case the idiot bartender doesn't give us the right dwarven village or she goes into hiding."

The footfalls behind her quickened, snapping leaves and branches. They were getting closer and, if she wasn't wrong, had split up, one on either side.

"Monut!" she hissed again, her eyes wide as she searched the trees, her dinner churning in her stomach from the disruption. She couldn't understand the man's obsession with her. She was just an ordinary human, nothing special about her other than she lived with dwarves.

The forest was dark, making it hard to see if she was heading in the direction of the small clearing they had landed in. No matter how hard she tried, she couldn't see the outline of an enormous dragon, but the heavy footsteps behind her were closing in. She dug in her toes. She needed to get as far away from the men as possible and look for Monut later. Her foot caught on a root, and she landed hard on her stomach. Winded, it took a moment to regain her breath. Her knees and elbows ached.

She spat the leaves that clung to her lips before climbing to all fours—only to be shoved down to the ground, a large form with stale ale breath pinning her down.

# CHAPTER ELEVEN

Returning to her room at the inn, Samara placed her headdress on the counter, eyeing it as she changed out of her costume. Since beginning their travels, she had discovered that the headdress in front of her was a perfect replica of the original diadem that the human princess had worn when she'd escaped annihilation. It was also exactly the same as the one Callista had worn from the day she met her. Somehow, Callista had gotten her hands on it. It wasn't the sorceress's to keep. It had been a gift to the human royals from elven monarchs. Embossed in dragon elf magic, it served as a symbol of the united and harmonious rule of the kingdoms. It currently sat on the senior sorceress's head, empowering her with its crystal magic to use against the people of the kingdoms and the dragons. The audacity amazed Samara, even though she shouldn't be surprised after how Callista had acted in the end. And to think she had almost been within reach of it while she'd stayed at the coterie. She would have had Ulrieg try to steal it before they left if she had known.

Images of the tortured dragons in the coterie building's underground flashed through her head, and shivers ran down her spine. She took that back. She wouldn't have had Ulrieg steal it. She wouldn't willingly risk his life.

Ulrieg jumped onto her bed next to her dress and fluffed out his wings before tucking them by his side. *You're kicking yourself for not knowing about the diadem. Aren't you?*

Samara nodded. "I would've tried to take it somehow if I had known."

The dragon lowered to his abdomen. *Well, now we have at least two reasons for returning to the coterie building as soon as possible.*

A deep sadness washed over Samara as her thoughts shifted to Paxton trapped in the orb. She nodded. "Who knows what that orb is doing to Paxton? Maybe Devi, Henriette, and Peadar could help him. But I still want to go back soon if they can't." Her brow pinched. "Hopefully, we'll have some luck." She changed into her dress and neatly placed her costume and headdress into the wardrobe. Her stomach growled. "I better hurry down to get some dinner."

Raucous laughter echoed up the stairs from the tavern below.

Her mouth pressed into a thin line. "I wish it weren't a popular tavern. I could do with a quiet night."

*I completely understand. You know how I feel about hanging around people.* He snorted. *But mixing with other people might do you good.* He exposed his vast array of pointy teeth in what Samara had learned was a grin. *Besides, your life was too sheltered before you joined the coterie. You were very naive.*

Samara rolled her eyes. "Yes, I know."

*Mixing with different personalities and cultures will be good for you.*

"Even if they hated the show?"

*Ha. Didn't you hear their response tonight? They loved it. I'm sure it'll make their night to meet one of the performers.*

She straightened a few items on the duchess. "I had a split second tonight when I thought I saw Mist in the audience wearing a large cloak with the hood on."

*And you didn't tell me!*

"You were busy with the stage effects, and I

wasn't sure. I kept an eye out to see if I spotted the person again, but either my eyes were deceiving me, or they were simply an audience member that may have had similar features to Mist. I didn't think it was necessary to tell you when I wasn't sure. It could've just been my nerves acting up. I thought we might see coterie members before now."

*You still should have told me. I would have had a good look around when I had a break. I also could have checked the cottages without anyone knowing. I'll have a look around the village tonight. Don't ever push away your suspicions.*

"I know. I'm telling you now because I'm not sure if I saw her." Samara sighed deeply, removed the brunette wig, and ran a brush through her hair as she gazed into the mirror. It amazed her how the magical pink still seemed extremely bright despite not continuing with the color magic required in the coterie. She was afraid that it might lead people to believe she was a current Sacred Flame coterie member. It must have been brilliantly bright during her coterie days. Sitting on the vanity table stool, she bundled her hair and tied it into a loose bun. Maybe that would make it less obvious.

She turned to Ulrieg. "Are you coming down, or do you have other plans?"

Ulrieg stretched. *I'll quickly scout the village to see if I can find this person, and then I'll go hunting.*

Samara rose and opened the window, giving him access to the outdoors. "Be careful."

He huffed and climbed onto the windowsill. *I'm more worried about you.*

She turned the handle, opening the door. "I'll keep an eye out in the tavern also."

As Samara closed the door, Ulrieg leaped out the window. Ruckus bounded up the stairs to greet her, riding on the scent of stale ale and rabbit stew, followed by Forgrac's laughter. She smiled. She hadn't heard that sound until they left the coterie. It was pleasant to see a different side of the dwarf. It was another sign that no one in the tavern looked like Mist. She was sure that Forgrac would know Mist's face anywhere. Samara hurried down the last few steps and into the tavern's light, halting at the number of people crammed into its walls. It seemed like the majority of the village's humans were there.

Following the sound of his laughter, she spotted Forgrac sitting on a higher stool, ale in one hand, his wife, Vassuda, seated by the other. The light from the overhead sconce highlighted his sizeable hooked nose towering over his bushy, dark-brown beard that he finished off with a straight cut. Several villagers encircled them, listening to every word the dwarf said. His eyes locked with Samara's, and he waved her over. She weaved her way to them. As much as Samara didn't want attention, she was always willing to be in his circle of friends.

"Hello, love. So good of ya to join us." He waved his arm broadly to a stool at the bar beside them. "You'll be happy to know that the food and drink are free for us tonight. The owner loved our play." His hazel eyes gleamed, accentuated by the shine of liquor.

Samara climbed onto the stool next to his wife.

Vassuda placed a hand on her back and leaned in to be heard over the din of the tavern. "Are ya hungry?"

She nodded. "Starved. I've hardly eaten all day."

The small female nodded and looped an auburn ringlet behind her ear. "That'll be the nerves. It'll get better the more you do it."

The dwarven female ordered Samara a bowl of stew, watching as the barmaid spooned a couple of large scoops into a bowl before grabbing a fresh portion of bread. Steam coiled up from the bowl, and the smell caused Samara's stomach to growl from neglect.

A large tankard of ale plonked in front of her, slopping over the side. "Here ya go, love. Ya deserve this." Forgrac reached across his wife, pushing the tankard closer to her. "Enjoy the spoils of your work." He winked.

"Thanks." Samara scooped up a spoonful of hot stew and blew on it, eyeing the people standing before the dwarf and his wife. She nodded politely, feeling her cheeks warm when their eyes traveled to her hair and narrowed. Facing the bar, she shoveled the stew into her mouth, allowing the rich flavors to distract her from the unwanted attention. She wished she knew the reversing spell to return her hair to its standard color. Instead, she had to wait until it grew out and faded naturally. That was the downside of leaving the coterie so early—she had so much more magic to learn.

The atmosphere around them dampened, and Samara met Vassuda's eyes before flashing them worriedly toward the humans. It didn't take the dwarf long to assess the situation and nudge her husband.

Chuckling, Forgrac playfully slapped the closest human with the beady, close-set eyes and burly brunette beard. "Ah, I see what ya gawking at and know what ya thinkin'. Don't mind her hair. It's only that color 'cause she used to be part of the coterie. She ain't anymore."

The man pulled at his oversized tunic, seemingly unconvinced.

"Do ya really think I'd be warnin' people 'bout the Sacred Flame coterie members if I traveled with one? Nah. I'd trust this one with me life." Forgrac slurped some ale from the refilled tankard before him, catching froth on his mustache as he eyed the humans' reactions. "In fact, she's actually proven it an' has saved me from the coterie." He stroked his tiny podgy belly and leaned back.

The woman placed her hands on her ample hips, her dress swaying around her when she leaned on one leg to contemplate for a moment before she let her arms hang by her sides. She had a beautifully soft face. Her plump cheeks were framed by loose blond ringlets that fell from her braid as she nodded once to the male.

Samara glanced over her shoulder between mouthfuls to see the two humans' shoulders relax and their gaze soften when they looked at Samara.

The beady-eyed male leaned toward Forgrac. "That's good to hear because we also wanted to tell you something, and the last thing we need is a coterie member listening in." His eyes flicked to Samara, almost looking apologetically.

Curiosity washed over Forgrac's face. "Oh. Really? What's that?"

Loud laughter cut through the air as Skorrig

entertained a group in the far corner, his limp rarely holding him back from a dramatic performance.

Samara leaned closer, trying to catch the man's response to Forgrac.

"I've heard rumors that a human lives in a dwarven village." He looked satisfied with his information. "Got it from a good source."

Forgrac cocked an eyebrow. "Is that unusual?"

The male looked disappointed. "Apparently, she's been living there her whole life. Even lives like a dwarf. The barkeep in a village nearby served her recently."

Both the dwarf's eyebrows pushed together. "And? I guess that's interesting, but I'm going to need somethin' a little more than that." He lifted his ale to his mouth, ready to take another sip.

The woman rolled her eyes at the man before leaning closer to Forgrac and Vassuda. "He's leaving out the part that she has an unusual mark between her thumb and forefinger."

Forgrac spluttered out his ale, coughing to the side. Once he'd managed to contain himself, he said, "Well, that would've been a better place to start."

"Yeah, well. Our informant isn't completely sure because the person didn't seem to think they were anyone special. But from what you said in your play, this could be worth looking into." The man held his ale cup to obscure his mouth from anyone watching.

# CHAPTER TWELVE

offers the weight of an iron wagon from the previous night's performance and bellies full from an early breakfast, the traveling show packed their carts and hit the road once again. This time, though, they were following the person's lead regarding what could be the royal birthmark. They didn't have an exact location, but the whole party was heading back to the Perpetual Vale. They had visited Forgrac's village and family before and doubted the human would be there, which left them with one less village to search.

Thankfully, they hadn't traveled too far from the dwarven area, as they had been performing in the human villages on their outskirts.

Last night's worry of thinking Samara had spotted Mist in the crowd had been for naught.

They'd seen no sign of her in the tavern, and Ulrieg hadn't spotted her or her crow familiar in the village. The relief was beyond explanation.

Samara sat next to Forgrac in the driver's seat. Ulrieg sat invisible on top, his talons resting over the front edge of the material cover of the cart as their wagons swayed along the dirt road leading into Mirwohr, the main village of the Perpetual Vale. Their trip through the countryside had them gazing at the trees and open plains, with the mountain-side in the distance. The dwarven-crafted steel wheels held the rocking wagon sturdily as Forgrac directed the horses along the main road between the few cottages and stalls.

Apprehension and excitement swirled through Samara's stomach. Though they were leaving behind the place she thought she might have seen Mist, each new place they visited brought with it another chance they might run into members of the Sacred Flame coterie. She and Forgrac would be on their most wanted list. They had both caused a lot of disruption during their final days at the coterie. Yet, it was a risk they were willing to take to find the missing royal. The sooner the royal took over the realm of Slosiaran, the sooner Samara could get back to the coterie to rescue Paxton from the orb's clutches.

Her mind was lost in her own thoughts, and her attention was abruptly pulled back to the present when Forgrac muttered, "Now that's an odd place to lie down."

Samara followed Forgrac's gaze to the dirt path not far ahead. A male dwarf lay in the middle of the road, his body convulsing visibly from several yards away.

She clutched at her upper arm, her fingers digging into her flesh as fear sank its claws into her. "It looks like he's been cursed."

Quickly, she studied the trees surrounding them, looking for any members of the coterie. Her search came up empty as the wagon rolled closer to the thrashing man. Dirt covered the back of his clothes, and leaves and twigs clung to the fibers. His face was contorted as though in pain. Sacred Flame coterie members were the only people she knew who could cast a spell like that. It was a cruel spell, its torment also touching Samara, igniting her worry over potentially spotting Mist in the audience the night before—even if it wasn't Mist's style to be discrete.

"Keep an eye out for any coterie members hiding in the bushes," she said.

"Of course." Like cumbersome storm clouds, Forgrac's bushy brows crowded his face.

*I'll scout the area.* A telltale breeze whispered

along the back of her neck as Ulrieg leapt into the sky, and the wagon rolled to a stop in front of the thrashing man.

The wagon following pulled in behind the first, and Skorrig watched as the others climbed out of the wagons to observe the delay. Arrows rattling in her quiver, her boots thumped on the dirt road as Samara jumped off the wagon and carefully approached the stranger. Before squatting by his side, she scanned the surrounding trees, looking for any sign of a coterie member or their familiars. She jumped when a crow cawed over her, but the creature didn't seem the slightest bit interested in her as it continued its flight.

*I can't see anyone nearby. Perhaps he's been like this for a while, or the coterie member is traveling by wagon or horse.*

Ulrieg's summary was the reassurance she needed to relax into remembering a method to pull the dwarf out of his nightmare. Her memory of the spells she had learned had grown fainter, and she knew she would have to start practicing her magic to keep on top of what she had learned. She pressed her hand against his sweaty forehead and muttered, "*Liborte.*"

Instantly, the man stopped thrashing, and his eyes slowly cracked open. Confusion washed over his face as he stared up at the sky. When his brown eyes finally landed on Samara's brilliant-pink hair, they filled with terror, and he sprang up, scurrying backward on all fours. "Please, don't hurt me!" he cried. "I promise I'll do what ya want."

"Friend!" Forgrac yelled, determined to be heard over the dwarf's panic. "There's no need to panic. She won't hurt ya. In fact, she freed ya from the torturous curse."

Panicked eyes flicked to Forgrac, instantly easing when he realized the person addressing him was a dwarf. Still, apprehension marred his features as he surveyed Samara. "Are ya certain? 'Cause it was people with hair like hers that put me here in the first place."

Chuckling, Forgrac climbed off the front of the wagon. "Of course." He sauntered to the man and held out a hand to help him up. "I vouch for her completely. I've been friends with her for a long time. Not once has she let me down."

Reluctantly, he grabbed Forgrac's hand and stood with his aid.

"Me name's Forgrac Copperfeet. That's Samara Wren." He indicated her with his hand before waving it at the accumulating audience. "These are our companions. We're all part of a traveling performance."

The man's shoulders relaxed more when he realized the group was mostly dwarves, and he nodded to the group. "Silut Goldhide is me name. Can ya tell me where I am?"

"You're on the path to the village of Mirwohr. How did ya get here, me friend?" Forgrac slapped him on the shoulder.

Silut's brow creased, and he gazed at the ground, scratching his bearded chin. "I don't really remember. But I do know that a couple of people with brilliantly colored hair placed hands on me, and the next thing I knew, I was woken up by you lot from what I was certain was a nightmare."

"Huh." Forgrac scratched his head. "Do ya remember what color their hair was?"

He shook his head.

"Honestly? I would have thought that you would remember a detail like that."

"Don't ya believe me?" Silut crossed his arms.

Holding up his hands in defense, Forgrac backed slightly. "I didn't say that. I was merely pondering your memory loss."

Silut chuckled, the sound nervous, and he shrugged. "Sorry. I guess feelin' lost has got me defensive."

"Totally understandable." Forgrac slapped him gently on the shoulder. "Do ya remember where ya from? Perhaps we can give ya a lift back to ya village."

He tugged at his beard on both sides of his face. "Unfortunately, no."

Vassuda shifted between Samara and Forgrac. "Ya poor dear. Ya should join us, then." Her gaze passed from Forgrac to Samara for agreement. "Don't ya think?"

Forgrac thumped him on the back. "Of course. Dwarves always help dwarves, for we know they would never betray us to the coterie."

Silut expelled rowdy laughter. "Of course, we would never betray each other to the coterie. Never would we want the life of a slave to befall one of our own." He wiped his brow as if dispelling sweat. "What a dreaded life that would be." He returned Forgrac's greeting, the thumping sound audible as he gazed across the group. "Thank you for taking me in, friends."

"Of course. Of course." Forgrac led him toward the wagons. "You must be tired. Would you like to travel in the second wagon? It has more space to sleep during travel."

"Ya too kind." Silut allowed Skorrig to show him to the back, accepting his aid to climb up before Skorrig helped himself onto the driver's seat.

Samara climbed up next to Forgrac on the first

wagon after everyone had retreated to their places. She heard Ulrieg settling into the wagon top behind them. "Is everything still clear?"

*As far as I can see. I followed the crow for a short distance but abandoned the pursuit when it seemed to be traveling straight to a destination far from here. It simply must have been a wild crow. Otherwise, there were no signs of a coterie member or their familiar.*

She worried her bottom lip. "I wonder how he got here. There aren't any buildings around."

*Nope. There sure aren't.*

Snapping the reins, Forgrac egged the horses into trot. "The poor guy must feel so lost. Imagine losing your memory, even about your loved ones. That would be terrible."

# CHAPTER THIRTEEN

Dust billowed to waist height behind the wagons from both sets of wheels as they entered the first village.

"Ah, Mirwohr, the main village of the Perpetual Vale." Forgrac took in a deep breath with a contented expression. "It's been so a long time since I've been here. It used to be me favorite place to perform an' trade. The fact that it's not far from home helped."

*Hmph. If this is the main village, I'd hate to see how tiny the small villages are.* Ulrieg dragged his talons over the wooden edge, grating on Samara's nerves. *Maybe we wouldn't even know they were villages.*

Forgrac chuckled. "Yes, it does look small, but it's not. The dwarves live within the mountain. We prefer the dark confines of a cave to a wooden cottage. The cottages are more for visitors along with some inns to stay in, an' the rest are primarily places to trade or do business with other beings."

*There's still not many places of business,* Ulrieg grumbled.

"That's because most of the dwarves work within the mines harvestin' the precious metal. Only a few of us decide to deal with other bein's." The dwarf pulled on the reins, redirecting the horses closer to the middle of the road.

Samara thought of all the times he'd had to sleep in the coterie building and work in the kitchen and garden, and a sadness washed over her. "You must have hated it at the coterie, then."

He placed the reins in one hand and rubbed his beard. "I didn't love it, but I had been workin' in the travelin' theatre for quite some time. That took some gettin' used to. I wouldn't be back doing it if I didn't love the theatre. I guess I'm a little more social than other dwarves. Though, I can say for sure that I don't want to return to bein' a servant. I pity the ones stuck servin' the coterie members, unable to leave." He shook his head, mouth turned down at the edges.

They drove past several stalls manned by dwarves, and uneasiness washed over Samara as the dwarves watched them roll by, their faces cold and unwelcoming.

She muttered, "If they're friendly to other beings to trade, then why do I feel like they want me to leave?"

Forgrac glanced at her and frowned. "Maybe it's your hair. Remember, It's still incredibly pink. Ya don't know how many of their family members have been taken as slaves for the coterie. Ya saw how Silut reacted when he first saw ya. Have ya got somethin' to cover it up?"

Samara rocked to the side, pulling her brown cloak from under her. "I've only got this. It's too hot to wear around here. I'm only using it for padding against the hard seat."

"Sorry, but I think ya gonna have to wear it 'til the locals realize ya not part of the coterie." Forgrac cracked the reins.

A thump landed on the carriage behind her, and she jumped, turning to find nothing.

*I've just listened in on the couple standing over on the left.* Ulrieg heaved a breath as he lay on his stomach. *Forgrac's correct. They're suspicious of both of you because of Samara's hair. They have no love for the coterie here. I don't know how you'll get past that.*

"Silut got over it pretty quick," Forgrac argued.

"And you were the one to get him out of it." Samara squeezed her hands together between her knees. "Maybe you should try talking to them, Forgrac."

With a sigh, he steered the horses to the side of the road and half climbed, half jumped from the driver's seat to the ground. He waddled toward the couple, bearing his best smile. "Good day, me friends." He set a foot into the outer boundaries of the cottage, eyeing the fine utensils crafted from metal and stone that they sold in their store. "These are beautiful pieces." He fingered one closest to him. "It's been many years since I've set foot in this lovely village."

The man stepped slightly in front of the female. "Is that because ya a slave for the coterie member?" He inclined his head in Samara's direction.

Forgrac pulled his head back and chuckled. "She ain't a coterie member."

The man raised his chin. "That color hair is a sign of the coterie sorceresses."

"True, me friend. True." Forgrac rested a hand on the man's shoulder. "But she ain't one anymore. I was a slave for them, but now I'm free, an' the sorceress works for me. I'm back runnin' a travelin' theatre, an' she is one of me actors."

The man's eyes narrowed. "Are ya sure ya ain't

working for her? I ain't seen a dwarf in charge before."

"Oh, I ain't in charge. That ain't how we work. We're equals." He indicated the rest of the dwarven crew before leaning closer to the man and lowering his voice. "I'd also be careful showin' such open disdain for the coterie if I were you. It's likely to get ya killed." He cupped his mouth. "Trust me, I'd know."

The dwarf's face turned wan as the woman nudged in front of him. "I've lost count of how many times that mouth of his has gotten him into trouble. One day, he's goin' to say the wrong thing to the wrong person, and that'll be the end of him." She rolled her eyes. "Especially since we had the senior member of the coterie from the border sniffin' around here not so long ago."

"Ya did?" Forgrac's eyes widened.

"Yup." She nodded enthusiastically. "An' he was lookin' for the likes of ya."

Forgrac's shoulders stiffened. "For me?"

She leaned forward and poked Forgrac in the chest with a stubby finger right above his rounded belly. "He described a dwarf that had escaped with one of the former coterie members. There was a handsome price on ya head too."

Forgrac rubbed the back of his neck. Samara

wondered if he was having second thoughts about why the two were shooting daggers from their eyes when they first arrived.

The dwarven woman raised an eyebrow. "It is ya, ain't it?"

Tension ran through Samara's shoulders. Perhaps coming here was a bad idea. Though, they had no other way to look for the lost royal. She focused hard on her connection with Ulrieg after hearing him take flight not long before. *Ulrieg. Do you see any sign of coterie members around or dwarves looking shifty?*

*Everything looks normal. I can't see any sign of strange activity. Though, I've only stayed briefly at Forgrac's dwarven village, not enough time to judge suspicious behavior.*

*Yet you used to stay around trolls.* She rubbed behind her ear.

*Yeah, I know. The trolls were dimwits, so it was easier to hide among them, and they lived above ground, not in caves with dank air.*

The woman's voice drew her attention back to the store. "Don't worry ya li'l self over it. I was jus' teasin'. Though, I'd love to know what ya did. We hate the coterie folk round here. They come here acting all high and mighty. Yet, all they do is take us as servants and boss us round." She waggled her head. "There ain't nothin' they've done to help us. Back when the human royals ruled the kingdom, it was a fair an' just system."

Forgrac rubbed his long hook nose. "Yeah, well, we kinda deserve their wrath. We stirred up a bit of a hornet's nest before we escaped."

The woman smiled. "Good for ya!" Her face dropped into a frown. "Though, I don't know that comin' here was such a good idea, seein' as they're already lookin' for ya in dwarven villages."

"We realize that. We've been travelin' all over. We came back because we heard that there's been sightings of a human who lives with the dwarves. Have ya seen them?"

The man glanced at his wife, and a knowing look crossed their faces.

The woman nodded. "That'd be Gibobo's girl. She the only human we know livin' with the likes of us. Gibobo used to work for a young human, helpin' her with chores durin' the final months of her pregnancy. She'd done a few jobs for the human's family for many years. Ya know how these humans only live a few years. Well, a coterie member went hunting for the girl's parents a couple of days after she was born. Who knows why? It don't take much to become the enemy of the coterie." Her face saddened. "They went and burned the cottage down with the parents in it. Gibobo was lookin' after the baby. Lucky. 'Cause that saved the girl's life. Gibobo an' Lozzeak have been lookin' after her since."

The woman placed items on the shelf and turned back to Forgrac. "She's a fine young thing. Made of the tough stuff. But there ain't nothin' special 'bout her other than livin' with the dwarves. Though she's become a mighty good blacksmith. That's because her pa an' ma are blacksmiths in a nearby village." She ran a hand over a few metal items lining the shop's shelves. "She made these. They come here every so often to trade goods."

"What village do they live in?" Forgrac rubbed his elbow.

"It ain't too far away." She glanced at the carriages. "I guess ya want to know the way outside of caves?"

"That would be best. This is our livelihood, so we gotta take it with us," Forgrac agreed.

The woman paced to the door of the shop and indicated past the shop across the dirt road. "See those mountains over there?"

Forgrac nodded. The mountain range looked huge even in the distance. It stood in a long line against the horizon.

"That's the edge of the Merciless Sanctuary. Their village and adjoining cave is on this side of that range."

Forgrac nodded. "Ah, is it Bhalwahrum?"

"That's the one."

"I haven't been there in a long time. Tell me, is the Merciless Sanctuary still a desolate plain?"

"Aye. It is. No one goes in there unless they have a death wish." She leaned forward and cupped her mouth to whisper, "I hear not even the coterie members dare to travel in there."

"I can't say I blame them. I nearly burned me nose off when I was young." She tapped the tip of her large nose.

# CHAPTER FOURTEEN

They met many disapproving stares traveling through the village as Samara remained on the wooden seat next to Forgrac at the front of the wagon. Despite her sweltering under the long cloak with the hood raised, the dwarves seemed to catch glimpses of Samara's hair color, instantly filling the dwarves with suspicion. The carriage swayed through the dirt street of Mirwohr, leading them to the next village. Though the dwarves lived in caves and were interconnected with other villages through the mountainsides, they also had a dirt path for visitors of other races to travel. It was only when the wagons were between villages that Samara welcomed the lack of stares, pulling off her cloak to gain respite from the sweltering heat it provided.

Skorrig drove the second cart behind them, filled

with the remaining traveling actors who didn't fit on the first, along with their newest accomplice, Silut. The trees grew thicker along the side of the road, giving them some much-needed shade from the sun. Samara leaned back, gazing up at the blue sky and taking in the few puffy white clouds that gave the sky character. Birds chirped cheerfully from the trees, often flittering just above them as they flew across from one side of the road to the other.

"How do you feel you're doing with the acting?" Forgrac clicked the reins on the horses, and they increased their speed slightly.

Samara swallowed. "It's nerve-racking, but I think I'm doing all right, though I'm afraid to say it out loud because you probably have a completely different theory."

A knowing smile crossed his face, and he ran a hand over his beard, pressing the burly strands together. "For a new person to the business, ya doing well. I realize ya probably nervous, but try to relax an' let the emotions rise from your belly, placing yaself into the character's shoes. Let them flow freely. Why don't ya practice while we're between villages?"

Samara's brows pushed together. "I've always thought the princess would have invited her attending dwarves to join her."

Forgrac flicked the reins down. "Really?"

She nodded. "From the rest of the play, I get the impression that even though it was mostly dwarves that served the human royals, the royals treated them with respect, unlike how the coterie treats the dwarves."

"All right, then. Give it a go. Let's see if it works."

"After you say that, they leave the princess with the dragon." She cleared her throat then trained her face to be filled with concern. "Wait! Don't go. Come with me. If you go back, you'll be in danger."

"That's good," Forgrac encouraged. "Now Dirana can say, 'We must go. Whichever way we choose, our families will be in danger. We can hide underground until the attackers have passed, then we will return to our families an' claim we weren't workin' the day of the attack.'"

Still in character, Samara grabbed Forgrac's hand and squeezed it. "Thank you for everything. May you and your families be safe for the kindness you have shown me."

Forgrac chuckled. "Wonderful! Now keep goin' like that. The more ya feel the words an' emotion, the better you'll become."

Samara repeated the lines.

"Good, good." Forgrac hummed a joyful sound. "Each time ya practice, ya sound more convincing.

Now ya jus' need to remember that when ya in front of an audience."

*Hmph! Sounds like a melodrama to me.* The canvas top of the wagon swished from Ulrieg's thrashing tail.

"An' one that should help ya find ya realm an' hopefully end the time of dragons hidin'.'" Eyebrow raised, Forgrac peered over his shoulder at the invisible Ulrieg.

*All right, all right! Then, I'll put up with a little over-the-top emotion for the dragons' sake.* Hot breath washed over the back of Samara's neck. *I guess it is kind of fun, and it seems to be getting better with each performance,* Ulrieg grumbled reluctantly.

The horses' clopping hooves on the hardened dirt road echoed back from the trees. Samara sucked in the smells of the forest. She had always enjoyed her time outdoors, listening to the birds and the wind whistling between the trees leaves. She missed the crisp smell of the pine forest near the coterie building. With her cape removed and her quiver resting at her feet between her and Forgrac, she enjoyed the breeze brushing against her face, pushing back strands of hair.

The trees thinned, and movement caught her attention as she spotted a dwarf, arms ladened with branches. She waved. The dwarf nodded in acknowledgment, though his dark eyes studied them warily under black bushy eyebrows as they passed. He threw his armful of branches onto a small cart and continued collecting more as he watched them progress down the road.

They passed several more dwarves, all dressed in brown pants and beige tunics tied at the waist with rope. The outfit appeared to be their standard work clothes. Each busy dwarf occasionally looked up with a wary expression while they collected branches in the woods. Eventually the trees thinned, giving way to open fields of grass speckled with herds of sheep and cows. The fields were occasionally spotted with dwarves attending to their animals. By the time the sun lowered beneath the mountainside, casting a colorful array of orange, purple, and blue, they reached several cottages on the outskirts of the village. The insides were dark, with shutters and doors closed, except for the local inn, which rested closer to the mountainside. Warm light spilled out of its windows and onto the dirt street, and the air was rich with laughter and merriment.

Two dwarves filed out the door, excitedly chatting as they stumbled along the road toward the mountainside, oblivious to the approaching carriages.

Forgrac directed the horses toward the inn.

*Wait!* Ulrieg's voice sounded strangely urgent, and his talons scratched on the top of the carriage as he pushed himself up to all fours. *I'm getting a strange feeling. I'll fly ahead and check it out. I think it would be good for you to stay here with the carriages until I have a look around.*

Forgrac pulled up the horses, and the carriage behind also slowed to a stop under the cover of a large tree that cast a dark shadow beneath the moonlit sky.

A soft breeze whooshed over Samara as Ulrieg launched into the sky in his invisible form. She had learned in the past that when the moon was so close to being full, she should never doubt Ulrieg's feelings. She tightened her cloak around her head and shoulders as the night's chill air cooled her skin.

An owl hooted from a distance, and her thoughts returned to Gray, the wild owl that had reluctantly played her real familiar for quite some time before Zofia had mistreated him. She hoped he was doing well after she released him back into the wild, saving him from more rough treatment from the coterie members. She had grown quite fond of him while he was with her, and he had become more like a pet before the unfortunate treatment.

Something caught her eye near the alehouse, and she squinted in that direction. A deep horror filled her as her mind registered what she saw. A ginger fox trotted across the road toward the tavern. She held her breath. Any sighting of a fox had her wondering if it was Ginger, Kaine's familiar. She would do anything to avoid interaction with the fox or Kaine. She could be overreacting from her worry about running into the coterie members, but she also didn't know if Kaine had passed all his tests. He'd shown loyalty to the coterie on her last day at the building. If he had passed all their requirements, he could be wandering the realms, either looking for her and Forgrac or doing the coterie's will. She kept her eyes on the fox. Thankfully, it didn't turn their way, even after it sniffed the air. They must have been downwind. Instead, it sat on the opposite side of the tavern.

A breeze swept over her, and talons clacked on the wooden molding at the front of the wagon top. *Pull the horses off the road as quietly as possible and find another place to sleep.*

"Why's that?" Forgrac softly tugged on the reins, directing the horses to pull the carriage in the oppo-site direction.

*I've just spotted Kaine from the Sacred Flame coterie inside, and his familiar, Ginger, is sitting outside the alehouse.*

"Are ya sure?" Forgrac asked.

*With brilliant-blue hair and a determination to touch everyone, I couldn't mistake him even from the back. I'd have to be color-blind. I was especially certain when a fox waltzed up to the tavern and sniffed the air before sitting as though it should be there.*

"So, that *was* Ginger I saw in the distance. I thought that was a fox!" Samara exclaimed.

*It certainly was. Good spotting with your human eyes.* Ulrieg sounded impressed.

Forgrac took them along the road until they were far enough away and spotted a semi-worn track slightly overgrown with new budding bushes. Branches thunked under the carriage and whipped against the wheels as the cart swayed roughly along the road. The path took them toward the mountain, and after they had traveled until the moon was higher in the sky, they found a small open plain to park the carriages.

With a firm tug, Forgrac pulled up the horses. "I hope this is far enough to keep out of Kaine's sights. That is one lousy human."

"I second that." Samara followed Forgrac onto the ground. "That's really annoying. I hope he's gone first thing tomorrow and isn't after the royal."

Forgrac grimaced as though he had sucked on a lemon. "That's a real worry. I really hope he's not."

"We're not strong enough to fight him." A deep

sadness filled Samara. "If he is there for the royal, we'll have to find a way to get her back. She's possibly the last royal, which is too much power to put in the coterie's hands." She rubbed the back of her neck. "I really hope that's not the case."

The accompanying dwarves climbed out of the back of the wagons, with the new member climbing sleepily out of the second.

Silut stood with his feet planted wide and stretched his arms to imitate a star, yawning broadly. "Ah, that is the best sleep I've had in ages."

Climbing off the front of the wagon, Skorrig stretched his hips. "I can vouch for that. His snorin' rocked the wagon more than the potholes."

Letting out an embarrassed chuckle, Silut rubbed his upper arm. "Sorry 'bout that. It's been a while since I've slept well."

A couple of the dwarves created a fire while Vassuda and Samara set to work making a meal for the group. The worry about the princess was etched on Samara's nerves, and she was glad for the distraction. The clatter of pots and a wooden spoon rang above the noises of the night creatures as they prepared a few rabbits Ulrieg had caught for them. Skorrig set to work preparing the rabbits before limping over to the fire and adding them to the pot.

Forgrac threw another log on the fire after

sending Silut in pursuit of more firewood. "What're the odds that Kaine is at the one village we want to visit?"

Pouring water into the pot with the rabbit, Samara stirred it. "I doubt he's there because of us. Our visit here was impromptu." She frowned into the distance. "Unless the people who told us about the girl with the distinct mark also told someone from the coterie. Then Kaine could be there because of us and the human."

Vassuda threw chopped onions, carrots, beans, and cabbage into the pot. "I have me doubts. They seemed genuine. It could all be a coincidence. It would be interesting to see how the dwarves of the village reacted to a coterie member being in their midst. They didn't seem to take kindly to Samara on our trip in."

Ulrieg briefly turned visible while Silut was away from the camp. He scratched the back of his head, his teeth showing menacingly. *I'm pretty sure they didn't appreciate his company. It was an amusing interaction. The dwarves in the alehouse were almost expertly avoiding his touch. It was like they knew what he's capable of.*

Forgrac slapped his thigh and huffed a laugh. "That's fantastic! I wish I coulda seen that. That's a true indication they distrust the coterie, right there."

"Did you see any sign of the human?" Samara stirred the pot, covering the newly added vegetables with the liquid.

*No. They were nowhere to be seen. But that doesn't mean they're not there.* Ulrieg lay on his belly, stretching his talons out before him. *I'll scout the area tonight to learn what I can and see if I can find the human. I might be able to work out what Kaine is doing there.*

"I don't want you putting yourself in danger." Cold worry washed over Samara. She set her gaze on him.

*I'm the only one who can do it invisibly. I'll keep my distance. That fox of his can be quite cunning.*

# CHAPTER FIFTEEN

An animal's screech echoed through the darkness, waking Samara from her sleep. Springing upright, she wiped sleep from her eyes and tried to get them to focus in the carriage's minimal light. Vassuda's monotonous snoring filled the tiny space, accompanied by Dorabrona's deep breathing. Blinking, Samara grabbed her bow and arrows, threaded them over her back, crawled to the back opening, and peered into the moonlit night. Forgrac's still form lay near the fire, slumped against a large rock, his chest rising and falling softly in a slow rhythm. The last of the flames still licked the remainder of a log, the crackles synchronizing with the crickets' calls.

*Ulrieg?* She called through their bond. *Is that you?*

Only the soft call of a cicada added to the crickets' symphony. Ulrieg must be too far away. The arrows clacked as she climbed out of the carriage and onto the ground. She stretched before pacing around the campsite, her eyes peeled for an unwanted guest.

Forgrac had volunteered to keep watch, but he must not have stayed awake long enough to rouse his replacement. It wasn't the best of moves when they knew a coterie member wasn't far. Samara placed another log on the fire and sat on the opposite side from Forgrac, allowing him more time to sleep as she took over the watch. Worry for Ulrieg ate at her stomach. Her only solace was that the moon looked almost full, which meant Ulrieg's sensors would be on high alert.

After a good search, she focused on the fire, entertained by the dancing flames and the crackle of burning wood. The orange glow took her back to the glowing orb of evil magic pulsing in the cave under the coterie building. That same evil orb had entrapped her beloved. The tumultuous magic locked in the sphere was eating away at the good in Paxton, devouring his magic and using it to build its strength. Paxton was in there because of Samara. She was certain of it—despite him saying he brought unfavorable attention to himself because of his curiosity and his research. The disturbing memories brought back with them the way Kaine had turned against her and tried to use his power of charm, accentuated through touch, to persuade her to tell him her secrets. She wondered if she would be in so much trouble if she hadn't been involved with him in the first place.

Crackling leaves and the snap of twigs pulled Samara from her thoughts as she sprang to her feet, nocked an arrow, and pointed it over Forgrac's shoulder. She expelled a breath, ready to release the bowstring until Silut's little form barged into the open. He halted with wide eyes when he spotted Samara.

He lifted his hands in the air. "It's only me. Sorry if I startled ya. Nature called." He looked sheepish. "Not much I can do about that. I was on me way back to continue the night watch."

Slowly, she lowered her arrow. "You're the one on night watch?"

Silut nodded. "Yep. But I couldn't wait any longer, if you know what I mean."

Samara screwed up her nose, indeed understanding. "I didn't think they would make the new person be on night watch."

He continued toward her. "I volunteered," he said proudly. "It was the least I could do after what you all have done for me."

Frowning, Samara nodded and sat on the log. "That's nice you offered to help."

"Of course." He sat next to Forgrac's sleeping form, studying him. "He looks so peaceful. That's why I left him here when I took over. Also, he looks like he needs the rest."

Samara stretched her legs out in front of her, not planning on going back to sleep. She was too worried about Ulrieg.

A snap to the left startled her, and she twisted to investigate, her eyes meeting the black beady eyes of a fox. Her shoulders stiffened, unsure if she had locked eyes with Ginger, Kaine's familiar, or a creature of the wild.

The fox froze, imitating a statue. Only its ears twisted, picking up any surrounding sounds. Samara scanned the trees, fear gripping her heart with the thought of Kaine lurking in the darkness of the thin forest. The fox's nose twitched, rising slightly, investigating the scent in the air. Her gut swirled, and bile rose in her throat. The fox seemed too used to humans to not be a familiar.

"Ginger?" Samara asked softly.

The fox bared her teeth, and her ears flattened before she turned away, trotting back toward the village.

Cold dread rippled down Samara's spine. That fox had a distinct way of sticking its nose into Samara's business and discovering her most treasured secrets. She had no idea how the fox had found them, but it wouldn't be good news for their traveling group.

*Ulrieg?* Samara tried again to call to her dragon and trusted familiar. She received no answer. They must be far from the village if he couldn't hear her. Hopefully, that meant it would take some time before Ginger could return to the village and tell Kaine where they were. It might give them enough time to escape.

"What's wrong?" Silut asked.

"It's that meddlesome familiar again," Samara hissed.

"The fox?" A deep frown creased his face.

"Yes. That sneaky creature is trouble itself." Rising to her feet, she shook Forgrac lightly. "Forgrac, wake up!"

The dwarf tossed and rubbed his nose roughly as he snorted his displeasure at being woken.

"Forgrac." Samara shook him again when he didn't open his eyes.

One eye slitted open. "What is it?" He suddenly sat bolt upright, eyes wide and scanning the surroundings. "Sorry, love. I fell asleep while on duty. Is everything all right?"

Samara placed a calming hand on his shoulder. "We're all safe for now. Silut took over. But I'm afraid Ginger's discovered us. We need to move."

After casting Silut a confused side glance, he climbed to his feet, stretching to his full height and attempting to rub the sleep from his eyes as he scanned the area. "Where is she?"

"She left, but I wouldn't be surprised if she's gone to tell Kaine we're here." Samara rubbed her temples.

Forgrac's eyebrows shot up. "Did she recognize ya?"

She nodded. "Yes, I'm pretty certain. I said her name, and she instantly looked disgruntled."

"I thought we went far enough away. The road we took certainly made it seem a long way, but now that I think of it, it probably ain't that far for a fox to cut through the forest." He rubbed his hands down his pants, his eyes taking in the carriages, the horses tied to a nearby tree, and the mountain range lining one side. "I know of a place we might be able to escape, but we won't be able to take the carriages and horses." He lowered his voice for her ears only. "Where's Ulrieg?"

Her eyes cast to the sky as if looking for the dragon before matching Forgrac's voice level. "I don't know. I've called him a couple of times, but I haven't received an answer. He might be out of range."

Forgrac peered over his shoulder at Silut as if seeing if he'd heard what they'd said. When he appeared unaware, Forgrac turned back to Samara. "Do ya think the others would be safe if we left? I'd hate to lose all our equipment if someone found it while we were gone."

"Maybe. Kaine should only be after us, so he might not do anything to them." Samara looked from one carriage to the other as though picturing the people inside. She eyed Silut, knowing he hadn't asked for the coterie's unwanted attention. She worried her cheek. "Though, I don't really know Kaine like I thought. It might be best if they all came with us."

"We betta wake them then." Forgrac waddled to the wagon with the men and set to work waking them as Samara concentrated on the female carriage, disturbing Vassuda's soft snore. After she filled them in, the females climbed out individually over the wagon's edge. Each one reluctantly rubbed the sleep from their eyes.

Forgrac met them near the fire, standing beside a confused and worried-looking Silut.

"What's the plan?" Skorrig sat on the large stone near the fire, warming his hands against the flames, sleep still evident on his face.

Forgrac surveyed the edge of the forest for a sign of Kaine or Ginger. "I'll check the edge of these mountains. I wouldn't be surprised if a small cave opens into the side. If Kaine comes for us, we dwarves should be much more adaptable to making our way through the mountain than humans. Even if I've been away for a long time, I'm still a dwarf at heart."

Dorabrona kicked some dirt over the edge of the flames, careful not to catch her nightgown on fire. "Sounds like a plan."

With Forgrac leading the way, they headed toward the mountainside, their pace fast for a group of people with short legs.

Samara had only been in the cave entrance at Forgrac's village, and the main meeting section was often carved bigger to allow for any larger folk who might be visiting. The tunnels she had seen leading to their private rooms were often carved to suit the dwarves, hindering unwanted visitors from passing through. Following the short beings through tunnels made for them would be interesting. She hoped she wouldn't have too much trouble fitting through. She gazed back toward the camp, spotting a lagging figure faintly outlined by the fire's embers that struggled to stay alight after being doused with dirt. It seemed one of the dwarves was struggling to keep up. She squinted and made out Skorrig's down-turned mouth, his eyes cast in darkness, giving him a sense of despair as he limped behind them.

"Forgrac!" she called. "Skorrig has fallen behind."

Quickly, Forgrac filed to the back of the group. "Skorrig, what is it?" He noticed Skorrig struggling to move his leg forward. "Aye. I keep forgettin' about how badly that minin' accident messed up ya leg. Can we help ya keep up?"

Skorrig released a disappointed breath and shook his head before waving a dismissive hand at him. "Nah! Ya go ahead. Me injured leg ain't gonna keep up with ya lot. I'm afraid that me long walkin' days are over. I'll stay back and watch the wagons."

"But we can't just leave ya here. I can't have ya sittin' all alone when trouble is undoubtedly headin' this way," Forgrac squeaked.

"I'll stay hidden behind the bush or somewhere they won't look." Skorrig shrugged.

"But the fox will be able to sniff ya out," Forgrac protested.

"If they're after the likes of ya, Samara, and

Ulrieg, then they ain't gonna follow me scent." He waved a dismissive hand at them again, his motion urgent. "Go! I ain't gonna be the reason ya get caught."

Forgrac placed a gentle hand on Skorrig's shoulder. "Stay safe." Then he returned to the front of the group and led them toward the mountainside.

# CHAPTER SIXTEEN

Moon high in the sky, Samara craned her neck searching for a sign of Ulrieg, worry gnawing at her stomach. He still hadn't answered her call. She hoped Kaine and Ginger hadn't found him. Her ex had probably honed his skills since she last saw him, and she knew from experience he wasn't afraid to use them.

Forgrac led them along the mountainside. All the dwarves' eyes stayed trained to the rocky crevices—using their expertise to search for an opening. They found a large crevice dug into the side, and the group followed the natural lining cutting into the mountain, removing them from the breeze that whipped along the rocky slope.

"I found one." Vassuda crouched, her head stuck into a hole that rose up to her shoulders.

Samara cringed. If that was how they entered the mountainside, then she would have to crawl into the entrance. She hoped that once they entered, the tunnel would open to a height that enabled her to stand. Each dwarf filed in after Vassuda, leaving Samara and Forgrac to be last. Uncertainty washing over her, Samara glanced over her shoulder.

"Go on, love. I'll be right behind ya." Forgrac placed a gentle hand on her upper back.

Still unsure, Samara yanked up her skirt to move it out of the way then shifted her quiver to her front before dropping to all fours, the stones digging into her knees and palms. She edged her way into the hole, the rocks already causing her knees to ache. Apprehension wrapped its cold embrace around her with the darkness. "How do you see in here?" she called back to Forgrac.

"Our eyes have adjusted over the generations. I wouldn't call it night vision, but we're not completely blind when it comes to weaving through dark caves."

Samara inched forward, skinning her knee on a rough rock. She groaned. She hadn't even made it completely inside the tunnel yet.

"Are ya all right, love?"

*Samara!* Ulrieg's voice was panicked.

*Ulrieg?* She shifted upright and knocked her head

on the ceiling of the tunnel. "Ow!" She rubbed the spot and edged her way backward. "I'm coming out," she called to Forgrac. "Ulrieg just called me."

*Where are you? I can't see you.* His voice rose. *Where are the rest of our group?*

*We're at the mountainside. We left our area in case Kaine came by. Ginger paid us a visit earlier.*

*Dragon moon! That's a relief for the rest of you. I was worried Kaine had done something to all of you. But it doesn't look great for Skorrig.*

Samara froze. *What do you mean?*

Watching her expression, Forgrac's face filled with worry. "What's goin' on?"

*Kaine and Ginger are at our campsite, and Skorrig is with them. It looks like Kaine's about to torture him for information.*

Samara held up a finger to Forgrac, indicating for him to wait. *But Kaine doesn't need to torture people to get information.* All feeling left Samara's face. Kaine must've fallen further under the coterie's influence.

*I guess he's acquired a taste for inflicting pain because I'm certain I'm not wrong.*

Wide eyed, she glanced at Forgrac. "Skorrig is in danger. Kaine has him, and Ulrieg said it looks like he's about to be tortured for information."

Forgrac's eyes widened. "Then we have to go back."

Samara shook her head. "No, I have to go back. You stay here." She controlled her face, making sure he didn't see the terror she felt over facing a coterie member again. The practice she had done to keep her magic strong felt inadequate compared to the continued advanced training the coterie members would receive. Sucking in a breath, she shifted away from the cave.

"I'm still comin' with ya." Forgrac clasped her wrist to stop her before calling into the mountainside. "Ya lot keep in there. Samara and me are headin' back to the camp. We're gonna check on Skorrig."

"Be careful!" Vassuda's voice echoed through the tunnel.

"Always, me love." Forgrac abruptly turned and traveled with Samara down the slight incline that merged with the mountain.

They weaved through the trees, ensuring they kept themselves obscured behind them as they walked the several hundred yards toward the camp. Samara's mind whirled with the spells she knew, especially ones that Devi had taught her in defense arts. She hoped it would be enough.

Her dress caught on some low-growing shrubs, and she gently pulled it free, trying to keep the leaves from rustling.

*There you are.* The branches swayed above her, and when she looked up, nothing was visibly sitting on the branch. *Nothing like sending your bonded into a panic.* The irony shone through in his voice. *It would've been nice if you let me know you were safe before taking off.*

*Sorry. I did call you, but you didn't answer. So the feeling goes both ways.* She pushed her mouth to one side.

*Hmm. I must've been a little farther than I thought.*

*Where were you?*

*I'll explain later. First, we need to help Skorrig.*

A noise not too far away made Samara pause. She indicated to Forgrac to be cautious then eased her head around the side of a tree. Small embers still burned dully in the firepit, and only a couple of feet away, Skorrig was trapped between Ginger and Kaine. The dull flame illuminating Skorrig's back. The side view of Kaine's chiseled face revealed a sneer, but the expression didn't succeed in marring his handsomeness.

*It shouldn't be that way,* Samara thought. His inner ugliness should be expressed on the outside. It didn't seem fair that someone so cruel at heart could look so handsome on the outside, when ones like Paxton were so attractive on the inside, yet the outside was dulled by plainness.

Kaine's brilliant-blue hair looked muddy under the firelight as he inched toward Skorrig. "You know. I could easily extract the information I want with a simple touch."

Skorrig stepped back, stumbling over his bad leg, barely keeping upright. He had a fresh ugly red cut on his right cheek.

"But that would be too easy and too painless." The sorcerer whipped his second knife from behind his back. "I'd rather give these a little practice. It's been way too long since they've drawn traitorous blood." He inched closer, and the dwarf stepped back again. "You're traitorous, aren't you?"

Skorrig shook his head. "N-n-no."

"Oh, but you are. Ginger said that this is the camp of a traitorous coterie member and a deceiving dwarf. Anyone in their presence is a traitor to the Sacred Flame—and me—and must pay the price."

He slashed at the dwarf, slicing open a gash along the arm Skorrig raised to protect himself.

The dwarf cried out, clasping his wound.

*Grrr. I'll rip him to shreds,* Ulrieg cried as the branches above Samara bounced and lifted.

*Ulrieg! Come back!* Samara cried.

Instead, Kaine shrieked in pain, and two bloody talon marks appeared along his back. "Where are you, dragon?" He searched the sky then flung out his hands. *"Petra!"*

Samara gritted her teeth, listening hard for a thud, to see if Kaine's stunning spell hit Ulrieg. No thud came, and she released her breath.

Kaine shrieked. "Hiding in your invisible form again, like the coward you are, dragon. Why don't you show yourself and fight with honor?"

*I'll show you coward!* More bloody gashes appeared on Kaine's arm, causing him to drop a knife. *Just because I don't have magic doesn't make me stupid.*

A gust of breeze from Ulrieg's wings pushed Kaine, and the sorcerer spun, thrusting his hands in that direction. *"Petra!"*

Branches of a tree snapped from an invisible force plummeting to the ground, and a thump reverberated through the darkness.

Samara held in a scream and stepped out from behind a tree. She drew an arrow from her quiver. *"Manictium,"* she whispered, spelling it as she nocked it, then she released it from her bow. Moments later, a satisfactory thunk sounded as it embedded into Kaine's backside. Instantly, Kaine's handsome face distorted, and random sentences spilled from his mouth as his body twitched.

With Forgrac struggling to keep up, Samara ran

down the slope heading for the spot she had seen the branches snap, finding Ulrieg visible and lying still. If not for the soft, warm breath from his nose that she felt on the back of her hand, she would have thought he was dead. Her relief was pushed away the second Forgrac called out to her, panicked.

"Samara!"

Whirling, she found Forgrac pinned against a tree trunk. Ginger, teeth exposed, was poised to strike. Reaching for an arrow from her quiver, she charmed it, whispering *"Petra,"* and fired it into the fox's hind leg. The fox yowled in pain and fell to the ground, unmoving.

Forgrac flinched then breathed a sigh of relief as he joined Samara. "How is he?" He squatted next to Ulrieg.

"He'll be fine once I get rid of this spell. I wish I had learned more before leaving the coterie. I have a feeling I'll need the information, not only now but also in the future." She stroked a hand over the side of Ulrieg's face, watching the dragon's wide eyes soften, and the dragon sighed contentedly. Seeing the positive reaction, she continued to stroke him with a tentative hand. If nothing else, she would make him feel loved until she worked out how to release him from the spell.

It was disruptive having Kaine wandering

around, shouting random sentences, but at the same time, it was one way to keep an eye on him. It was reassuring to know that he hadn't managed to knock the arrow out and regain his normal mentality. Until Ulrieg was released from the spell, she needed Kaine and Ginger to be preoccupied.

She racked her brain, determined to remember the different spells Devi taught them during her classes. The first one that came to mind, she attempted. *"Mendamora."* She waited. She didn't have too much hope for it, as it was a healing spell for minor injuries, but it was worth a try. Nothing happened. She tried the next, *"Childora."* Again, the calming spell wasn't what she thought would work, though Ulrieg's eyes calmed, even when she didn't stroke his face. She hoped the next one would work, as she was running out of spells she knew. *"Liborte."* That would release someone from being lifted up in the air against their will or manhandled.

Ulrieg stirred, his legs kicking out to the side before he rolled and stood, shaking himself off. *About time! That was scary. I hate being under their spells.* He shivered then glanced at Ginger, who remained still. Kaine continued to stomp noisily around the forest floor, the moonlight illuminating his distorted face. *Well that serves them right. Let's get out of here before they come to their senses.*

A twig snapped behind them, and Samara reached for an arrow.

172

# CHAPTER SEVENTEEN

"Got you!" The man's knee dug deeper into Emelyne's back, pinning her down.

"Why are ya doin' this?" Emelyne croaked, struggling to talk with her lungs squashed.

He huffed. "I have people looking for someone with markings like yours. If you turn out to be the one they want, it'll be a big payday for us."

"That's ludicrous!" she cried. "Ya mistaken!"

"That's a risk I'm willing to take." The man shifted his weight to bare down on her.

Emelyne struggled. All of her training with swords and the muscle she had built from blacksmithing made her strong for a female. Still, she didn't know how to get herself out of her situation, especially when the men were well-built brutes and she was pressed flat against the ground on her stomach. "Monut!" she yelled, not caring if the men thought she was crazy.

One arm was yanked behind her back, and she struggled as they pulled the other to meet it, clasping her firmly around the wrists.

"Monut!" she called again, lifting her head off the ground and searching the darkness around her. Twigs and dried leaves clung to her cheek, and she ignored them, determined to find him. The dragon said he would remain close, but she couldn't see or hear him anywhere.

"Give me a something to secure her with!" the man pinning her down yelled at the other.

The companion yanked loose the rope around his waist and squatted beside the larger man, helping to secure her. He pressed the rope to her wrists, wrapping it around them several times.

No matter how much she struggled, she couldn't knock the men aside. She attempted to pull her hands apart, only to be rewarded with the sting of rope burn. "Mon—"

Her call was interrupted by a cry as the man on top of her was yanked away with the force of a cannon and thrown through the trees. He crashed through the branches for several moments before finally coming to a stop. A large thump sounded beside Emelyne, and she glanced up to see a large claw planted near her shoulder as the companion was lifted from the ground and thrown in the opposite direction from the first.

*Are you all right?* Monut's hot breath washed over Emelyne's back as she fumbled to stand without the use of her arms.

"Yes, thanks." Struggling to catch her breath, she brushed her cheek on her shoulder, removing the twigs and dried leaves from her face before wrestling with her restraints.

*Turn around. I'll see if I can get that for you.*

Emelyne shifted so her back faced the dragon, and he dragged a talon against her rope, sawing until the restraint thunked to the ground. She rubbed her wrists. They ached from her attempts to escape, and she wouldn't be surprised if the rope had left a mark. "Thanks again. I wish I knew what that was all about. Who would have thought that grabbin' a quick meal at the tavern would cause so much fuss?"

*You weren't in there long. I barely managed to find a decent meal and had to swallow it fast when I heard you call. Do you know why they restrained you?*

She shook her head and rubbed her hand over the mark she couldn't see in the darkness. "They did seem strangely interested in this birthmark." She held it out for Monut to see.

The dragon lowered his head, its outline barely visible in the darkness, as warm breath washed over her hand. *Ah, yes. This is the mark that has your parents worried. I apologize. I shouldn't have brought you out and put you in danger like this. It was very unwise of me.*

Emelyne frowned. "Don't apologize. We were both hungry, an' I wouldn't mind meetin' more humans. Though, less like those two."

*Hmmm.* Monut growled. *I was afraid you would say that. Yes, we are both here because we were hungry, but I didn't know you were in danger until it was too late. This is unacceptable.* Under the dull light of the moon, his eyes sank into darkness as his brow furrowed. *To avoid this happening again, I offer you my bond.*

Emelyne's brow mimicked the dragon's. "What? I don't know what that means, but in any case, ya don't owe me anythin'."

*In truth, I've grown rather fond of you, and it would be an honor to be bonded with you, not just because I didn't know you were in danger.*

She placed a hand on the soft part of his snout, the dragon's natural warmth instantly heating her body. "That's really sweet. I like ya a lot too."

*Then I offer you the bond of a closer friendship.*

Emelyne cupped his nose in her hands and

rested her forehead against his snout. "That is honestly so sweet an offer I'd be stupid to not accept."

*Then it is done.* A deep warmth radiated through her forehead, heat rushing to her birthmark hand and back through her palm into his nose.

She pulled back, eyes wide. "What jus' happened?"

*That was the bond. Soon you'll be able to speak to me through your mind.*

Emelyne didn't understand exactly what that meant, but her heart warmed, especially when thinking about Monut. It was like their souls were connected. She stroked his snout. "It feels good."

*Ah, ha. I have not found a human like you before. You're the first one I've bonded with.*

"Then I feel privileged." Emelyne still didn't understand the extent of what had happened, but she had known and trusted Monut for most of her life. Her adoptive parents had introduced her to him when she was young, in case they had felt she was threatened.

*First, I'll teach you to speak directly to me through the bond.*

"A lesson already? That was quick," Emelyne jested.

*An important lesson.* He focused on her. *Now, try to*

*think something in your mind. Imagine you are saying it to me, but keep your mouth shut.*

*I wish I had magic so I could fight the coterie members, especially if they tried to hurt ya.*

Monut's eyes widened. *That was really good, but think it louder, and put more energy into it. I could barely hear it.*

Emelyne focused hard, keeping her eyes on Monut. *I mean it. It doesn't seem right that a dragon ya size an' might could be defeated by them just because they have magic.*

*You got it.* Pride filled his eyes. *I agree with you. It doesn't seem right.* Monut lowered to the ground and extended a wing. *Climb on.*

Careful not to walk on his membranes, she climbed up his wing and onto his back, sitting just before his wing joints and clasping onto his neck. "What's so bad about me wanting to spend more time with humans?"

*Nothing. Except for the danger it can put you in, like tonight.* Wings unfurled, he launched into the air and stroked their enormous length, lifting her high into the sky.

The dull light of the tavern disappeared into the distance, and Emelyne flicked her braid over her shoulder as she faced forward. A cool breeze brushed against her face, sweeping the loose dark strands of hair back from her cheeks. She smiled, taking a deep breath as the troubled thoughts of the night left her. "I could get used to this." As soon as the words were out, she wondered if they sounded arrogant. "I'm sorry. Is that rude? Because I only meant this is fun, not that I want to control ya an' expect ya to take me everywhere."

Monut chuckled. *Relax. It's not how the bond works. Many years ago, it was common for a dragon of my size to allow a human or elf to ride on their back. It was how many battles were fought.*

"Even against the members of the Sacred Flame coterie?"

*Especially against the coterie or their minions.*

Emelyne's mind spun. In one night, her world had expanded immensely. "Ya know, not everyone in that tavern were like those men. The bartender was nice and seemed to want to protect me from whatever those men were trying to do. Maybe there are a lot more people like him."

*Maybe. Only time will tell.* Monut banked and headed for the mountainside encasing the Merciless Sanctuary.

A strange whirring sound buzzed through Emelyne's mind as the dragon fell silent. She frowned then broke into a smile. "I know this whole bondin' thing is new to me, but I get the sense ya not tellin' me somethin'."

A deep rumble echoed through her mind. *Hmmm. Perhaps I bonded with you too soon.*

"What? Nah." Emelyne shook her head. "Am I wrong?"

*It is not that. You are quite perceptive.* He beat his wings in long steady strokes before gliding toward the desolate plain. *It pains me to say that, in this case, I'm not at liberty to tell you. It is something you will find out soon, I hope. For I don't want to keep things from my bonded. It is a dragon's shame to do so.* He tilted a wing and corrected course toward the crevice where the other dragons met. *I hope you can forgive me in this one instance. I believe you will find out at the right time.*

Her brows pushed together. "That's rather cryptic."

*I apologize. A lot is resting on this secret being kept.* He landed near several dragons. It seemed that most had returned from their hunt and were settling in for the night. The baby playfully skittered between the resting adults.

She sighed. "All right. If that's the way it has to be, I'll let ya off… this time. Ya have been trustworthy in the past, even without a bond."

He held out his wing, and she climbed down his

side. Her boots thumped as they landed on the desolate ground.

The little dragon raced up and nudged her side.

She laughed and wrapped an arm around his neck. "I guess I can forgive ya for stealin' me dinner." He made a chirping sound and ran back to his mother, snuggling in by her side.

Emelyne turned to Monut. "Don't ya usually fly around at night?"

*Normally, many of us would take the opportunity to fly under the cover of darkness, but tonight we have been warned that the coterie member and his familiar are near. It isn't worth the risk to be out there longer. As you can see, most of the dragons have already returned from their hunt.* Monut circled on the spot before making himself comfortable on the ground. *No. Tonight we have risked enough by going out to hunt. We will spend the rest of the time tucked within this crevice. The power of the coterie is too great. Even a large dragon like me can be overcome by their magic.*

As Emelyne eyed the dragons settled within their area, a cool breeze washed over her. It was hard to believe that such large, majestic creatures could be overpowered. A shiver passed over her from the cold and the thought. The coterie must really be something to contend with.

Monut stretched then coiled into a tight circle.

*Come. You are cold. Lie within my boundaries.* He indicated the inner curve of his body. *I can keep you warm and will protect you from any threats for the night.*

Warmth washed through Emelyne. She could get used to her bonded dragon offering her refuge. She stepped between his large legs and lay on the ground, resting her head on his front talons. As soon as she settled, her world was encased by a large membranous wing, wrapping her in a warm cocoon.

Tension coursing through Samara's veins, she jumped to her feet, ready to attack, only to find the newest member of their group standing behind her, eyeing the visible Ulrieg.

"Silut! You startled me!" She pressed a hand to her heart, unconsciously shifting to block his view of Ulrieg. "Where did you come from? Weren't you with the others?"

Ignoring her questions, the dwarf moved to the side to see past Samara. "Is that a dragon? I ain't seen the likes of them. I heard there may be a few in hidin', but I ain't seen one for meself." He cocked an eyebrow.

It was too late. The damage had already been done, and Samara's shoulders caved. She moved aside, exposing Ulrieg. "Yes, this is a dragon called Ulrieg."

"He looks vicious." Silut stayed carefully out of reach.

*Nah! I'm cute and cuddly with super-soft horns. Pfft! People these days!* Ulrieg shook his head.

Ulrieg's speech stunned the words right out of Silut's open mouth.

Samara squatted beside the dragon. "He's only vicious with sarcasm—unless you threaten someone he cares about."

Silut's face relaxed slightly, though his eyes remained wary. "Ya seem kinda attached to him."

"I am, especially at the heart." She placed a hand on Ulrieg's shoulder, avoiding the many spikes.

With a puzzled look, Silut turned his attention to Kaine, who thrashed around, clearly uncomfortable with whatever horror he was living in his mind. "What did you do to him?"

"I've placed him in a madness spell until we can get away. He had intentions of harming our group, especially us three. I've also stunned his familiar." With a tilt of her head, Samara indicated the prostrate fox not far from Forgrac.

Forgrac nudged Ginger with his foot, and she didn't move. "It was either them or us. I know which one I'd prefer. Ya know from experience how horrible they can be to ya."

Silut nodded a grim acknowledgment. "Yes, I do. They are ruthless when they want to be." The color seeped from his face. "What's the plan now?"

*We must get moving,* Ulrieg said as they started toward the carriages.

Forgrac cast a sidelong glance at Ginger passed out under the tree. "We'll have to move the carriages before Kaine and Ginger return to normal. Did ya have any luck at the village findin' the human?" He looked at Ulrieg.

"What human's this?" Silut attempted to keep up with Forgrac and the dragon.

Ulrieg paused, his height smaller than the dwarf's, though his vast array of horns and red eyes made him look fierce. *One that is in danger from the coterie,* he answered, keeping strangely cryptic, before he addressed Forgrac. *No. There was no sign of the human. I got a strange sense coming from the other side of the mountain. I couldn't investigate because I was trying to work out where Kaine and Ginger had gone. It's a good thing I came back.*

"Yes, it is. I'm sure Skorrig will be very grateful." Forgrac fell in line with the dragon. "Do ya think it's safe for us to go to the village?"

A cloud of steam shot out of Ulrieg's nose.

*That's a huge risk. I don't think Kaine's business is finished there. It's possible he was distracted by our arrival.* A dark shadow passed over them, and the dragon paused, his eyes darting to the sky. *What was that?*

"What was what?" Forgrac craned his neck to glance up.

Samara stood next to Ulrieg and tried to follow his gaze. Other than a few puffy white clouds illuminated by the almost full moon, she couldn't see anything.

*Something passed in front of the moon. It seemed enormous. I don't know how you missed it.*

"I ain't see anythin'." Silut craned his neck.

"It was probably a cloud," Forgrac mumbled.

*Honestly! Don't you think I would know the difference?* Ulrieg narrowed his gaze on the actor.

Forgrac threw up his hands. "Now there's the snarky dragon we know and love." He chuckled. "All right, all right. Keep ya talons on. I get that if anyone should know, it'd be ya."

"I can't see anything, Ulrieg." Samara spun on the spot, scanning the sky.

The horns on his forehead bunched as he scowled. *It was quick. I think it's gone now. I don't know what it was, but my gut tells me I should investigate. I think it has something to do with what I felt at the village.*

The dragon turned invisible, disappearing from their sight.

Silut stopped in his tracks. "Where did he go?"

*The same place I've been the whole time you've been with us.*

The dwarf frowned at Ulrieg's snarky reply.

"Do you want us to do anything, Ulrieg?" Samara asked.

*How are your mountain-climbing skills?*

Eyeing the jagged incline, Samara grimaced. "More like rock-climbing skills. That's pretty high and steep."

*Then if you can stop Kaine and Ginger from going into the village for a day or two, it's probably best if you leave the rest of the dwarves in the mountainside and head to the village to see if you can find out more. I'll look for you there when I figure out what's drawing my attention.*

Samara worried her lip. "What should we do about them? I don't want to leave Kaine wandering around like that."

"Why not?" Forgrac grunted. "He wouldn't think twice about leaving you like that, or worse." Placing his hands on his hips, he turned to assess the sorcerer and his familiar then huffed. "Maybe this will do it." He wandered to the men's carriage and pulled out a long coil of rope, looping it over his head and across his body. "Give me a hand, would ya?" He addressed Silut then grabbed Kaine's arm as the raving sorcerer tried to pass him.

The second dwarf grabbed Kain's other arm.

"Let's press him against that tree over there." Forgrac nodded to a tree with a trunk bigger than Kaine's waist.

Once Kaine's back met the tree trunk, facing away from any direction they might take, Forgrac set to work securing the sorcerer's hands behind the tree and tightening his waist against the trunk with the rope. He then wrapped a piece of cloth around Kaine's mouth. "There. That'll stop him from usin' any spells to get him outa this mess." He then yanked the arrow out of Kaine's backside.

All consciousness returned to the sorcerer within moments, his blue eyes suddenly registering what was going on around him, and his brow creased in a frown. He tried to speak, but his words came out muffled around the cloth in his mouth.

"Good! That'll keep ya busy while we get away." Forgrac stood in front of him, grinning. "Ya so lucky that Samara has a bigga heart than you an' me. I would have left ya wanderin' in ya tortured state."

Kaine's frown didn't lift as Forgrac, Silut, and Samara returned to the carriages and helped Skorrig into the back.

"I'll go get the other dwarves." Silut wiped his hands on his pants.

"Are ya sure?" Forgrac asked.

Silut nodded. "I'll check that they're all right while you lot do whatever ya need to do."

Samara climbed up to the driving seat with Forgrac as he steered the horses to the village of Bhalwahrum. The carriage rattled and swayed along the dirt road.

Forgrac peered back at the spot they had tied the sorcerer. "At least with Kaine secured, we should be safe to head to the village for a while. Hopefully, us leavin' the others in the mountain will protect them from any danger. I'd rather it be jus' us. I'd hate to put Vassuda in danger. That would haunt me for the rest of me life."

The sun slowly rose in the east, bathing the land in a golden glow when they turned the corner in the road. Weariness washed over Samara as she took in the warm light shining on the walls of the few cottages and the inn above the alehouse, defining the area before the entrance to the dwarves' mountain home.

A few dwarves wandered the street, slowly preparing for the day's work, ready for any visitors calling in to trade or purchase goods.

Forgrac breathed in deeply, letting out a

contented sigh. "How I love mornin's like this at me village. As much as I like to travel with the actin' group, this is the part I missed most. I like the fresh outdoor air, not the dank, dark mountain walls of our home."

Samara rubbed her arms, trying to ease her goose bumps. "After trying to crawl through the tiny tunnel, that is something I can understand. Though, I've always preferred the fresh air and open spaces."

They rolled up to the front of the alehouse and secured the horses to a post, helping Skorrig out of the back before pushing through the large double door. Other than the barkeep, the place was empty, the stale stench of ale overwhelming. Light cracked through the opaque glass windows, highlighting the dust floating through the air. Skorrig's limping gait drummed on the wooden floor.

The barkeep wiped a table with a dry cloth, the short, stocky dwarf's skirt swaying with her aggressive movements. A long ginger braid fell over one shoulder, dusting the top of the table. "Can I help ya?" She rubbed her fluff-covered jawline with a sleeve, her eyes wary as she took in Samara's brilliant-pink hair. "Are ya with that other coterie member? 'Cause he was supposed to pay me husband for the extra night of rentin' the room, but it seems he skipped town, leavin' us out of pocket."

She swept one fist onto her hip, holding the other hand out. "If so, I'd appreciate it if ya pay for what ya colleague owes me."

Samara frowned. "No, we're not with the coterie. If anything, we're trying to avoid them."

The woman huffed, flicked her long braid behind her back, and placed her second hand on her hip. "That'd be right! No one is with the coterie when money is due."

Samara pulled out a few hard-earned coins and placed them in front of the lady, hoping to create some goodwill. "Does this help?"

The woman eyed the coin then snatched it up, tucking it into a purse hanging around her waist. "It'll do." She hurried over to the fire burning behind the bar and stirred the pot.

The smell of freshly made porridge filled Samara's nose, making both their stomachs rumble noisily.

Forgrac sniffed deeply. "Any chance that the coin covers the cost of some breakfast also? We've had kinda a rough night."

Wiping her hands on her apron, she huffed defeat. "All right. Take a seat." She served three bowls of porridge and placed them on the bar.

They wasted no time occupying the stools and dug into the food.

The warmth of the porridge filled Samara's stomach, warming the chill from her bones. "Thank you. This is delicious."

"It ain't hard to make. Ya probably coulda made it from the contents of ya carriage." The woman's skirt swept over the floor as she went back to wiping off tables with the dry cloth.

Skorrig slurped a spoonful of porridge and chuckled. "Ya wouldn't say that if ya had tasted Samara's cookin'."

Samara chuckled and nodded. "True. I'm not the best cook. But Forgrac is spectacular."

They gulped down several spoonfuls of porridge as the dwarven woman continued to clean up the mess left from the night before.

"Busy night, last night?" Forgrac asked between bites.

"It's oft busy nights round here. The miners are big drinkers. Always been that way in this village. They work all day swingin' that pick an' wash down the dirt for the rest of the night." She shook her head. "Not even the coterie sorcerer killin' one of our villagers could stop this lot from drinkin'." She eyed Samara as though watching for her reaction.

Samara cringed. "I'm so sorry. What a terrible thing to do." She attempted to ignore the woman's stares and hoped Forgrac or Skorrig would spark up more conversation. Being dwarves, they would probably have more luck getting information out of her.

Swallowing his mouthful, Forgrac dropped his spoon into his bowl. "That's terrible. Was he provoked?"

The woman shook her head. "The girl was only standin' in his way for a wee moment. It was uncalled for."

Forgrac nodded. "That it was." He wiped his mustache with his forearm. "What was the sorcerer here for?"

"He says he was after a new blade for his throwin' knives he carries on his back." She dropped the cloth behind the counter, poured three tankards, and placed them in front of the trio before picking up the straw broom propped in the corner behind the bar.

"Thanks." Forgrac took a sip from the tankard near him. "An' do ya think that's all he was here for?"

"That wouldn't be surprisin'. The metal mined from our mountain is good quality, known throughout the land. Not only that, our blacksmith, Lozzeak, an' his daughter are known for their quality work round here."

Nodding, Forgrac swallowed his mouthful. "Ah, yup. I've heard of him. I didn't know he was from round here or that he had a daughter." He took another swig of his ale and let out a loud, contented sigh. "That's good brew."

The barkeep swept the dust out the door and placed the broom back in the corner before washing up a few missed tankards from the night before.

"Tell me, I've heard a rumor that there's a human livin' in these parts. Have ya seen her?" Eyes peering curiously over his tankard, Forgrac took another sip.

The barkeep pretended to be busy scrubbing around the basin as her eyes flicked up to Samara, then to her hair, before she straightened her face and set back to work. "Don't know of any human round here. Funny how these rumors can fly an' twist the truth. Mayhap they got confused with a visitin' human. We get a fair few, ya know, especially to visit the blacksmith. Maybe it was a regular visitin' human." She glanced quickly at Forgrac, her eyes uncertain, as though seeing if her lie was accepted as truth.

"Ain't that the truth?" Forgrac gave Samara a knowing grin before leaning back and stretching his arms and legs. "Sounds like we're gonna have to have a little look round this famous village an' see for ourselves the quality work this blacksmith does."

The barkeep's eyes widened for a split second before she straightened to look impassive. "I'm afraid he ain't open this early. It could be a long wait."

"That's all right. We can wait." Forgrac rested his chin on his hand, looking pleased with himself.

*Samara, are you in the village?* Ulrieg's voice pulled her attention away from the barkeep.

*Yes, I'm in the alehouse at the moment.*

*Good. I have something I need to tell you. You'll never guess what I found.*

# CHAPTER NINETEEN

Emelyne stayed with the dragons a couple more nights, eating the food her ma prepared for her. The days were scorching, drenching her with sweat even under the protection of Monut's wing. No matter how much water she drank, it was never enough. Thankfully, the nights passed by without incident. She even managed to save her meals from the baby dragon.

At the start of a new morning, way before the sun burned the desolate land, Emelyne's mother finally brought news that the coterie member had disappeared. Together, in the dark, they went back to her village with Monut accompanying them to the entrance of the mountain for protection. She wasted no time in getting back to the workshop to help her pa.

When Emelyne left Monut, a strange ache filled her heart. The feeling was hard for her to grasp, as it brought with it a sadness for returning to her adoptive parents—an unusual experience. She loved her ma and pa and loved working with them. She thought that perhaps it might also be partly because she missed her friend, Thiznabo, and returning to the village without her would be terrible.

*Do not fret, my bonded. What you sense is normal when bonded separate, plus it's mixed with grief for your friend. I feel the separation too.* Monut's voice crossed their bond instantly, filling her with warmth.

*I promise I'll visit ya soon,* she communicated back —another thing that felt strange to her. Speaking that way felt like Monut read her thoughts, except for the extra effort required to focus on him and reply. She liked the warmth, the additional companionship that came with being bonded to him. It was a part of her made whole that she didn't know had been incomplete. In a few short hours, her life had taken on a surprising loss and enrichment.

Back in the blacksmith shop, she hummed as she hammered the metal she was molding, doing her best to not focus on the spot where Thiznabo had fallen. Her friend had been moved, and her parents said her body had been looked after.

The sun barely peeked over the trees of the

distant forest, slowly lighting the window to the east that they'd cracked a few inches to form a cross breeze with the open door. She always loved the early hours and the fresh crisp air that came with it. Though she had grown up with her main home in the cave, she never grew tired of the smell of trees and the sounds of the birds chirping in the distance. The early-morning crow of the rooster from the nearby farm amused her. She had heard that the humans always lived above ground, and she wondered if her human heritage was the cause of her love for the outdoors, when the people she grew up with often preferred the caves.

Beads of sweat formed on the back of her neck, and she wiped them away, catching sight of Lozzeak as he sleepily wandered into the workshop and splashed cold water from the bowl on the bench over his face.

"Mornin', Pa!" she called, halting her hammering for a moment.

Lozzeak grumbled, "Ya always too darn cheerful in the mornin's, love. I don't know how ya do it. The sun's too bright an' hot most of the time."

Emelyne wiped new beads of sweat off her face. "Ya work next to a furnace. What are ya talkin' 'bout the sun bein' too hot? Besides, this sun is mild compared to the Merciless Sanctuary."

He plastered his auburn hair back from his face, leaving traces of water through the front strands, and shook out his cheeks, causing weird sounds to exit his open mouth as they flapped against his teeth. After jumping on the spot and swinging his arms, he grabbed a small leather bag off the bench. "Here. Ya ma sent this for ya."

She took the bag and opened it, and the aroma of freshly baked bread wafted out. Her stomach growled. "Thanks, Pa." She sat on the stool near the bench in front of the window and set to work devouring her simple but tasty breakfast. Her ma always sent Emelyne freshly made bread in the morning. From what she'd been told, her ma used to cook for her birth parents.

A bright color caught her eye across the street. Worry washed through her that the sorcerer had come back to collect his new knife set. She glanced over to see a tall female—at least taller than a dwarf—walking up the road, dressed in a beige traveling dress with long sleeves and a rope tied around the waist. Emelyne couldn't quite see if her ears were pointed like the elves she had heard about or if they were rounded like a humans. Though, she could definitely see her brilliant-pink hair.

Her cheeks turned numb. "Pa?"

"Hm?" He looked up from inspecting his next project.

"Is it true that the only people with brilliant-colored hair are from that coterie ya told me 'bout?" Her eyes didn't leave the strange woman, who appeared to be searching for something.

"Yup. That's right. Why?"

"'Cause there's a woman over there that ain't a dwarf an' has brilliant hair."

He waddled over to her, a deep frown on his face. "Has she got an animal close by?"

Emelyne placed her bread on the bench and pressed forward to look on either side of the woman down the road. "I can't see one."

Suddenly, the woman crossed the road, heading directly for their blacksmith shop.

"Quick! Ya gotta get outa here," Lozzeak hissed.

"Won't she see me through the windows an' open door?" Emelyne cried. "Besides, she don't look that dangerous."

"Looks are deceivin' when it comes to magic users. Ya saw what happened to ya friend." He swatted a hand at the taller workbench more central to the shop. "Squat behind the bench. At least then she won't see ya from the window." He waved his hand rapidly, urging her to hurry, before charging out the door and slamming it shut behind him.

"Good day, miss. You're up extremely early. Can I help ya?" His voice was faint but intelligible through the closed door.

Emelyne froze, images of what happened to Thiznabo torturing her mind. Her father had done the same thing. Even though he told her to hide, she couldn't quell her anxiety, and she peeked through a slit in the open shutters. The young woman blinked and threaded a strand of hair over her ear, exposing a semi-angular tip. She didn't look much older than Emelyne, but it was always hard to tell when they had elven blood, even if it was mixed with human. She was quite attractive, with more petite facial features than Emelyne, and her expression held an innocence. It had to be a persona. The appearance went against everything she had heard about the Sacred Flame coterie. Though Emelyne still couldn't see her familiar, from what she had heard, they always had one.

The woman answered Lozzeak's question. "A friend of mine said I should see what is in your blacksmithing shop. They said I would find something of interest in there."

Lozzeak's shoulders were still, almost stiff, yet his voice carried all pleasantness. "Oh. That was nice of them to recommend me shop. But I'm afraid it ain't open yet. Ya see, we aren't prepared for new visitors at this time of mornin'. It's a right royal mess. Perhaps ya can call in later today."

Small frown lines creased the woman's forehead. "Oh. What time will it be open?"

He chuckled, sounding embarrassed, and tugged at one of his beard's braids. "Well, it should be ready for ya 'bout lunch. Ya see, it's in a state of disarray."

The young woman looked disappointed and almost like she didn't believe him. Though, unlike the male, she didn't seem annoyed or about to attack.

Lozzeak continued, as if trying to sweet-talk her. "If I had known that someone as important as a member of the coterie was in the village, I would have tidied up sooner."

The woman tugged at a strand of her hair, and she seemed to hesitate. She worried her bottom lip. "I'm not from the coterie. I left them not long ago— not long enough for my hair to change color."

He balked, looking hesitant about whether to believe her or not, then seemed to decide to play it safe. "I'm sorry. I can't open the shop for ya. Perhaps ya can call back later."

"All right. I will. I want to see your product. I've heard rumors of its quality in many villages I've visited." Mouth downturned, the young woman turned away, heading farther down the street.

After making sure she was committed to walking away, Lozzeak trekked back inside and locked the door behind him, breathing a sigh that sounded like relief. He peered over his shoulder at the woman then frowned.

"What is it, Pa?" Emelyne crept out of her hiding place and squatted behind him, peering out at the street.

A dwarf with a dark-brown beard cut straight and thick hair hurried after the woman.

"That's odd."

"What is?" She shifted to get a better view but remain hidden.

"That the dwarf is headin' toward her." He waited until the dwarf caught up to her, placed a hand on her back, and almost keeled over from lack of breath. "An' keepin' company with a former coterie member." He watched longer. "An' he's not actin' at all like a servant to the woman, but more like a friend."

The woman glanced back at the blacksmith shop, and Emelyne ducked. She hoped she was quick enough to not be seen, only glancing up a few minutes later when Lozzeak said it was clear. Emelyne watched as they disappeared around another building, then she stood tall when they were out of sight.

Lozzeak looked up at her. "In any case, we have to get ya into hidin' again. I know ya only jus' came back, but even though she says she's ain't with the coterie anymore, I don't trust anyone with brilliant-colored hair, even if I can't see a familiar. It's jus' not worth the risk with ya here."

"It's not worth it with anyone here." Emelyne placed her hands on her hips. "I can't believe ya jus' raced out there to approach her after what happened to Thiznabo." She whacked him on the shoulder. "Me heart nearly stopped from the worry."

His face shifted, and he looked pleading. "I know no one is safe, but can ya please jus' go an' visit Monut again?"

Emelyne's heart sang over the thought of visiting Monut, yet the feeling was muddied by the idea of leaving her parents to face danger without her again. "I'm happy to go visit the dragons, but will ya stop doin' stupid things like approachin' the coterie members if I do?"

He threw up his hands in defeat. "I promise. I'll only talk to them if it's safe."

She nodded and gathered a few items. Things had happened so fast, she hadn't even had a chance to tell her ma and pa that she had bonded with a dragon. After all the fuss over the coterie members, she didn't know how they would take it. Maybe they would think that he was her familiar and that made her a potential for the coterie. Her mind whirled. Maybe that was the reason they were so protective over her. They thought she might be recruited. The coterie didn't accept dwarves as sorcerers, only humans and elves or mixed. She was happy with her reasoning as she prepared to make a dash to the mountainside cave, making sure she remained obscured behind buildings. Then she remembered that coterie members had to have magic, and she had none. She would have to argue that point later.

Her pa brought her mind back to the present. "You'll understand soon why we need ya to keep out of their sight."

"I'd feel better if you an' Ma came with me."

He nodded. "I know, but I have to get these knives made for the sorcerer before he comes back. I promised him somethin' special to keep us safe an' distract him from killin' anyone else." He peered out the window and checked down the street. "I'll stand watch in case they come back this way."

# CHAPTER TWENTY

*Y*ou can't give up so easily. The human girl is in there. Ulrieg passed over Samara as she turned away down the street, Forgrac hurrying to catch up with her.

*I can't just barge into his shop, even if I know he's lying.* Samara looked up when she felt a breeze pushing down on her from above.

*Why not? What's he going to do? He's only small, and you have magic.*

*For one, it's not very polite,* Samara argued.

*Pfft!* Ulrieg snorted. *Who needs to be polite when the realm's future is at stake?*

Samara looked condescendingly up at the roof of the cottage next to her, where she imagined Ulrieg sat. *I'm not going to win any friends by barging into their place. We want to gain their trust, and that's not the way to do it.* Samara spotted Forgrac approaching her, and she waited for him. "Where's Skorrig?"

Forgrac placed a hand on her shoulder as he caught his breath. "I left him in the alehouse. He can rest his leg in there an' keep an eye out for the human."

"Good idea." She indicated for him to walk with her. "I'll catch you up on everything soon. I don't want to talk right now in case others can hear us."

Forgrac nodded, falling into stride next to her as she continued along the street.

*And two, didn't you see the size of his arms and legs? He's massive. It's probably from all his years working as a blacksmith. She's probably very muscular for a human female as well.*

*But she's the one,* Ulrieg argued. *It's worth the risk.*

She placed her hands on her hips. *How do you know?*

*Dragon moon! I'm getting to that part.*

*Well, come on then.* Samara took the corner around one of the cottages and out of view of the blacksmith.

*You'll never guess what I found on the other side of that mountain.*

*Get to the point, Ulrieg.*

*The Merciless Sanctuary.*

*Yes, that's what we were told.* Samara kicked a rock impatiently.

*Don't you remember? We passed it when we traveled with Callista to the Paddosha Palace. She said it's so desolate that not even members of the Sacred Flame coterie go in there.*

*So, it's a horrible place. And?*

*I'm rubbing off on you, aren't I? Listen to how snarky you're getting.* Ulrieg chuckled.

*Ulrieg!* Samara warned.

*All right. So, because the coterie even refuse to go there, it's a perfect hiding place.*

*But they said no one could survive in there, it's so desolate.*

*That is true. No one, can. But it's a good place for certain types of dragons.*

Samara's step froze mid-stride, and she looked back at the building she just passed. *Are you saying what I think you're saying?*

*Yes. There are dragons hiding in there. About twenty, I think, after a quick glance. Not only that, there's also a really large dragon with them. This morning, before the sun rose, I found them just in time to see a young human female exit a cocoon he had made with his wing, probably to protect her from the harsh desert night. I followed her and a dwarf who had gone out to meet her for quite a distance. They were accompanied by the large dragon until the people entered the mountain. I flew over the mountain and waited in the village cave until I saw the human exit it. When I followed her outside, she went into the blacksmith's building before setting to work.*

*That's great that you found some dragons that are safe and the human, but that still doesn't make her the lost royal,* Samara argued.

*Except, while I was waiting for her to walk some distance so I could follow her, I remained invisible and hung around the dragons, listening to their conversation. They were all discussing her and how she was the lost princess and that they wished that her adoptive parents would tell her.*

Samara frowned. *So you're saying that she doesn't know she's the lost royal?*

*Seems so.*

*But how would she not know?*

*I guess we'll find out. There must be a good reason.*

Some dwarves traveled down the street toward them, but when they saw Samara ahead of them, they crossed to the other side.

Samara sighed. "I wish my hair would change back to its natural color quicker. It's proving to be a hinderance more than anything." She filled Forgrac in on the conversation, keeping her voice to a whisper.

The dwarf froze in disbelief before rushing to

catch up. "I wonder if the other dwarves know she's the princess."

"I don't know. First, it'd be interesting to see if any of them confess to having a human here." Samara eyed the dwarves on the other side of the road.

Forgrac looked doubtful. "Often these dwarven villages are tight-knit. They're not always trusting of outsiders, especially ones who aren't dwarves." He chuckled. "It's actually a brilliant plan by her adoptive parents. The dwarves won't give information away to strangers."

"Let's try that theory," Samara called over her shoulder as she headed across the road, heading straight for the dwarves who tried to avoid her. "Come on, Forgrac."

Forgrac hurried to catch up with her as Samara started the conversation.

"Good morning," she said cheerfully.

The two dwarves—dressed in long pants and short-sleeved tunics covered in dirt, as if they had just come from a shift at the mines—half-heartedly muttered, "Mornin'."

Samara smiled. "I heard a rumor that a human is living in this village. Could you please tell me where I can find her?"

The dwarves' broad shoulders tensed, and their faces dropped, their lips pressing together.

"It's very important," Samara added, hoping to bypass their tight-lipped nonresponse.

The dwarves shook their heads, and the one with protruding ears swiped down his arm as if busying himself with cleaning up.

"Nah. We ain't seen no human. This is a dwarven village. No humans would live underground with us."

The second dwarf laughed. "Ain't no human that can live in caves like we dwarves do. It makes them go mad." He circled a finger near his temple and crossed his eyes.

Samara couldn't miss how nervous they sounded. "All right. Thank you. I guess I'll just have a quick look around this lovely village then leave you to it." She turned as if to go back toward the blacksmith's.

The first dwarf shifted to stand in her way, his face nervous. "Seein' as this is ya first time in the village, I suggest ya see the candle shop down the road. They make amazin' candles that shine brightly, even in our deepest caves." He pointed in the direction behind Samara, the opposite way from the blacksmith's.

Samara was about to turn to play into the dwarf's hands when she saw a human female, attractive with a sturdy build, peek out of the blacksmith's window. She ducked quickly and dashed past another window toward the mountain, then disappeared through a door at the back of the store. Samara eyed the larger cave exit from the mountainside that the two dwarves before her had exited recently. It was much larger than the small entrance her accompanying dwarves had ducked into the previous night, and she assumed this hole was the main entrance to the village's cave home.

*Did you see that, Ulrieg? The human just ducked into their cave.*

*Sneaky! So sneaky I missed it. I'll follow her.*

In order to humor the dwarf in front of her, she turned and looked for the candle shop cottage. She smiled sweetly at the one that suggested it. "Thank you. I'll have to have a look at them before I leave. That's so sweet you recommended it." Rubbing her chin, she asked, "Tell me, have you heard of the lost royal?"

Both dwarves looked shocked, but the first one answered. "No. I didn't know there was still an existin' royal."

Eying him as inconspicuously as she could, Samara thought he was telling the truth. "Oh, because there's a rumor going around that says a human frequenting the dwarven areas has the same mark on her hand that the royals have had for the last several generations." When all she received in return was confused looks, she said, "Never mind." Then she spun to slowly walk in the direction of the candle store, indicating for Forgrac to walk with her, as the dwarves continued heading in the opposite direction.

Forgrac kept pace with her. "What are ya up to?"

"I was seeing if the dwarves here would lie to protect the human from someone who looked like they were from the coterie. They definitely protected her, but they don't seem to know about the missing royal. They may be putting the two together now." She gazed over her shoulder at them. "Though, while I was talking to them, the human female dashed through the blacksmith's shop into the cave. I think she thought we couldn't see her."

"Then why are we headin' this way an' not the other?" Forgrac threw his hands out to the side.

"Because I want to lose these dwarves before I go snooping around their home. Besides, I sent Ulrieg after her." She leaned back, checking to see how far the two dwarves had gone around the corner. She couldn't see them anymore. "We should be clear to head to the cave now."

They reached the entrance of the cave without being interrupted. It seemed it was too early for most dwarves to be above ground. Forgrac led Samara into the entrance with more confidence than Samara felt. When they entered, it took Samara's eyes a few minutes to adjust to the dullness. The farther they traveled from the entrance, the darker it got with only a few sconces burning on the wall to illuminate the area with a dull light. When her eyes adjusted, she searched unsuccessfully for the human. She was nowhere to be seen. Several tunnels led from the main front room that was approximately twice Samara's height. At least she didn't feel claustrophobic that time, even if there was no sign of the human.

*Ulrieg, I've lost her.*

*Don't worry. I'm on her tail. I don't think you would like to follow her where she's gone so far. It's tiny and cramped.* Ulrieg grunted as though he was having trouble passing through an area. *I'll let you know later where she went.*

Emelyne wove her way through the tunnels to the other side of the mountain. She thought she had managed to get to the cave without being seen by the female who looked like she was from the coterie. The female had seemed nice but had been very persistent about coming into the smithy. At least the female hadn't killed her pa like the male had taken Thiznabo. She shook her head at the thought. Her pa's stubborn streak could have gotten him killed.

She passed the mining section, grabbed the final sconce before the tiny tunnels, and crouched low to thread her way through the remaining passages. The flame flickered eerily on the dark stone walls, adding to her nervousness. She hadn't had to travel to the other side of the mountain so many times as she had over the last week. Scratching from behind startled her, and she struggled to turn quickly in the tight space to investigate the cause. Her heart leaped, as if ready to race the rest of the way without her, as she threaded the sconce through her legs, trying to not let the flame catch on her clothes as she twisted to look back. She couldn't see anything. Shrugging off her uneasiness, she pressed forward, telling herself it must be the echo of her shifting to get through the tight spaces every time she heard another noise she was unsure of.

Finally, she saw the light at the end and squinted as her eyes strained to adjust to the bright sunshine reflecting off the arid land. The sun beat down on the dry soil not far from her, raising beads of sweat almost instantly. She reached for the canteen she'd grabbed on her way there and took a sip, aware she would have to be sparing, not knowing when she could leave the harsh side of the mountain. After a while, she headed to the right to travel the distance to the dragon area. She kept in the shadows, glancing over her shoulder to make sure those sounds she heard weren't anyone following her.

It was hard to believe it was only that morning her ma had told her it was safe to go home, as no one had seen the sorcerer all night. And she was already going back to the dragons, leaving more work for her pa to complete on his own. It was annoying that the female who said she wasn't from the coterie had arrived, as her pa had a lot of work for her to do. At least one good thing came of it—Monut. Her heart hummed. He would protect her. The joy almost had her skipping through the Merciless Sanctuary. In her fit state, it didn't take her long to reach the dragons' area and find them all curled up in the shadow that the early-morning sun cast over the mountains.

*Monut! I'm back.* Several feet still separated them.

His large brown eyes slowly opened and focused on her. Warm affection passed through his gaze, and she couldn't help smiling, as she returned the warmth. *As much as I'm ecstatic my bonded has returned, what brings you here so soon?*

She hurriedly explained, *Another person with brilliant-colored hair has arrived at the village. A female, half-elf and half-human. She wanted to enter the smithy, but Pa sent her away so I could escape. She said she ain't from the coterie, but Pa ain't takin' any chances.* Reaching the dragon, she stroked the side of his face, his head enormous against her hand.

A soft rumble sounded from his throat. *It is better that you are safe here with us than taking any risks.*

A noise like someone was clearing their throat sounded behind her, and Emelyne spun, her eyes wide as they landed on a black dragon. His eyes were a glowing red, and long angry horns spread gener-ously over the ridges of his small body. She had never seen the black dragon before. He looked fero-cious, scarier than Monut had looked the first time she'd seen him. He wasn't tiny, but she estimated that his head would only reach her waist.

Monut raised his head to catch a better look at the dragon.

*Monut! Is this a new member to ya group?* The uncertainty in her voice was palpable.

The black dragon puffed out steam. *All right. You can wipe the frightened look off your face. I've been told I look scary, but I'm here as a friend, even though I've turned up uninvited to your secret hideout.* The black dragon moved as though he was the one speaking directly into their minds. *I must give you credit. This is a brilliant hiding place. Not even the Sacred Flame coterie members are game to come here.*

*Why are you here, friend?* Monut's voice held a hint of warning as he tilted his head to one side as if taking in the new dragon, his movements cautious. *Are you after a safe place to hide? We always welcome new dragons to join us if they adhere to our guidelines.*

The black dragon huffed a laugh. *No, I'm not here to stay. I'm here for you.* He looked directly at Emelyne.

Monut rose to his feet, his teeth exposed,

instantly blocking the black dragon from her. *What do you want with her?*

The black dragon seemed undeterred despite the sheer vastness of Monut's size in comparison to his, and he shifted to see Emelyne clearer. *We mean you no harm.* He spoke directly to Emelyne. *We've traveled a long way and believe you are the one we're looking for.*

"Me?" Emelyne placed a hand on her chest, uncertain.

*Yes.* The dragon nodded, but something in his face seemed as though he struggled to hold back a retort at the simplest of comments. He took a deep breath, which seemed to contain his apparent impatience before answering. *We're looking for the lost royal, and we have heard rumors that indicate it may be you.*

Emelyne laughed, slapping her hand on her thigh. "Ya got the wrong person here. I ain't no royal. I'm just a regular human, other than bein' raised by dwarves."

A murmur passed through the dragons behind her, and she spun to look at them, her confusion growing as she peered at their faces. Monut shifted, and when she spun back to face the little red-eyed dragon, she caught sight of Monut's raised scaly hackles.

*Who is spreading such rumors? You must not believe everything you hear.* Monut stood firm.

The black dragon remained nonchalant. *All right, all right. You don't need to get your talons twisted.* He rolled his eyes. *I know your size is impressive compared to mine, but there's no need to show it off.*

Monut growled, and he seemed to grow in size.

The strange black dragon huffed and lowered to the ground, as though annoyed in his defeat. *Look. Let me start again. My name is Ulrieg. I've been told I'm not the best at first impressions and I'm a bit rude.*

"That's an understatement!" Emelyne scoffed.

He shrugged. *I am what I am, and I enjoy it.* He exposed his teeth, which looked like he meant it to be a grin. *I'm not our first choice for approaching you. It would have been a lot better if one of my companions had talked to you first, but my bonded is being avoided like the plague because she has the markings of a coterie member.*

Emelyne took a step back, her cheeks turning clammy. "You're with the pink-haired woman at the village?"

Monut looked as though he was ready to pounce on the small dragon but balked at the last moment.

The dragon seemed to see Emelyne's fear and lowered flatter to the ground to remove all signs of a threat. *Don't panic. Let me explain. She was with the coterie not that long ago, but she bonded to me accidently quite some time ago, and we had to hide it.*

He disappeared, and her eyes widened with fear.

He reappeared in the same spot. *I told you not to panic. I'm trying to demonstrate to you what happened.*

Emelyne shifted, rubbing one foot against the other. It took all her effort not to back away.

*My accidental bonding with her instantly made her an enemy to the coterie. She was painfully naive to their ways, and I educated her over time. Despite all this, she stayed there, as I remained invisible, helping to rescue dragons the Sacred Flame coterie members captured and tortured. Not too long ago, our bond was discovered, and she was captured after she set a dwarven servant free from their entrapment. She still looks like a coterie member because it will take a while for the color to leave her hair.* He smirked. *But trust me, it's a lot duller than it used to be.*

*Why are you after the royal? I heard only the coterie members were after her.* Monut didn't move from blocking the dragon's path to Emelyne and looked uneasy as he weighed the information.

The small dragon looked directly into Monut's eyes. *Our plan is to help the royal return to their rightful place and run this realm. We know it won't be easy, but we want to help return this kingdom to the way it should be, not let it be run by the coterie.*

The muscles in Monut's jaw relaxed. *You're awfully vocal about something that could get you and your companions killed by anyone supporting the Sacred Flame coterie.*

Ulrieg gave a sardonic smile. *I don't know about you, but my experience is that anyone who's a friend of the dragons or is a dragon tends to not support the coterie. Especially since the coterie have made every effort to either kill us, ban us, or make our realm disappear to everyone outside of it.*

Monut sat back. *That is very true. I apologize for doubting you.*

Cyrra pushed forward. *Yeah, don't mind him. He's very protective of the princess. It's kind of his family's legacy, plus it's grown since he bonded with her.*

Emelyne gawked at the brown-striped dragon. "Cyrra, what are ya talking about?"

A guilty look crossed the outspoken dragon's face as she caught Monut's glare. *Um, you still need to talk to your ma and pa, Emelyne.*

Ulrieg crept a couple of steps closer, his body trembling with excitement. *Can I have a look at your hand?*

Emelyne frowned. "Why would ya want to look at me hand?"

*The royal heirs are rumored to have a birthmark imprinted between their thumb and forefinger. It was a blessing given to the original escaped princess by a water dragon,* Ulrieg explained.

Emelyne scoffed. "I have a scar in that spot, but I got it as a child, playin' at me pa's blacksmithin' workshop. It has nothin' to do with bein' a royal." She yanked off the leather blacksmithing glove and held her hand closer to the black dragon.

Ulrieg met Monut's eye. *With your permission, I would like to accompany your bonded back to the village to have that discussion with her parents and to meet my bonded and her dwarven companion.*

Monut looked as though he was about to say yes when Emelyne placed her hands on her hips and interrupted. "Shouldn't ya be askin' me, not him?"

Ulrieg turned to her. *Yes, of course. I was getting to that. But I kind of fear him more than you. He's just a little bit bigger than me, in case you hadn't noticed.*

Heat rushed into Emelyne's cheeks. "Ha. Of course." A realization hit her. "Wait! When you say ya bonded, does that mean ya her familiar?"

*In all its oddity, it does.* A strange look passed over his face. *It was more of a shock to me than her, as I knew how much the coterie hated our kind, but in saying that, we are a good match, and she has proven she is nothing like the coterie members.*

With her eyebrow arched, Emelyne glanced at Monut. "Do ya think I can trust him?"

Monut nodded. *I should think you can as much as any other dragon here.*

# CHAPTER TWENTY-TWO

Having come across too many tunnels, Samara and Forgrac found a dark corner in the main foyer of the dwarven mountainside home and sat, backs pressed against the cold stone walls and backsides turning numb against the hard stone floor. The dank, musty smell added to Samara's discomfort, reminding her of the time she and Kaine had been captured by the trolls and she'd met and bonded with Ulrieg. At least the latter was a pleasant thought, though her life hadn't been the same since. It had become filled with uncertainty and danger when her eyes had been opened to the Sacred Flame's real actions.

Samara shifted to try and find a more comfortable position. "I thought there would be more dwarves in this area."

Forgrac shook his head, barely visible to Samara in the flickering fire from the metal sconce on the wall not far above him. "Probably everyone is already doin' their work for the day, either in the mines or out in the village front. An' I'm sure the mothers an' fathers not workin' are busy lookin' after their li'l ones."

Time ticked by, their eyes constantly checking the tunnels for any sign of movement from the human. Instead, a dwarf walked into the main room and spotted them sitting off to the side. The stocky man wandered over to them, deep creases lining his forehead as he approached.

"What are you doin' here?" He placed his hands on his hips, his eyes passing over Samara's hair, and a flicker of uncertainty passed over his face. "We don't usually like outsiders enterin' our mountain home without a local accompanyin' them. I'm sure ya understand."

"Yes, of course." Forgrac groaned as he shifted awkwardly to stand. "We're hopin' to catch up with a friend."

One of the dwarf's bushy dark eyebrows raised. "Oh. Who?" His eyes turned suspicious and raked over Samara's hair again.

Forgrac cleared his throat. They were waiting for Ulrieg and hopefully the human girl, but they couldn't tell the dwarf that. "I'm afraid I can't remember their name. That's a bit embarrassin'!" He chuckled.

"Well, ya can't be that good a friends with them if ya can't remember their name. I suggest ya wait outside in the village front, so as ya don't upset the rest of the village." He swept his arms as if pushing them outside.

Reluctantly, Samara climbed to her feet, and they exited the main room of the cave together, squinting against the harsh sunlight they were no longer used to. It had been a long night, and their eyes were already tired and bleary.

"I suggest that ya go to the alehouse an' meet ya friend there. Most of the folk end up there at some stage durin' the day," the dwarf said.

"Thanks." Forgrac leaned against the mountainside. "But if it's all right with ya, we'd like to stay here an' catch some sunshine until they turn up."

The dwarf eyed him. "You're a strange one, ain't ya? Most dwarves prefer to be out of the sun." He shrugged. "Suit yaself. As long as ya wait outside of the mountainside. Me apologies if this upsets ya, sorceress." He inclined his head toward Samara.

"Oh, ignore the color of her hair. She ain't with the Sacred Flame coterie," Forgrac explained. "She left them not long ago."

The dwarf looked as though he wasn't convinced. "Is that so? Well, good day." He turned and headed down the street.

When he had traveled out of earshot, Forgrac huffed. "Travelin' bunions, love! It's harder than I thought to convince these dwarves that ya ain't with the coterie. It feels like they only tolerate ya presence because they feel they've no other choice."

Samara placed a hand on his shoulder in an attempt to calm him. "That's probably a good sign for us and this kingdom overall. Hopefully, the princess has headed over to the other side of the mountain, and Ulrieg can convince her and the dragons. Surely, if anyone can get through to dragons, it will be another dragon."

They sat on a large stone nearby, their eyes slowly getting used to the bright sun. The smell of baking bread wafted on the soft breeze, and though they'd had breakfast not long ago, it made Samara's mouth water. She had taken for granted all the fresh food she used to get at the coterie that had become rare while on the road. If possible, she would pick up some freshly baked bread before they left.

Her thoughts traveled to the carriage still left at their camping spot and their dwarf companions hiding in the mountainside with Kaine tied up not too far from them. Her stomach fluttered for a different reason. "I hope we catch up with the princess before Kaine escapes his restraints. I'd hate to be here if he decided to return to the village."

"Yup. Me too. I didn't think it would be this hard to talk to fellow dwarves, but clearly, the coterie has instilled much doubt into the different villages over the years I've been trapped in Wraeyanor an' servin' the coterie." He shook his head. "I shoulda known that it would end badly with the coterie involved, even if I was down to me last year. When do they ever do anythin' that is good for the people an' not self-servin'?"

Samara rubbed his back. "You tried to do it the peaceful way, and that shows your true character."

*Samara!*

Samara's back stiffened when she heard Ulrieg's voice. *I hear you. Is everything all right?*

*We're on our way out of the mountain. Can you meet us in the main cave room?*

*We were there but got kicked out. We're waiting just outside the entrance. Who's with you?*

*The princess, though she doesn't believe she's royalty. She only came with me because I convinced the dragons. We need to take her to see her adoptive parents and convince them to tell her the truth. She does know that you're not with the coterie, but I don't know if she believes it.*

Samara pushed her lips to one side. *Hopefully, together, we'll get through to the father better than I did this morning.*

"Are ya talkin' to Ulrieg?" Forgrac's hazel eyes studied her face.

"Yes, he's almost here." She relayed what Ulrieg had said.

"Fingers crossed, they aren't too stubborn to see the tru—" He silenced himself when the young human female exited the mountainside.

The human's eyes fell on Samara's pink hair, and a nervous tension flashed through the muscles of her wide jaw.

Samara stood and studied her up close. She was possibly the same age as Samara, and there seemed to be a naivety in her eyes, though she also had a cautiousness that Samara knew she hadn't had when she'd first joined the coterie. "Hello. I'm Samara, and this is Forgrac."

"Hello." Forgrac grinned, trying to appear friendly.

The young woman wrapped one gloved hand around the other, and strong muscles rippled under her long sleeves. "I'm Emelyne."

Samara hadn't seen her up close before and quickly assessed her, taking in the muscular build, much stronger than other females she had known, elven or human. Though at the same time, she was thin. If it weren't for all the muscles, she could even qualify as petite. The years of working as a blacksmith had certainly made her strong. She attempted to break the ice and get past the young woman's apparent nervousness. "I hear you've met my companion, Ulrieg."

Emelyne's eyes darted around, as though she was looking for eavesdroppers, before lowering her voice. "The little black dragon?"

Samara nodded, keeping her voice low. "The one that's invisible right now."

Nodding, Emelyne stepped slightly closer. "It ain't widely known 'bout the inhabitants of the Merciless Sanctuary."

"Understood." Samara nodded.

"Do ya mind if we go to ya family's shop an' speak to ya with ya pa and ma?" Forgrac asked, his eyes landing on a female dwarf that had just exited the bakery.

Seeing Emelyne with the bright-haired woman, she called, "Is everything all right wit' ya, Emelyne?"

The young human nodded and waved. "Aye. Thanks. Brilliant day to ya." She turned to Forgrac. "Agreed, it's best if we found some privacy. Come." She led the way to their blacksmith workshop and barged through the door, inviting Samara and Forgrac in after her.

The blacksmith whom Samara had tried to convince earlier to let her in turned white, lowering the piece he was working on to the bench as he gripped his hammer. His knuckles bulged under his gloves, his eyes widening as they darted from Samara to his adoptive daughter. "Emelyne. What's the meanin' of this? Are ya all right?"

Emelyne waved a hand at him and removed her gloves. "Relax, Pa." She closed the door behind her, and her ma emerged from the corner, grabbing a hammer as she approached. Her wide jaw set, pushing out at her furry chin line. Though she was shorter, the mother clearly spent many hours inside the forge as well, making her another person to contend with.

Samara marveled at how the female dwarf looked almost as strong as her male counterpart. It was clear they all worked regularly at the blacksmithing shop. If she didn't have magic and Ulrieg, along with the knowledge that she wasn't there to hurt them, she would squirm under their scrutiny.

"Greetings, friends." Forgrac stepped in front of her. "We aren't here to cause you any harm."

"Then why are ya here with the coterie member?"

the mother hissed, raising the hammer higher. Despite the threat the coterie members posed to the dwarves, they weren't backing down when they thought their adoptive daughter was in danger.

Reluctantly, Samara braced, ready to call up a spell to defend themselves.

# CHAPTER TWENTY-THREE

Emelyne understood what her parents were going through. She was having a hard time dealing with it herself. If not for the little black dragon convincing Monut that he was on their side, she wouldn't have brought the dwarf and his ex-coterie member into her parents' shop, even if the pink-haired girl's familiar was a dragon.

The black dragon turned visible in the corner of the room, and both parents started.

Emelyne shifted between her parents and the newcomers. "Ma and Pa, relax. They have somethin' they want to discuss with ya, an' as ya can see, they travel with a dragon. The dragon has convinced Monut that they are on our side." She shrugged. Her parents had always told her to trust Monut's judgment. "Though, what they claim is a far stretch, an' I think they're at the edges of crazy."

Her parents lowered their hammers slightly, and with faces filled with curiosity, they moved closer to the visitors.

Her pa eyed Samara. "Ya the one who tried to gain access to our workshop earlier."

The ex-coterie member nodded. "Ulrieg told me that Emelyne was in here. As you can see, he has the ability to be invisible. That's very helpful for many reasons, especially when trying to discover information."

Her pa grunted. "That explains why ya were so persistent." He indicated himself. "I'm Lozzeak, an' this is me wife, Gibobo."

He placed his hammer on the bench nearest him, and Gibobo followed suit. He eyed Ulrieg in the corner. The dragon seemed to be keeping his distance so as not to scare them, a sensible approach, as his red eyes and excessive horns were unnerving.

"What can we do ya for?" Gibobo leaned her back against the bench, close to her hammer, her hands resting on the benchtop.

Forgrac glanced at Samara.

The young ex-coterie member took the lead, tugging at her brilliant-pink hair. "As you can see, I was a member of the Sacred Flame. In my last days with them, I traveled with the head sorceress to the Paddosha Palace."

Gibobo stiffened, and the young sorceress smiled with understanding.

"It was there that I saw the head sorceress's true colors. I was ashamed and embarrassed over the way she acted toward the villagers there." She sucked in a deep breath, as if trying to clear awful images from her memory. "While I was there, Ulrieg and I came across a young couple who were hiding a crystal from the head sorceress, Callista. They died at her hands for taking the crystal's location to their graves."

Emelyne thought she saw the young sorceress wipe a tear from her eye, and her apprehension softened further.

"While we were with the couple, they told us that they knew of a hidden royal who has the right to rule the kingdom of Slosiaran."

Emelyne twitched under her gaze and watched her parents' expression, unable to read their faces.

"While I was away, Forgrac was imprisoned by the coterie senior members after rescuing some dragons, and I was caught rescuing him from the underground. Long story short, we escaped with help from my beloved, who is now paying the price." The young sorceress closed her eyes briefly, as a tidal wave of heartache washed over her face. "Since we escaped, we have been roaming with a traveling actors' group in search of the lost royal."

"Why?" Lozzeak pulled at his belt in an effort to make himself feel comfortable. "What do ya think ya can do if ya find them?"

Forgrac and Samara exchanged glances. "We hope to help them return to their rightful place to lead this kingdom. We think it's time the people started rallying to fight back against the Sacred Flame's rule."

"Ain't that madness!" Gibobo exclaimed, her eyes darting protectively toward Emelyne.

Forgrac moved in front of Samara. "We know it ain't gonna be easy, but if we can get the people residin' at the base of Paddosha Palace to support the royal, we have a possibility to rebuild it quietly, gatherin' up more followers. Especially if the dragons hidin' in the Merciless Sanctuary decide to gather more dragons to help."

"If the coterie members don't hear 'bout it first an' stop it in its tracks, killin' everyone and all dragons involved," Lozzeak argued.

"Yes, it's a risk." Forgrac spread his arms, palms out. "But we have to try. Don't ya think?"

Lozzeak folded his arms across his chest. "An' what does that have to do with us?"

Ulrieg shifted forward, his gaze intense, and the two parents flinched. *I think you know very well what that has to do with you. I've talked to the dragons in the wasteland, and they have confirmed our suspicions. I have seen the mark on her hand.*

Gibobo shifted uneasily, fiddling aimlessly with her hammer.

Ulrieg continued, *It seems Emelyne doesn't know anything about the meaning of the mark, nor does she know of her family heritage, and the dragons said she needs to hear it from you.*

Emelyne scoffed. "Do ya hear how ridiculous his proposal is? I ain't no princess or royal. I'm just a human livin' in a dwarven village."

Ulrieg's red eyes landed on her. *And why do you think your parents hid you every time a coterie member came to the village?*

"Like I said, it's just because I'm a human living in a dwarven village." Emelyne indicated the town. "As ya can see, there ain't any humans livin' here but me. It don't take much to arouse the coterie's suspicions, an' they are quick to punish." Tears blurred her vision. "Me best friend died simply because she got in the way of a stupid coterie member with blue hair."

The young sorceress gasped. "I'm so sorr—"

*That's not surprising coming from Kaine,* Ulrieg interrupted. *I can't say a single nice thing about him.*

Samara glared at him, and the dragon looked sheepish.

*There I go again, being abrupt. My sweet bonded will always let me know,* he said sarcastically, exposing his teeth in what looked like a nasty smile. He faced Emelyne. *I'm sorry about your friend.* He shook his head. *Though, I've got to add that you're as naive as Samara was when I first met her.*

Emelyne was speechless.

*I didn't think that was possible. Haven't you ever wondered what happened to your real parents?* Ulrieg turned to her dwarven parents. *Are you going to tell her?*

Gibobo shook her head. "She's not old enough to know all of this yet."

Ulrieg scoffed and waved a wing at Emelyne. *She clearly has the maturity of an adult, even if she is young. I would class that more than how old she is.*

Lozzeak sighed and rubbed a hand across his braided beard. "Gibobo, it's time. There ain't no way ya can keep this from her now."

Resignation washed over her face as Gibobo pressed forward and took Emelyne's hands in her own stumpy ones, running a thumb over the birthmark between her forefinger and thumb. "What they say is true. I knew ya birth mother was a descendant of the royal family. I saw the mark on her hand, as had many others in the human village round her. I kept it a secret an' helped her in her final days of the pregnancy. Only days after she had ya, a member of the coterie arrived at the village. We knew it was too late for her, but she pressed ya into me arms an' made me promise to look after ya. Thankfully, the coterie member didn't know ya existed. From that day on, I kept ya hidden in this village, an' made sure ya wore gloves every day to cover ya mark. Boy, did ya make that difficult in ya younger days." She chuckled.

Emelyne's mouth fell open. She couldn't believe what her ma said. "Ya can't be serious!"

Gibobo shook her head. "I'm deadly serious. An' as for Monut, he has known all along. I had to hide ya a few times and stumbled across Monut when I rushed through the mountain to get ya away from a visiting coterie member. At first, he scared the life outa me, but he convinced me he was a descendant of the great dragon who protected the first princess who escaped the palace with the help of dwarves, my ancestors, when it was being attacked."

Emelyne's legs felt weak, and she leaned against the wall. It finally made sense to her why they told her to hide every time a coterie member was nearby. "Why did ya keep it from me all this time?"

Gibobo fiddled with her hands. "We didn't want to put any pressure on ya while ya were young. Especially, since we never knew if ya would be the one to rise. An' we didn't want ya to know, in case ya told ya friends an' the word spread, puttin' ya in danger. Ya know how much children like to tell secrets."

Emelyne pulled at her long braid as she paced a few feet. "How am I supposed to rule a kingdom an' convince people to follow me? I ain't got the first idea how to be a royal. I ain't had hardly anythin' to do with humans."

"If we find the royal's true believers and people who are tired of being under the coterie's rule, I think they would support you the best they can," Samara said.

Emelyne scoffed. "That ain't much comfort. Where do I even start?"

The black dragon snorted and scratched a talon on the stone floor. *Just think about what the blue-haired sorcerer, Kaine, did to your friend, then you'll find the motivation to rebuild your kingdom and rise against them.*

A strange fire burned in Emelyne's abdomen. "I think ya might be right."

"Well, there ain't no way ya ma an' me are goin' to let ya do that on ya own. We'll pack our things and support ya the whole way." Lozzeak glanced at his wife, and she nodded.

"But ya got ya shop here and ya livin'. I imagine there ain't any money in the royal coffer. It'll more than likely be stolen. An' it'll be dangerous. I can't have ya puttin' yaselves in danger," Emelyne protested.

Gibobo placed a hand gently on her arm. "We ain't gonna leave ya to do this without the most committed support. An' there ain't nobody who'll support ya more than us. Ya'll probably find all the dragons will follow ya too. At least I know Monut certainly will. They've all been waitin' for this moment."

Ulrieg cleared his throat. *A dragon would have to be stupid to not support anyone willing to go against the coterie. Our lost realm depends on it.*

Forgrac wrung his hands. "I know this is outa the blue, but we really need to get movin' quickly. The blue-headed coterie member that was in ya village yesterday may come back any moment an' discover ya. I don't think he knows about Emelyne, but I wouldn't want to risk it. He's a nasty one and definitely a loyal member of the coterie." His eyes connected with Samara's and the young sorceress nodded, her face pale.

"Righteo. I was gonna get his throwin' knives breathed on by the dragons, 'cause that's our secret for our divine weapon makin'." Lozzeak grinned. "Now, I ain't gonna do that. I'll just leave it here in the shop, and he'll never find us to ask why it ain't our normal quality."

"Yes, we don't need the coterie getting any powerful weapons. They are enough to deal with because of their magic," Samara agreed.

As everyone moved, Emelyne's heart thumped wildly. Her mind was stuck in a daze, unable to completely process everything that was happening.

"Emelyne!"

Her ma's voice sliced through the haze in her mind, and she blinked, focusing on Gibobo.

"Go to our cave and pack up ya bag with as much as ya can, includin' a bit to eat an' drink. Then go to Monut. You'll have to learn how to ride him so we can keep ya out of sight." Gibobo squeezed her arm.

Satisfaction washed over Emelyne. "Actually, he's already carried me. I haven't had a chance to tell ya. It was fun. He also bonded to me to keep me safe after our little trip."

Gibobo's jaw dropped.

*Then, nothing will stop him from coming with you,* Ulrieg confirmed.

A softness washed away Gibobo's shock as she smiled. "He probably doesn't want to fly out until he has the cover of darkness. We'll pack the rest an' head out in a wagon with these two an' their companions. Plus, we'll take as much metal as we can."

*I'll find you once I make sure Samara and Forgrac get to their group and collect the other wagon all right. I assume you and Monut don't know where to go. When I come back, I'll show Monut and the others the way,* Ulrieg said.

# CHAPTER TWENTY-FOUR

After giving Lozzeak and Gibobo instructions on where they had camped, Samara, Forgrac, and Skorrig traveled back along the rocky road with invisible Ulrieg flying overhead and Skorrig singing boisterously in the back of the wagon. A few too many ales while he was waiting had dampened the fear of the coterie and what anyone thought.

As soon as they arrived, they checked the surrounding trees, finding them bare with no sign of Kaine. Forgrac raced ahead, scooped up the rope they had secured Kaine with, and held it out to show Samara as her larger strides closed the gap until she was a few paces away.

"He got loose." His bushy eyebrows hovered low over his eyes as he scanned the area around them. "Ginger ain't here no more neither."

Weariness washing over her, Samara placed her hands on her hips and undertook an investigation. All she really wanted to do was sleep. It had been a while since she had, but she knew it wouldn't be getting shut-eye anytime soon. "To be honest, I'm not surprised. After I removed the spell, he could use his magic, so getting out of a few restraints wouldn't have been very difficult."

*I've done a quick scout. I can't see them anywhere nearby.* The tree above her bounced a few times from Ulrieg's weight.

"I hope Lozzeak and Gibobo get here quickly. We need to get movin'. We don't know if he's plannin' to come back or if he's headed to the village to collect his new weapons." Forgrac tidied the rope and carried it as he headed to the area where they had left their belongings.

They pushed out into the small clearing with the wagons. The sun was already past the midday peak, heading for the trees on the western side.

Silut emerged from the edge of the trees. "Ah! Ya back!"

The four spun to face him, startled by his sudden appearance.

Deep creases marred Forgrac's face. "Didn't ya join the others?"

He waved a dismissive hand. "I didn't find them,

so I thought I'd wait on the edge of the trees to stay safe until ya came back."

"What do ya mean ya didn't find the others? Are they all right?" Forgrac's frown deepened.

Silut scoffed. "I'm sure they're fine. I don't have the best sense of direction, so I ain't very good at findin' things."

"Yet you seem to keep finding us all right." Samara climbed the first step to the back of the wagon.

"Oh. I wouldn't look in there. It's a right royal mess." Silut clenched his teeth.

Samara peeked through the material covering the remaining wagon and gasped.

"What's up?" Forgrac paused a few feet away from the male's wagon, his full attention on Samara.

Silut shrugged. "I told ya."

Samara pulled her head out of the wagon so he could hear her. "The inside is a mess. It looks like someone turned everything over to search it."

Forgrac rubbed his beard. "Can ya tell if anythin' has been taken?"

Samara shook her head. "I don't think so. It's a bit hard to tell at this stage."

Skorrig peeked into the wagon. "Ya. It's jus' as bad as Silut said." He then wobbled to the edge of the extinguished firepit and lay on the ground.

Silut nodded. "I've been tryin' to clean it up since I discovered it like that but haven't had much luck so far. I haven't been with ya long enough to know how ya like things."

Hurrying to investigate, Forgrac approached the wagon. "Do ya think it was Kaine? It wouldn't surprise me if he was lookin' for evidence of our next destination."

"I wouldn't put it past him." Samara attempted to straighten a few things.

Forgrac pushed the material door aside and let out a whistle. "Well, they definitely ransacked it. And they sure made a mess."

"I'll set to cleaning it up. Did you want to get the others out of the mountain? We need to head out as soon as we can." Samara pulled out a piece of clothing, one of the stage clothes, and folded it, placing it gently aside before reaching for another. "After my effort of getting in the mountain, I think you should be the one to get them."

"Smart thinkin'. Hopefully, they haven't gone too far in." His feet thumped on the ground when he climbed down from the wagon, and he brushed his hands on his pants. "Ya be careful out here. Kaine could be anywhere."

*I'll scout the area regularly until you come back.*

The wagon rocked slightly as the invisible Ulrieg

took off, capturing Silut's attention. "What was that?"

"Oh, that was probably jus' Samara stompin' round the wagon," Forgrac said before facing the other direction to talk to the invisible Ulrieg.

"Don't ya have to find Emelyne?" Samara stood to stretch her back before humping over to clean up more.

*I only need to get to them by nightfall. That still gives me plenty of time.*

"All right. Then keep a good eye out."

Silut gazed strangely at him. "What are you talking about?"

Forgrac shook his head. "Nothing! I'm just egging meself on."

Silut frowned. "Are you talking to the dragon?"

"All right. You caught me. I guess it's a little easier to tell since you know he's around."

Silut's mouth thinned. "You don't need to keep him a secret to me anymore. I've seen him. I understand if you need to keep him a secret to everyone else, though."

"Oh, no. The other dwarves know about him. It's only newcomers we keep him a secret from." Forgrac chuckled and slapped the other dwarf's shoulder. They headed toward the mountainside in the direction of the small tunnel.

By the time Samara had finished straightening the first wagon, the whole crew was waddling down the small slope toward the wagons.

"That didn't take long," Samara called.

"Luckily, they were waiting near the entrance. I've still got a lot to fill them in on." Forgrac led them to the firepit.

Samara grabbed some bread and fruit from the wagon and stepped down. "Wingless flight! I forgot to get some fresh bread from the village before we left." She looked at the hardening several-days-old bread and sighed before giving the food to Forgrac to distribute among the dwarves.

"Not much we can do 'bout that now, love." Forgrac handed out the food as he filled in the rest of the group. When he finished, he instructed a couple to feed and water the horses before preparing them to pull the wagons.

The rumbling of wheels and the clopping of hooves sounded down the road, and Samara turned to spot Lozzeak and Gibobo riding toward them.

"That was quick," Forgrac called to them when they pulled up their brown horses a few paces away. He grabbed the horses' bridles and stroked their noses.

"We tried to be as quick as we could. We didn't want to be caught by the coterie member in case he got suspicious." Beads of sweat gathered on Lozzeak's forehead, and he wiped them away with a stocky arm. "It's gonna be interesting livin' above ground all the time without the shelter or me shop."

Forgrac chuckled. "I understand. It took me a while, but now I love it. I even find meself wonderin' at times how we dwarves do it. It's mighty good of ya to support ya adoptive daughter like this. I hope ya feel the same as me about the daylight quickly."

After one of the male dwarves took over tidying the wagon, Samara joined Forgrac to look up at the blacksmithing couple. "Are you ready to keep going? The coterie member was out here before we went to the village. We don't know where he's gone, and he could come back any time now."

Lozzeak nodded. "Since hearing that, me energy just tripled. We're ready to get outa here."

Forgrac clapped his hands, grabbing the team's attention. "All right, everyone. It's time to leave."

The group climbed into the wagons, and Forgrac and Samara sat at the front of the first cart.

*I'm leaving for the Merciless Sanctuary. We'll catch up to you tonight. It'll be interesting to see if all the dragons come.* Breeze washed over Samara as invisible Ulrieg took off into the sky. *Stay sharp.*

*You too. Let us know if you spot Kaine or Ginger.*

Slapping the reins against the horses, Forgrac led

them along the road, all eyes wary and searching for any sight of Kaine or Ginger as they followed the dirt road through the woods.

Weariness tugged at Samara, strengthened by the sway of the wagon, though her adrenaline fought to get them safely to Paddosha Palace Village. She had only been there once with Callista, the time the head sorceress had revealed her true colors, so Samara hoped she remembered the way. At least she had Ulrieg to help guide her from the sky if she got off track. Hopefully, they would reunite by nightfall, if they didn't run into trouble.

The sun edged toward the west, its hot rays beating down on them. Samara wiped her forehead with her sleeve and wondered how the other drivers were doing.

Eyes squinted against the bright sun, Lozzeak had wet patches staining his chest and underarms as the blacksmith led his horses close behind. His red hair looked like it had come alight with the rays of the sun, making the dwarf appear like a burning candle sitting on top of the wagon seat with his fair skin. It would be a big change for the blacksmithing couple, who were used to staying indoors or in a dimly lit cave. It was a testament to how much they cared for their adoptive human daughter. Emelyne was lucky to have been taken in by such a caring couple.

Samara's mind moved to her own family. In all their travels through different villages, they still hadn't found Paxton's family, or hers. She could only hope that meant that they had found an off-track village in the human realm of Slosiaran, away from the general reach of the coterie.

If all went well, they should only have to bear the outdoor travel for the day.

# CHAPTER TWENTY-FIVE

Emelyne grabbed her things as her ma instructed and headed through the mountain to the Merciless Sanctuary on the other side. Her mind remained shrouded in a haze, still unsure what to make of her newfound information. *Monut, I'm on me way back. Ma and Pa have explained everythin', an' we have a lot to talk about.*

*Oh, my bonded, I feel your burden. It's a lot to process, isn't it?*

Monut's voice in her head filled her with warmth and a strange kind of security. Her boots clacked softly on the stone, and the small torch she carried cast her shadow along the floor and walls, chasing her as it tried to keep up.

*Especially when you thought you were destined to live*

*a quiet life in a small dwarven village being a black-smith's daughter. I have longed to tell you for so long, but the time wasn't right, and I thought it would be better coming from your parents.*

*Ya've known this whole time, an' ya didn' tell me?* Emelyne slapped the wall beside her, the cold stone biting into her palm.

*Yes.* His voice was sheepish and lined with guilt.

She didn't know how to react. It was daunting. It seemed like a lot rode on her shoulders. A quiet life working in the blacksmith workshop would have been preferable. It seemed like she didn't have a choice. Though, there were some important things she'd learned from her adoptive parents over the years, including a high distrust of the coterie and a solid work ethic, along with treating others with kindness—something she had learned that the coterie members didn't do. And as much as she didn't want to give the little black snarky dragon credit, he was correct—watching the coterie sorcerer kill Thiznabo had put a fire in her belly. She couldn't let that go unpunished. Thiznabo hadn't even gotten to go out with dignity. A sword fighter as good as Thiznabo should die by the sword, in battle. She stored the anger for the future and let her mind travel back to current events. *Ya know, it's kind of annoyin' that me newly bonded didn't tell me. I thought bein' bonded would mean we would tell each other everythin'.*

*You are correct. We should be more open to each other. That is a large part of being bonded.*

Pushing through to the Merciless Sanctuary, she spotted Monut's large form approximately a hundred feet away and hurried her footsteps, glad to see he had come to greet her.

The large dragon's back straightened, his strong eyes spotting her instantly. He hurried toward her, the ground thundering with his hurried footsteps until he stopped in front of her. He spotted the bag slung over her back. *Is everything all right?*

"Other than me world bein' rocked to the core, I guess it is." Her shoulders sagged. "We're leavin' today to head to Paddosha Palace. Are ya up for an adventure?"

*I will go wherever you go. I will protect my bonded in whatever way I can. And it's my honor to aid and protect the royalty of Slosiaran as my ancestors did.* He lowered to his abdomen.

Emelyne's lips pushed to the side. "I ain't gonna want ya to do that. That's embarrassin'—havin' a big dragon followin' me everywhere—as much as I love ya company. Talk about standin' out in a crowd! Jus' make sure ya open with me from now on. I ain't want no more secrets."

Monut's eyes clouded with what looked like guilt. *I know. I promised I would keep it from you until your ma and pa thought you were old enough to understand and could possibly take on the responsibility. I did not want to keep it from you, but I knew it would be a lot for you to wrap your mind around. Forgive me for holding this from you? I promise I will no longer keep anything from my bonded.* He lowered his head to the ground.

Emelyne couldn't stand the guilt that lurked in his eyes. She touched his nose. "I understand. Even now, I find it hard to process."

He extended his wing. *Would you like to climb on? It will be a quicker trip that way.*

Warmth filled Emelyne. She didn't mind walking, but riding a dragon, even if it was on the ground, was an opportunity too good to pass up. Scrambling up the hard ridges of his body, she sat in front of his enormous wings as he furled them by his side and trudged along the ground toward the crevice that the rest of the dragons hid within.

Distorted dragon figures slowly sharpened through the haze as they approached. The baby played near his mother, pretending to fly and chasing his tail as a way to pass time waiting for the hot sun to disappear and be replaced by the cover of darkness, giving the dragons freedom to stretch their wings. Clouds of dust gathered around him, slowly settling on the older dragons resting nearby.

Cyrra spotted Emelyne and Monut and bounded up to walk along with them. *Welcome back. That was a quick trip away. Is the sorcerer back again?*

A low rumble crawled up Monut's throat. *She finally knows the truth. It looks like we could be leaving tonight.*

*Tonight!* She leaped from side to side. *That's exciting and scary at the same time. We'll be much more exposed out of the Merciless Sanctuary.*

*Yes, that is true. But if we want our children to grow up free, we need to start the groundwork to bring this kingdom back to the way it was and out of the coterie's hands. Maybe then, we'll find our realm, Dragoria. It hasn't been seen in so long.* The enormous dragon gazed wistfully at the sky. *With any luck, we will see it in my lifetime.*

They joined the other dragons and settled down for the rest of the day, waiting for the cover of darkness. Emelyne curled up under the protection of Monut's wing. Sweat beaded on every part of her skin, soaking her clothes to the point of being uncomfortable. It was hotter than laboring in front of the forge. She didn't know how the dragons tolerated it, though their bodies seemed to withstand temperatures that would be fatal for humans. Sitting, she tucked her knees to her chest and pulled out her canteen, taking a long drink of water she had collected from the running river not too far from the village. The water cooled her insides as her eyes drooped from the heat.

Something black appeared in the corner of her eye under Monut's wing, and she jumped, pressing her back against the large dragon's side. Heart thumping, she turned to spot Ulrieg, the little black dragon, teeth exposed in a vicious grin.

*I'm here.* He extended his wings and conducted a mock bow.

"Ya coulda made yaself visible before ya came under Monut's wing. Shattered anvil! Me poor heart. After all the hidin' and runnin' I've been doin'…" She shook her head, holding a hand over her chest.

Monut's wing lifted, bringing with it a brush of slightly cooler air, and he peered underneath. *Where did you come from?*

*Why, from the other side of the mountain, of course.*

The large dragon growled at Ulrieg's snark. *If you go near my bonded, I expect you to be visible until trust has been built.*

The smirk wiped off the black dragon's face as he addressed the much larger dragon. *I apologize. I must admit it is a gift I greatly appreciate and use often. I didn't mean to cause the princess any unwanted stress.*

Monut released a long stream of steam from his nostrils, but let it be. *Why are you bothering the princess this time?*

*I came to tell you that the others are heading out. I'm here to help direct you to the Paddosha Palace, if you don't already know the way.*

The gray dragon inclined his head. *Very well. I have never been to the Paddosha Palace. It fell in the time of my ancestors.*

Ulrieg sat and straightened his back, almost as if he was reporting for duty to the larger dragon. *I will lead the way while following the progress of the ones on land. It is ironic that the head sorceress, Callista, took Samara there, and of course, invisible me as well, to collect a significant crystal. We bypassed the Merciless Sanctuary on the way.*

*You have been here before?* The scales on Monut's forehead puckered.

The black dragon shook his head. *I saw it from a distance. We traveled from the border of Wraeyanor, spotting the Merciless Sanctuary on our distant left. We had no idea that it would hold any life. He tilted his head toward Emelyne. How is your bonded holding up with the news?*

"If ya wanna know, ya should ask me yaself." Emelyne crossed her arms.

*Of course, of course. I was asking your dragon because I'm certain he's not as naive as you. It's hard to fathom once you know what is really going on under the coterie's rule.* Ulrieg rolled his eyes. *And I'm certain Monut isn't that clueless.*

Monut opened his eyes, and they hardened on the smaller black dragon. *You've got a nasty streak, don't you? You can keep it away from my bonded. If you can't say something nice, don't say anything at all.*

The little black dragon grinned, and Monut rose to his feet, extending his wings to tower over him. Ulrieg snorted a defeated breath. *I've been told I'm a bit nasty. It's just the way I am. I don't mean anything by it.*

Emelyne placed a hand on Monut's leg. "It's all right, Monut. I can handle a little snark. It'll be the least of me worries when we leave here. It ain't how I expected me life to turn out."

Ulrieg tilted his head. *Trust me, my life didn't turn out the way I expected either. Accidentally bonding to an enemy was a huge shock to me, but she has proven it wasn't a mistake.*

"Yeah, well, that's another shock. I didn't expect to be bonded to a dragon." She gazed up at Monut and smiled. "But I kinda like it."

*It goes both ways.* The large gray dragon's posture softened as he looked at Emelyne, though his eyes were still sharp when the looked at the smaller dragon. He glanced over his shoulder at the other dragons as he spoke to Ulrieg. *We'll fly out under the cover of darkness. I'd be surprised if the other dragons don't come with us. It's what they've wanted all along.*

# CHAPTER TWENTY-SIX

When the last light disappeared from the sky, the dragons from the Merciless Sanctuary set off on their trip toward the Paddosha Palace. Emelyne mounted Monut by climbing up his ridges and sat just before his wings. She wrapped her legs around the base of his neck, her hands clinging to his protruding scales and horns. The cool breeze whipped across her face, shooting strands of loose hair from her braid over her shoulders.

The moon rose slowly in the distance, gradually growing closer with each beat of the dragons' wings. Monut's wings whirled a monotonous rhythm, lulling her into relaxation. The thrill of being on a dragon's back and riding alongside all different types of dragons was difficult for Emelyne to describe. She had never felt anything like it before the other night and had never thought she would. Dragons of all different sizes and colors traveled together above the few clouds scattered throughout the sky. Below, villages appeared small, with a few lights from sconces sprinkled through the darkness. If anyone were to look up just as they passed over a clear patch of sky and see the dragons flying above, it would be an extreme stroke of bad luck.

The strange black dragon, Ulrieg, guided the group of dragons. It was surprising how fast he could fly for a dragon a fraction of Monut's size, yet he was still far slower than the larger dragon.

They flew for several hours, occasionally taking breaks when they came across forests with a small plain in the center, giving the dragons a pause to catch their breath.

When they landed on their fourth stop, Cyrra approached Ulrieg. *How much longer to go? My wings ache. I don't know how much more I can take.*

Ulrieg grumbled. *I should have realized just how unfit you dragons had become. Didn't you stretch your wings regularly at night? How can you call yourselves dragons if you can't fly a decent distance?*

Cyrra screwed up her nose. *Wingless flight! I was just asking. We're not used to flying so far after having to hide in the Merciless Sanctuary. Of course we stretched our wings every night. We couldn't resist it.*

*Be patient, Cyrra,* Monut said. *I realize you're sore. But just think of the reward of where we're going. And if we can get the palace working, as we expect, to help Emelyne rule us, we should have much more freedom. Just keep that in mind, and that will give you strength.*

Emelyne's shoulders slumped. "All this pressure! Everyone's expectin' me to do somethin' fantastic. I've hardly even been around humans, let alone led them or know how to act the way they do." She pulled out her bag and started eating some of her reserves that she had packed in haste that morning.

The dragons turned their attention to the trees, looking for animals they could catch and devour. An owl hooted in the distance, quickly realizing it was the wrong move with a clearing full of dragons as the horde stampeded toward it.

After a while Ulrieg came racing into the center. *Quick! Everyone to the sky and up behind the clouds. Someone's coming through the forest.*

As every dragon obeyed Ulrieg's request, Emelyne packed her things and quickly jumped onto Monut's back. Joy flooded her when he lunged into the air. If whoever it was had seen the dragons, they wouldn't have had a chance to do anything about it. Unless they were a magic wielder, the dragons would have been long gone. That time, they were lucky.

The night wore on, and they passed two more stops. Fatigue settled over Emelyne. She was glad that she caught a little doze beneath Monut's wings in the desert, or she wouldn't have made it through the night.

Another village sprawled below them with a few remaining lights flickering from the night watch. With her human eyes, it was hard to see the village well in the darkness when Ulrieg led them to land in a forest not far away. Several soft thuds accompanied them as the dragons touched down.

*Dragons.* Ulrieg stood as an anchor to their circle, the dragons giving him their attention. *This is our final stop. The village of Paddosha Palace is just on the other side of the forest. You may have seen a few of the lights burning in a couple of the buildings and on the outskirts of the village. I think it is best to wait here until Samara and the others arrive. I don't think Emelyne should walk into the village by herself. They don't know that some dragons are still free—or they didn't seem to when I visited them last. So we'll wait here.*

*In this case, I think your decision is wise.* Monut inclined his head.

The red-eyed dragon seemed to appreciate Monut's support. *Please, rest up or hunt within the forest. Do not travel far or continue to fly above the village. The last thing we need is for the villagers to panic, thinking they are about to be attacked by dragons. The morn isn't too far away.*

The dragons slowly dispersed. The majority, too worn out from their long flight to go hunting, opted to rest instead.

Emelyne slowly climbed down Monut's wings and landed on the ground, her boots thudding against the soft dirt. She quickly grabbed the last few bites in her pouch and took a sip from her canteen before packing it away and snuggling against Monut's side. The large dragon was warm compared to the cool breeze of the early morning, and light had just started to peek over the horizon.

When day broke, she had managed to catch a few hours of sleep and climbed out from the protection of Monut's wing. She stretched, arching her back before she decided to let the dragons rest further as she wandered through the forest. She wanted to see if she could find some berries or something to eat as a way to stay entertained and nourished until the rest of the crew arrived.

Emelyne strayed some distance from the dragons, staying within the boundaries of the forest. A fox caught her attention, and she started to follow it, becoming disconcerted when its eyes landed on her and returned her stare for quite some time. Its actions led her to wonder if it was from the sorcerer who had visited her village––the one that had killed Thiznabo. She hoped it wasn't, because they had flown so far. It seemed impossible that the fox could have followed them unless it traveled by magic. She didn't know if they could do that.

When the fox continued to move, she followed it through the forest, keeping her distance and an eye out for any sign of a brilliantly blue-haired male. It led her for quite a while, and she pushed aside branches as she tromped through the forest. Eventually, they ended up at a chicken coop on the outskirts of a farm.

Still uncertain whether it was a wild animal or the sorcerer's fox familiar, she stayed within the forest boundaries and squatted behind a tree, eyeing the animal as it scoped the chickens.

The fox shifted out of sight, so she shuffled along the ground, her boots stomping on a twig and releasing a loud snap. She quickly moved her foot and scurried farther, only to stop when a boot sounded behind her.

"Stop where you are."

Emelyne paused and turned to find a human man dressed in farmer's clothes with a nocked bow pointed directly at her.

"What are you doing scoping my house?"

She moved to face him properly and stand, but he pulled the bowstring tighter.

"Don't you dare move, or you'll end up with this inside of you."

She met his eyes and knew that he meant business.

# CHAPTER TWENTY-SEVEN

After no sleep the night before, Samara's group needed to rest inside a thicket of trees away from a village. They had decided to stay away from civilization in case they ran across a coterie member. At that stage, they didn't want to rouse suspicion and give away their whereabouts to the coterie. They were too close to rebuilding Slosiaran to its former glory.

At first light and after a few hours' sleep, Ulrieg had left the dragons in a safe place and backtracked to find the crew to direct them toward Paddosha Palace Village as he rode invisibly on top of Samara and Forgrac's wagon. The crew ate their breakfast on the road, not wanting to waste time.

A few hours passed before the outskirts of Paddosha Palace Village rolled into view. The magnificence of a royal village was lacking in the destroyed buildings along the main road. Not remembering the buildings in that condition when she visited, Samara wondered if they had been destroyed since she'd left the coterie—by Callista or her minions visiting the village to rain down terror until the villagers gave up the location of the crystal that would finish the head sorceress's collection of power crystals in her office.

Samara eyed the village, pondering the best way to proceed. "How do you think we should introduce the princess to her village?"

Forgrac rubbed his chin. "Wouldn't they be ecstatic that the princess has returned? I'd jus' tell them straight out."

*Sure. And risk them thinking you're lunatics, causing them to reject her straight away. That's a great idea!*

Glancing over his shoulder, Forgrac cast the invisible Ulrieg a scowl. "Grumpy dragon. It was jus' a suggestion. What would ya do?"

*For a start, I would think they would be worried that it would make them a bigger target for the coterie—probably something they couldn't handle, judging by the state of the village. But I could be wrong.*

Stretching her legs in front of her, Samara expelled a breath. "He could be right. The coterie has brought so much torment and heartache to this village. They may not be happy that the princess has returned. We should probably play it by ear. Let's have a quick look around before we get Emelyne and show her through the village."

"That sounds reasonable." Forgrac pulled on the reins, directing the horses to follow the road.

"I think we should probably leave the crew on the outskirts until we know it's safe. Callista did make it clear that she would torment the village until the crystal was found, and it looks like she kept that promise." Samara rested her elbows on her knees.

Forgrac pulled up outside one of the old abandoned buildings several hundred yards from the main village and tied their horses to posts. The building looked to be an old inn. It was disheartening to see so many destroyed buildings in what used to be the human kingdom's prized village.

After telling the rest of the crew to stay behind, Samara headed off into the village with Forgrac and invisible Ulrieg as companions. They traveled up the cobblestones, heading toward the ruins of the Paddosha Palace.

While they traveled through the main street, a mixture of grief and something else flooded through her, as she remembered the last time she had come to visit with Callista. It was there that Callista had revealed the true evil that lay within her, treating the people in the worst imaginable way. Callista took many lives during that visit, including Samara's two newest friends, Loys and his wife, Sela, who had helped her and Ulrieg take the crystal and hide it. They had also told her about the princess. She hoped others in the village lived on the hope that the royal would one day return to rebuild their kingdom.

As she walked through the streets, she received many odd stares when they saw her brilliant-pink hair. Many people scurried in the opposite direction to get away from her, trying not to make it seem obvious, believing that she represented the coterie. Again, she wished that she knew the magic spell to undo that brilliant color. It would make life much easier to blend in and pretend she had never been part of the Sacred Flame. The village still looked ruined from when Callista had come. It almost seemed like the village lived in poverty, unable to afford the repairs. At the same time, it appeared the people took pride in their town, despite what seemed to be a lack of resources.

Forgrac's feet shuffled along the pavers and dirt road as he tried to keep up with her slow stride going up the hill toward the Paddosha Palace. As a light sheen of sweat glimmered across Samara's forehead and neck, her breathing growing labored from the hill's ascent.

They entered the village and stopped at a market stall to buy a few supplies for the group. The display was dismal, as though the village supplies had diminished even further since she'd been there last. She paid a higher price for the items than in the past, but they needed the supplies to prepare the night's meal. It wouldn't surprise her if the vendor had charged them more because they were strangers to the villagers.

The store owner gave them the change and packed the groceries in a box while he eyed Samara and Forgrac, gaze curious and weary. He even searched over Samara's shoulders, undoubtedly looking for her familiar.

*I'm not sure how this will go. These people seem rather unfriendly.* Invisible, Ulrieg followed them, staying out of the villagers' way. *It may take a while to make some friends here.*

Samara squinted at the man. "Is there a problem?"

The shop owner trembled visibly and fell to his knees, bowing. "I apologize. I didn't recognize you at first. How may I be of humble service, honored member of the coterie? I have not seen any sign of the crystal your leader seeks, but I will serve you in any other way I can if you spare my shop and my family."

Samara's face fell. The people remembered her from when Callista had destroyed a large portion of the village. But she had stood back and not actually participated in Callista's destruction.

She shook her head and reached out to help him off the floor. "I'm not here to destroy anything, and I'm not here for the crystal."

The man flinched before eyeing her with confusion.

A loud ruckus sounded in the village square, and Samara quickly grabbed her things and turned. Forgrac grabbed the change from the bench along with the supplies they had purchased, and they headed to the door, curious as many along the street filed up to the village square. They joined the large crowd that had already gathered in the center, all looking at something at the front. Samara slowly edged through the mob with Forgrac, trying to reach the source of the commotion.

*Dragon moon! This is not good. You won't believe what's happening.* The distress in Ulrieg's voice was palpable. *I told her to stay put. Does she not listen? How stupid is she to go and wander around?*

*What is it, Ulrieg?* Samara was still trying to push her way to the front. After weaving around many people, she finally broke through the human barrier with Forgrac squeezing in behind. At the front, facing the crowd, Emelyne knelt, her hands secured behind her back.

A man towered over her, dressed as a farmer, his bow and arrow pointed at her as he pushed her forward, so she almost fell on her face. "Look what I found trying to steal my chickens and scoping out my farm!" the farmer yelled to the crowd. "We should lock her up and punish her for stealing our goods."

"Hang her!" a woman yelled. "It's hard enough to get our own food these days without someone stealing it."

Emelyne looked up, exposing a black eye. Her face look bruised. Her hard shoulders caved in resignation. "I didn't steal anything!" she yelled to the crowd. "I was only following a fox. I was trying to see if it was a coterie's familiar. The fox was scoping the chickens, not me."

"I didn't see a fox!" the farmer yelled. "I only saw you about to attack my chickens. I've never seen you before, and you're not carrying any supplies. You *were* scoping my farm. You're just lying because you got caught and don't want to face the punishment. Our village has had a hard enough time without people stealing our food." He turned to face the villagers. "Let's lock her up and vote by tomorrow morning to hang her or not."

Samara's heart thundered against her ribs. That was not the way she wanted to start Emelyne's introduction to the village that belonged to her by birthright. She couldn't let them harm her.

As it was, Emelyne had more muscles than the farmer from her years as a blacksmith. Clearly, she had come without a fight, for the farmer didn't have a bruise on his body.

Hands raised in defense, showing her innocence and cooperation, Samara pushed through the crowd to the front to stand near the farmer. "I vouch for this woman." Samara addressed the entire village. "She's with me, and she does not need to steal food. I just purchased some from the local market, as you can see." She pointed to the box that rested at Forgrac's feet at the front of the audience. "She came separately, but she is with us. We just arrived this morning, and we were going to meet up with her. She was probably trying to find her way to the village."

When the villagers saw Samara's hair color, loud gasps sounded through the crowd, followed by a muffled murmur.

The farmer backed away a few steps, lowering his arrow as Samara walked near him.

"I don't have the crystal, and I don't know where it is. I'm sorry," he said.

Samara paused, realizing the fear the villagers must feel because of her clear coterie markings. She held up her hands again. "I'm here in peace. Relax."

"Weren't you with Callista, the head sorceress?" someone yelled from the audience.

A deep sadness washed over Samara. "I was, yes. And I did not like what I witnessed. It was the first time I had seen her act that way."

"Have you come here to punish us again?" someone else yelled.

"No. I'm not here to continue what Callista started. In fact, I'm actually here to do the opposite. It's been quite a while since I was here last, when Callista sentenced a couple to death." Samara took in the crowd, assessing her best move.

*Tell them you brought Emelyne to help restore the damage Callista caused.*

"She has come with me to help restore the village," Samara tried.

"Pfft! What, you'd have us spend all our coin so the coterie can destroy it again?" someone called.

"Yeah. That would probably be you!" another shouted.

Samara was surprised at their open defiance toward someone they believed was a coterie member. At the same time, it was possibly a step in the right direction. They had a mixture of fear and a severe hate toward the coterie, probably because of the unfair treatment Callista had dealt them, all to find the crystal. But she didn't know how to get them to believe her. *Ulrieg, I don't think I can get through to them. Do you have any better ideas?*

# CHAPTER TWENTY-EIGHT

Knees aching from the stone ground, Emelyne stayed put. The farmer's arrow remained trained on her as Samara attempted to reason with the crowd, though Emelyne could tell that she wasn't getting through to them. They had too much distrust for the coterie and Samara because of her history with them and their village. Emelyne was confident she could tackle the farmer. She knew the right movements to disarm people with arrows after the many times she had practiced with her best friend, Thiznabo.

With each minute that passed, her knees throbbed more. She wanted to shift, but every time she moved the slightest bit, the farmer pointed the arrow at her, and she didn't want to cause any disruption. He was already upset enough, along with the villagers seeing Samara. She would rather win them over through cooperation and showing them that she wasn't someone to fear. Though, it seemed as though it would be a feat to get them to trust Samara.

Over the short time Emelyne had been in contact with her, she had learned to trust Samara and believed she was who she claimed to be. She stood for rebuilding the kingdom and wasn't on the coterie's side. The fact that she was also bonded with a dragon helped. Emelyne had seen their connection. It looked very similar to how she felt with Monut.

She scanned the crowd before her, the ones who had circled around calling for her prosecution and possible death over what they thought was her theft. Their faces were hungry—hungry not just for a new life, but also for food.

Her eyes traveled over the buildings and the streets, and her heart ached for the people. The buildings had been all but destroyed. They were still habitable, barely, and were in desperate need of attention. The poor little village around the palace had been brought to ruin over the last hundred years without the royals to lead and defend them. It was probably held together with a thread of hope.

No wonder they distrusted outsiders. It would take a lot of work to earn their trust, if she managed to get out of her predicament and somehow get them to believe her. In some ways, she thought she would probably be better off if Samara weren't trying to save her. She was a human, after all, and she had no magical powers. She might've been able to reason with the farmer, and the villagers, eventually, proving she wasn't guilty.

Movement caught her eye, and she glanced over at two small figures shifting between the crowd. Uninhibited by the humans who stood at least a head higher than them, Gibobo and Lozzeak elbowed their way to the front. Their eyes remained fixed on Emelyne, worry creasing their faces.

A flicker of joy ran through Emelyne's heart on seeing that her ma and pa had made it to the village, yet the last thing she wanted was for them to see her in such a predicament. She knew they must be so worried seeing their adopted daughter face persecution for something that she didn't do. The glares they garnered didn't seem to bother them as Gibobo charged out in front of Emelyne and faced the crowd. Lozzeak stood by her side, keeping an eye on the farmer with the arrow.

Gibobo clapped her hands, calling all the attention to her. "Villagers of the Paddosha Palace. It's true what this ex-coterie member says. This is our adoptive daughter, an' we are the reason she speaks like dwarves an' not like a human. I can guarantee that she is well fed an' doesn't need to steal chickens from ya farmer. Can ya not see the muscles on her body? She is extremely muscly an' fit, an' she ain't too thin." Gibobo pinched Emelyne's biceps, holding her arms slightly away from her body before turning her attention back to the crowd. "I don't see any of ya lookin' as muscly as her. Ya all thin an' look like ya starving. Ya village is a wreck. Ya have nothin' here that we want to steal, not that we would anyway. I promise ya that we're here to help. We don't want to take from ya. We hope to help ya rebuild this place, make it look nice again, how it should look. If ya let her go, we offer ya the skills of three talented blacksmiths, meself, me husband, an' our adoptive daughter." She indicated Emelyne.

"Together, let us make this village of Paddosha Palace the envy of the human realm once again." Gibobo turned toward Samara. "An' as for this sorceress, yes, she is a sorceress, an' yes, she was part of the coterie. In the short time we have known her, she has earned our trust." She paused for dramatic effect. "Why does she have our trust?" She turned and faced the audience, taking in their faces. "Because we have seen her treat dragons kindly." She studied each and every person in the crowd intensely. "Have ya seen any member of the coterie treat dragons kindly? I bet ya haven't. They usually capture dragons an' torture them an' persecute them, makin' them a very rare breed. Not only that, she has also treated every dwarf that she has talked to kindly. This ain't the way the coterie would act."

Someone from the crowd yelled, "And how are you supposed to trust her after only knowing her for a little while? It's easy to pretend that you like someone when you really don't just for appearances."

Lozzeak placed a comforting hand on Gibobo's upper arm. "I agree. This can be done, an' people do pretend to be somethin' else to win over ya trust. But I don't believe this is the case with this sorceress."

Samara raised her hands, silencing the crowd as the murmur rippled through it. "If it makes you feel any better, I will leave these lovely people with you, and I will leave the village. Over time, hopefully, they can win your trust, but do not push them away because of me. They can offer you skills that will help you rebuild this beautiful place. I have things I must attend to, and if you still do not trust me by the time I come back, then I will not stay. But at least give them a chance. You don't have much more to lose, judging by the state of this village."

"We have no qualm with dwarves!" someone shouted, "but you, sorceress, it will take a lot more than a few words to get us to trust you. If these dwarves are honestly as good as they claim, then they can stay. They can stay in the ruined castle, in any of the rooms there, though it is advisable that they try and find their own food, for our supplies are getting low. We have been robbed by the coterie, and we also have very few farmers, which is why this farmer was so upset to have his chickens watched."

Samara held up her hands. "I will leave. I will give you time to sort out whether you trust them or not, and hopefully, I can help rebuild the realm from another place. I will also see if I can find you farmers to help build up your crops and pastures. In the meantime, I hope you remain safe away from the coterie's scrutiny."

"Is it true what they say?" the farmer asked Emelyne.

"We are talented blacksmiths who make quality items with metal, and we can certainly help you rebuild this village," Emelyne said.

The farmer lowered his bow and shoved the arrow back in his quiver, then looped the bow over his shoulders before helping Emelyne to her feet.

Samara nodded at her before turning and heading away from the crowd. Forgrac remained behind, watching the group. The crowd seemed to shift when she left, satisfied that Emelyne and her family would help rebuild the town.

"You can start work tomorrow," a man in the crowd said to the three blacksmiths. "We'll show you where the smithing shop is, so you know where to begin at first light. We haven't had a blacksmith in a very long time."

The farmer led them toward the blacksmith forge, showing them the empty, run-down shop not far from the square's center.

Pa nodded. "We'll clean this up tomorrow and get it set up, ready to start our work in full. We look forward to helping all of you, and so does our adoptive daughter."

"Are you not going with Samara?" Emelyne asked Forgrac, who had walked with them.

He shook his head. "No. I believe Samara intends to take the dragons to a special place and keep them safe until this village is rebuilt."

"What about Monut? Will he stay close?" Emelyne hadn't heard from him for a little while, possibly because he was out of range.

"I'm not sure." Forgrac said. "That'll be up to him. I'm sure if he goes, he will not leave for long if he is truly bonded to you."

"He is, and I assume he will stay around." Emelyne looked wistfully toward the forest.

"Yes, the bonded don't like to travel too far from their precious one," Forgrac said.

"Where will Samara take all the dragons?" Emelyne asked.

"She's taking them to a secret place I cannot share with you. But do not assume she knows little. I assure you she's working hard to bring this realm and the others back to their full potential so the coterie will fall."

In one way, Emelyne wished she could travel with Samara and see more of the realms, and in another, she knew that she had so much work to do where she was—to rebuild the Paddosha Palace and to bring it up to full strength—if they were to have any chance of going against the coterie.

# CHAPTER TWENTY-NINE

Reading the crowd before her and listening to their comments, Samara could tell that she wouldn't win them over. They still distrusted her deeply after her time in the village with Callista. She didn't blame the people of the Paddosha Palace. Callista had managed to destroy the village further overnight, wreaking havoc and killing several residents. If Samara were one of the villagers, she wouldn't have trusted her either. Once Gibobo and Lozzeak had approached the crowd in defense of Emelyne, Samara chose to take a step back.

When she saw the villagers release Emelyne in exchange for professional help to rebuild their village, she said goodbye to Forgrac, encouraging him to stay in the village. He could perhaps help them restore it, help build it with other dwarves, or take the opportunity to entertain them when they rested at night. He had no reason to go with Samara right then.

Emelyne and her parents certainly had their work cut out for them in rebuilding Paddosha Palace Village and also gaining the villagers' trust. It was probably best that they didn't know she was the princess just yet.

Samara left them and wandered to the nearest forest with Ulrieg to meet the other dragons hiding there. An idea had come to her of what she should do with the dragons. They would not be safe, a mere twenty of them, stuck in the forest nearby. She would have to take them to safety, and she only knew one place that would keep them safer than any other in all the realms. Ulrieg kept watch above her in his invisible form, scouting the area and making sure that no members of the coterie surfaced nearby.

When Samara arrived at the forest, Cyrra jumped. *Oh, wingless flight! You scared me.* Cyrra's eyes were wide with panic. *All sorts of noises have been coming from this forest, from all different animals, and who knows what else.*

"It's okay, Cyrra. It's just me," Samara said.

*Thank goodness!* She spread her wings, showing off her brown-and-beige stripes. *I mean it's nice being out of the Merciless Sanctuary and its threat of starvation or dying of thirst in a dry, desolate area. Instead, the forest is full of life. But that means people have reason to visit and hunt there.*

Samara touched her snout gently. "I understand."

Monut wandered up to her, his thundering footsteps slightly rattling the ground. *Have you seen Emelyne? I can't find her, and I can't connect with her through our bond.*

"Yes, she was captured by a farmer—" Samara started, only to be interrupted by a deep roar from Monut. She held up her hands, trying to calm him. "It's all good, my friend. The farmer thought she was trying to steal his chickens, but they managed to find their way out of it with her parents' help. They are in the village now."

Monut snorted a plume of steam. *They'd better not harm her.*

"I don't believe they will. I left because I didn't think I was helping the situation. Rather, I was making it worse. But I think the people are keen to rebuild their village again. They are tired of it being so run-down and wrecked by the coterie," Samara said.

*And what will you do?* Monut lowered his head to her level.

"I want to take you dragons to the safest place I know," Samara said.

*And where is that?* Monut asked, confusion on his face. *The Merciless Sanctuary is the only place that has been safe for us so far.*

"Yes, but I know of one other place where the dragons will be much safer, and only Ulrieg and I know about it."

*Where is it?* Cyrra stood close to Samara, dwarfing her, though her height was much shorter than Monut's.

"Believe it or not, Ulrieg and I think we have found Dragoria, and I managed to open a small window in the barrier. I left it there last time, but I do not believe that anyone else has found it since we left. Which means that the coterie doesn't know it's open. They probably can't sense the hole in the barrier. I have opened a few between the different borders now, and they still haven't been closed."

Cyrra jumped excitedly from foot to foot. *Oh, can we go? Can we go, please? Can we go? I definitely want to see Dragoria.*

Monut looked taken aback, confused, as Samara smiled at the stripy dragon's enthusiasm. *Are you sure it's Dragoria? You'd better not be getting our hopes up over nothing.*

Samara smiled. "We're fairly certain. The paths to the realm are rather run-down. We have opened it to the Slosiaran side of the realm only. We haven't gone in because we have much to do, and there's not much point in me going into Dragoria. We need to get this realm up and running then maybe find some dragon elves. Hopefully, there will be some guardian dragons left in there."

*It all sounds too good to be true.* Monut had a wistful look in his eye. *I should stay here with Emelyne, to make sure she is safe.*

"I understand." Samara moved closer to Ulrieg at the thought of being separated. "Maybe we can take you and Emelyne there once the village is mostly fixed."

It was an overcast day, the sky full of clouds without a single patch of blue.

Samara looked up. "Do you think we can travel today with all this cloud cover?"

*Once we get to the cloud cover, we will be safe, but we need to get up there first.* Monut craned his neck to look at the sky.

"Then let us prepare. Surely, if we take off, there will be nothing to catch us. It would have to be some powerful magic to knock dragons out of the sky. But there is one problem. I want to show you where it is, but I cannot ride Ulrieg. I would have to walk, and that would take weeks to get there."

*Don't be ridiculous. Since Monut has to stay here to look after Emelyne, you can ride me,* Cyrra said.

Samara nodded. "Thank you, Cyrra."

*But I won't be able to carry you for long. I'm not really a human-carrying dragon.* She squatted and indicated for Samara to mount.

Apprehensively, Samara climbed onto Cyrra's back, and the dragon flapped her wings before running to take her up to the top of the tall trees. Staying within the trees lining the plain, she kept within the cover of the forest. With Samara's body weight, they jerked from side to side, and they dipped with each wing beat. It took Cyrra extra flaps of her wings to remain steady in the sky with the weight of a person on her back.

After about half an hour, Cyrra lowered herself to the ground. Samara could feel Cyrra's heart thumping on the back of her thighs where they were hooked around the dragon's neck and pressed against her as she attempted to land. The landing dragon wobbled from side to side, and Samara's legs were unable to catch her balance and hold the drag-on's neck as they found the ground. Cyrra's chest thudded onto the ground from the force, and Samara was flung forward, landing in a bush not far from them.

"Are you all right, Cyrra?" Samara climbed out of the lantana bush and brushed the leaves and twigs off her clothes.

The beige dragon nodded. *I'm fine. I'll have a few minutes rest then I'll give it another go. I'll get it. Just wait and see.*

True to her word, a small amount of time passed, and Cyrra lunged into the air with Samara on her back.

*I need to go a bit higher to see if I can steady out.* Cyrra flapped harder, taking Samara just above the trees.

Samara tensed, digging her fingernails into Cyrra's scales and trying to get a good grip. Even with the added height, the dragon's flying was still unsteady. It seemed to work quite the opposite. Samara was scared. She did her best not to show it.

*Are you all right, Samara?* Ulrieg's concerned voice was a welcome distraction.

*Sure. I'm doing great!* Samara clenched her teeth as Cyrra jerked in all different directions.

*You know I can sense your feelings, right?* Ulrieg exposed his teeth in what was supposed to be a smile.

Samara was too preoccupied to look. *I guess you could say I'm a little scared.*

*Wingless flight!* Suddenly, Cyrra plunged, her wings unable to stabilize her as the ground shot up to meet them.

*Samara!* Ulrieg screamed.

There was nothing Samara could do. She didn't know any spells to cushion her fall. She closed her eyes, thinking her time had come. Ulrieg's panic through their bond didn't help calm her. Her hair whipped toward the sky. The breeze screamed in her ears. Terror pulsed through her veins. She wanted to do so much more with her life that was about to be cut short.

Something firm thumped against her side, followed by a sharp object dragging along her leg and up her dress as she was thrown in another direction. Her eyes sprang open, only to be met by Monut's large gray chest. He had grabbed her in his talon and held Cyrra upside down with the other. Cyrra's wings dangled helplessly.

Steadily, Monut lowered Cyrra and Samara gently to the ground.

When the ground bore Samara's weight, she breathed a sigh of relief. *Thank you, Monut.*

Monut stood over them, making sure they were all right.

His black horns bunched together in a frown, Ulrieg approached them. *I think you'll be better off walking, Samara.* He shook his head. *I'm sorry I'm not big enough to carry you.*

Samara climbed to her feet, stamping the ground to remove the dirt and leaves and trying to clear the fear at the same time. "You may be right, Ulrieg. I have no qualms about you not being able to carry me. It's very rare that it would come in handy." She checked her leg for blood, but Monut's talon hadn't broken the skin.

*Hmm.* Monut sauntered by her, his feet thudding against the ground with his heavy weight. His talons dug into the soft dirt, leaving scratch marks behind. *I think I should fly you there. That way, I will know where Dragoria is. Then I should fly you back, unless you plan on staying in Dragoria with the dragons.*

"What about Emelyne? Shouldn't you be near her?" Samara asked.

*If things settle down and she is no longer in danger, then I shall fly you there. I think it's the best option. I do not wish to stay there. As much as I would like to see Dragoria, I know that I should be close to my bonded to defend her, if need be, and be by her side to give her strength.*

"I would appreciate that, Monut," Samara said. "I think then we will cover much ground quickly, so I can get on to the rest."

# CHAPTER THIRTY

Samara climbed onto Monut's back, and he leaped into the sky with Ulrieg leading the way. The rest of the dragons followed, with Cyrra flying close to Monut. For a patch of time, they were exposed to all the villages below and the Paddosha Palace, but they flew in the opposite direction while they ascended quickly into the cloud cover. Samara peered over Monut's side, and her limbs trembled, weakening her hold. After her experience with Cyrra, flying made her nervous, even with Monut's steady wing beats.

Monut dashed through a puffy white cloud like a large cotton ball, halting any vision for Samara within a few feet. She grabbed tightly around his neck with nothing to hold on to but his scales. He rose in what seemed like an endless climb, while precipitation washed her face, until eventually they burst through the clouds with no one above them. It was only a big fluffy layer below them, looking like a large comfortable bed to sleep on.

Ulrieg turned visible the second he passed through the clouds, showing them the way. They flew south of the human realm, heading to where they had opened the barrier. All the dragons kept up, even the baby dragon, for the baby dragon wasn't much smaller than Ulrieg.

Above the shield of the clouds, they flew quite some distance until eventually the clouds tapered off. Ulrieg quickly scouted the area and led them to land and hide in a rock formation until nightfall. Strong hues of orange, blue, and pink painted the sky as the sun retreated for the day. It wouldn't be long until darkness engulfed the land, giving the dragons a blanket to hide behind as they headed farther south.

Weariness engulfed Samara as they rested. She had slept little over the last few days, and exhaustion's obsessive claws sank into her flesh. With her back pushed against a large rock, she feasted on a few nuts and dried fruit, ready to settle in for a quick rest. The sound of scraping talons pulled her attention to the side, as Cyrra approached her.

*Why are we hiding so much if you used to be part of the coterie. Can't you fight back and defend us?*

Samara finished her mouthful then took a deep breath. "I wish I were that powerful. I have learned some magic, and I can do a few magical things with my arrows, but I have not learned as much magic as I should have because I left the coterie early."

*Why?*

Samara took a sip from her canteen, the water cooling her parched throat. "Because I couldn't leave the dragons defenseless. I realized the coterie was capturing and torturing smaller dragons under the coterie building. I had to help them, and so did Forgrac. We were both found and had to run. It was no longer safe for us to stay. Now, unfortunately, I don't have access to any kind of magic learning materials, and I wouldn't have a chance of standing against the coterie, especially more than one member at a time—even if I gave it my best."

*Are we seriously going to Dragoria?* Cyrra's voice trembled with excitement.

"From what we could see, I think it was Dragoria. Obviously, I hadn't been there before, and neither had Ulrieg. But it had the markings of what used to be the great dragon realm, and Ulrieg was at the height of his moon peak, so he had high senses, just like he does now." Samara stretched her legs in front of her.

*If that's the case, there should still be dragons there. Shouldn't there?* Cyrra tucked her wings by her sides.

"I would think so. I don't believe they exterminated all the dragons. They just sealed off the realm so nobody could find it and no dragons could get out." Samara threw another handful of nuts in her mouth.

*Haven't the guardian dragons got magic?* Cyrra asked.

"I honestly don't know too much about guardian dragons. In fact, I didn't know such a thing existed as a guardian dragon, or any dragons, until I bonded with Ulrieg, and that was a shock. What we learned in the coterie had nothing to do with dragons. It was almost as though they never existed until I discovered them under the building where we were schooled," Samara said.

*Oh, that's terrible. That must've been a shock.* The stripy beige dragon wrapped her wings around herself.

"Yes, it definitely was. And it took me bonding with Ulrieg to open my eyes to the ways of the coterie." She rested her head against the rock and looked at the darkening sky.

Cyrra yawned and shuffled away, curling up in a

space between other dragons. The dragons rested in a circular form in a little opening between the rocks. The baby was playing and eventually collapsed in a deep sleep while the others rested, catching up on energy to be ready for another flight in the night.

Samara's eyes were droopy, and she adjusted to be more comfortable against the stone with Ulrieg curled up next to her. She was almost asleep when a stone skittered across the ground from a direction where no dragons rested. When she spun, she saw a human standing just on the edge of the dragons, frozen on the spot. His eyes were wide as he studied each of the dragon forms before he slowly backed away, cursing under his breath.

Quickly, Samara jumped to her feet. The last thing she needed was for a coterie member to be nearby and the human to go tell them about the dragons. She raced after him, only to find he had disappeared. Ulrieg joined her, turning invisible as they went on a search through the rocks and then toward the forest, trying to follow his tracks.

*Ah, gotcha!* Ulrieg sounded excited.

*Where are you, Ulrieg?* Samara asked.

*I'm just a few paces away, on your left.*

Samara quickly hurried in that direction.

*No, the other left! Wingless flight!*

Feeling her ears heat knowing she deserved his

snark in that instance, she quickly changed direction to find Ulrieg pinning the human against a tree, intimidating him with his deep-red eyes and his teeth exposed in a snarl. In combination with his multiple horns all over his body, he looked rather vicious and ready to attack.

The man thrashed underneath the pressure. "Please, don't hurt me. Please, please, don't eat me!"

"He won't eat you unless you intend to tell the coterie where we are." Samara stood beside her dragon, facing the man.

The guy huffed, looking rather nervously at Ulrieg's teeth only a few inches from his neck. "I don't know any members of the coterie, and I didn't know dragons still existed. But what I do know is that I don't want to be eaten by them. I've heard they're vicious creatures and will tear somebody apart in a matter of seconds."

"Ulrieg doesn't eat people, and neither do these dragons. You are safe with us, as long as you don't inform the coterie," Samara said.

The man raised his hands and pressed his back harder against the rock. "There is no chance of that."

Ulrieg leaned back and eyed the man curiously before he snorted out a plume of steam, causing the man to flinch against the hot air.

Ulrieg lowered one front leg to the ground, his

talons tapping on the hard dirt. *We're actually friendly. We don't eat people,* Ulrieg spat. *That's a disgusting thought. I'd rather eat a deer or rabbit any day. How could you think such a disgusting thing? Oh, that's ridiculous!*

Samara nodded, placing her hands on her hips. "I have been friends with many dragons, and none of them have wanted to eat me."

The sky was almost dark, and the dragons were preparing to take off again.

"That's good to know," the man said. "If you don't mind, I'll just go that way." He pointed in the direction farthest from the dragons, but Ulrieg didn't let up.

"Feel free to go, but please, remember, do not tell the coterie about this group. We do not need them to be captured and tortured," Samara added.

The guy cringed, then from behind a rock stepped a familiar face, causing Samara's steps to falter.

# CHAPTER THIRTY-ONE

"Samara is that you?" The tall male human before her looked as astounded as Samara felt. Dressed like a farmer, with a beige tunic and long brown woolen pants, Paxton's father moved next to the human they had been pursuing.

Samara struggled to move as her mind processed the shock. Out of all the people she expected to see, he was at the bottom of the list. He was so far away from where she had last seen them.

Paxton's father turned and saw Ulrieg pinning the first man against a rock. "Ulrieg, what are you doing?"

Ulrieg slowly backed away, removing his talons from the man and landing his four feet on the ground. The angry-looking dragon almost appeared embarrassed as his eyes darted from side to side. *Oh, this stranger stumbled across our little camp of dragons. So we were making sure that he wouldn't run back to tell the coterie where we were. You know, all in a day's work, trying to make sure we stay safe.* He brushed his front talons together as though wiping away the evidence.

Paxton's father moved closer. "This man won't endanger your dragons, and he's definitely not someone who would support the coterie. Like us, their family has been threatened by the Sacred Flame, though they don't have a child there anymore. Apparently, his son died recently, while under the coterie's care. But instead of just stopping their benefits, the coterie also threatened them."

Samara knew only one person had died recently in the group of apprentices.

She took in the new man and observed his face, recognizing similar features to Blade. She squinted. After consideration, she had little doubt that he was Blade's father, even if she hadn't known Blade long. She remembered his lifeless face staring up at her before Paxton had been gracious enough to bury him in a coffin of roots. She swallowed. "Your son was Blade?"

The man's face turned wan as he nodded.

"You knew him?" Paxton's father asked.

It was Samara's turn to nod.

"Did Paxton know him too?" Paxton's father ran a hand through his brunette hair.

Guilt swept through Samara as she nodded. She didn't think he would know about Paxton's demise yet.

"What is it?" Paxton's father twitched uneasily. "Is Paxton all right?"

Samara shook her head, and a tear trickled down her cheek. "I'm so sorry. Things went south for me after I returned to the coterie base, and Callista took me hostage. Paxton helped me escape, but as we were almost out of there, one of the sorcerers took Paxton and put him inside this evil orange orb that sits under the coterie building." She hugged herself, watching the pain on Paxton's father's face. "I don't know if the orb is going to kill him or try to turn him evil. I haven't managed to get back to see if a couple members secretly working against the coterie have been able to free him. Not knowing is tearing me up inside." By then, Samara's cheeks were wet. "I have a few more things to organize in Slosiaran, then I'll do my best to ensure he is released."

A mixture of grief and anger passed over Paxton's father's face. "Then you must come to get me when you go."

Samara shook her head. "There is no use going

unless you have a death wish or have learned strong magic."

He sighed his annoyance and threw his head back. "Then what can I do to help you get to him quicker?"

"At this moment, I'm not sure." Emotions whirled through Samara as she eyed Paxton's and Blade's fathers. She clasped her elbow and squeezed, trying to force away the additional tears over remembering, once again, where Paxton was and how little she had done to help him so far, putting the restoration of the realm before Paxton's wellbeing.

Ulrieg took over the conversation for her, his head tilting as he observed Paxton's father. *What are you doing out here? And how on earth did you two run into each other?*

"We have been wandering around, looking for a place to settle, a place that we can build up and earn a living. It has been hard, and we've been on the move. We ran into each other on the road," Paxton's father said. "But not only that. We ran into another family also doing the same thing. They are a very large family and could use help getting set up quickly."

Samara wondered about her own family. She hoped they were still safe. "Are you staying far from here?"

Paxton's father shook his head. "No, we're not. We're looking for a place to set up a farm, and we still must buy the produce and animals to run it. We have some coin, but not much. Setting up a few farms will be tricky. I don't think that we have enough. So, we have a long way to go and a long struggle ahead."

"I think I know how you can help me. I know of a place where you can settle that needs farmers." Samara brightened.

"I think all of us would be very grateful," Paxton's father said, and Blade's father nodded.

"I must lead the dragons somewhere safe first, but then I'll come back. While I'm gone, I need you to prepare to travel again. I know of a village that lacks farmers but has the land to be farmed, just not the knowledge to do so," Samara said.

"Are they open for more people coming in? Because so many villages have turned us away saying they're too full." Paxton's father looked unconvinced.

"I believe this place is very open. They are lacking in food, as the village was destroyed by the coterie, so it won't be completely safe. We have to be wary of the coterie, but you will be with people who I'm sure would appreciate your efforts."

"Where is it?" Paxton's father looked puzzled.

"It's Paddosha Palace."

The men gasped.

"Are you sure they'll take people like us?" Paxton's father asked.

*Pfft!* Ulrieg rolled his head dramatically. *They are desperate for help.*

"What about halflings? Do they accept them too?" Paxton's father furrowed his brow.

"They have accepted the help of dwarves. I certainly don't think they will discriminate against halflings," Samara tried to reassure him. Though she hadn't seen any there, she knew if Emelyne had her way, they wouldn't care who helped.

"Will dragons be there?" Blade's father eyed Ulrieg cautiously.

"I'm certain Ulrieg would return with me and probably Monut, who is a very big dragon." Samara gestured with her hands. "But don't be afraid. He's already bonded with someone very important and won't hurt you, either, unless you threaten his bonded. Did you bring anything with you?" Samara asked.

"No, we could not fit much through the hole to get into this realm, so we only brought ourselves and our talents, with very few belongings."

Samara held her quiver strap that looped across her chest. "Please go back and tell the others to prepare for departure. We'll meet you back here. I'll return as soon as I can to collect you and show you the way to Paddosha Palace Village and introduce you. They don't appreciate me because of the color of my hair, indicating that I'm a past coterie member. I traveled there with Callista once, when she was quite violent with the villagers, and they haven't forgotten. But I do have people there who will help you settle in," Samara said.

*Samara, is everything well?* Monut asked in her mind.

Samara looked at Ulrieg. *Can you convey to him that we are fine, that we have just run into a couple of families who need our help and we'll be back soon?*

"All right. The sun is going down, and we have to return to the group. They are deep in a thicket of trees, and we need to help them prepare whatever food we have," Paxton's father said.

Samara nodded. "Meet us back here tonight so we can find you on our way back. If someone waits here, we will collect you and take you to the Paddosha Palace Village. But for now, the sun is setting, and the dragons need to fly under the cover of darkness. I don't expect it to take too long traveling by dragon-back."

# CHAPTER THIRTY-TWO

The monotonous tone of the hammer banging against the steel they were crafting on the anvil rang through the blacksmith shop. They had been there at least a week, and Emelyne was slowly helping build different parts of the village. It would be a long, tough road to get the village back up to its past magnificence, reflecting the image of the Paddosha Palace. Then they had the daunting job of rebuilding the palace itself, if everything went to plan. She had watched the dragons fly off on the first day of her time in the village. She didn't know where they were going, and she wished she could have gone with them. Many of them had become her friends, but she had to stay, and they deserved a safe place to hide.

Because they had so much work to do, they had

taken Silut on as an apprentice to teach him the blacksmithing trade. No one else wanted to work with them initially, but they hoped that would change over time. They had too much work for the three of them, plus Gibobo, to finish. Silut paused to take a break, his breaths labored.

"Samara said they found ya on the road bein' tortured by a spell." Emelyne hadn't talked much to the dwarf. "That must've been awful."

Silut wiped his brow. "Aye! That's for sure. One of the coterie members did it to me. She surprised me, as her hair wasn't bright colors like they usually are. It was pure white. She left me there fightin' for me life."

Emelyne's chest caved. The poor dwarf must have been beside himself. So far, she hadn't heard anything good about the Sacred Flame coterie, except for Samara. "Did she take ya from a village, or did she spot ya on the road?"

"She grabbed me from the outskirts of me village. She scared the life outa me. I'm too frightened to return." Silut fiddled with the hammer's handle.

"What did ya do for work? It doesn't look like ya had a physical job. Ya get exhausted too quickly."

"Do ya mean like now?" Silut flashed a grin and wiped the sweat off his cheeks.

"Yes."

"I used to run the inn and tavern for our village."

"By yourself?"

A cloud passed over Silut's eyes as he shook his head. "With me wife an' two small kids."

Emelyne blinked. "What happened to them?"

Silute's shoulders caved. "I ain't got a clue. We got separated, an' I don't know where they went."

"I'm so sorry." Emelyne placed a hand on his upper back. "If ya ever run into them, they are welcome to join us here."

Silut grunted, the action taking the words out of her mouth. "Well, we better get on with it. These bars ain't gonna make themselves. Can ya show me what to do next?"

Emelyne was shocked by the sudden change of conversation but held onto a piece of steel, indicating to Silut how to hit it and how to mold it with the hammer against the anvil. Then she handed him the hammer. She held the steel with her left hand as he banged consistently against the piece of metal, trying to shape it as she had instructed him to do. But as she held it, Silut missed the spot and hit her hand instead. His aim was still off, being that of an apprentice. Emelyne dropped the piece of steel and swore under her breath, wringing her hand, trying to bring the feeling back into it and shake out the pain.

Horror clear on his face, Silut dropped his hammer, ignoring his work as the hot metal started to cool. "I'm so sorry, so sorry. Oh, I'm so sorry." His face was pale with worry as he watched Emelyne try to shake it out. He had hit hard, though it wasn't as hard as Emelyne would have hit with her muscular strength, but he was still quite strong and stocky for a dwarf who hadn't worked a physically demanding job.

Emelyne took off her glove to inspect what damage had been done, hoping she didn't have any broken bones. She twisted her hand this way and that.

Silut grabbed it as well. "Is there anythin' I can do?"

She shook her head then flipped her hand so the back faced up.

"Is that what I did to ya hand?" Silut looked pale as he pointed to the crescent-moon-shaped scar.

Emelyne shook her head. "No, that's just a scar I got when I was a child. It's been there for as long as I can remember."

Silut's brow furrowed. "That's an interesting scar."

Emelyne shrugged and tried to ignore the comment as she gave her hand another quick inspection, working her fingers to get rid of the stiffness. After a couple of moments she shrugged, slipped on her glove, and pulled it tight. "It should be right now. Let's get back to it. We can't afford any downtime."

The dwarf nodded, firing up the kiln again, then he picked up the steel himself and started to hammer it again. He continued hammering, his job on that one almost complete when Emelyne's father called her.

"Can ya help me with this for a bit, love?" he asked.

She raced over, turning her back on her apprentice, knowing he should be adept enough to finish what he was doing.

Their first job was a nice metal gate to go along the edge of the village, one that hopefully they could put up to stop looters from stealing. Everyone entering and leaving would have to speak to the person on guard. They would put people on duty at the edge of the village and make sure the fence was built the whole way around, enclosing the built-up area. The big piece would go right in the middle of the gate, and Emelyne's father needed a hand holding the very large piece of metal so he could mold the swells, welding them to other parts to make them steady and strong—stronger than any gates they had seen in other villages. They never used swells in dwarven villages, but it seemed important to have them for the gate of the Paddosha Palace Village, especially with all of the adversity the coterie had brought in.

Emelyne helped him sculpt the curves, using her gloved hands to hold the mostly cooled metal. It was still too hot to hold with her bare hand as they straightened it out and wound more curves through it. He made it several feet wide, enough to cover many of the bars that would run across the gate. He fashioned the wavy lines, then they set it aside before they started to work on another item.

Emelyne didn't know what her father had started to design. His pieces of metal were strangely shaped, making it hard for her to identify what he was creating. After working for quite some time and watching him mold it, when he had finished about a third of the design, she realized what it was.

"Are ya makin' a dragon?"

The image looked much like Monut's head.

"Yes, I am. I figured it would be a good sign to have on the front of the village, one that would support the princess."

Emelyne shushed him, staring over her shoulder toward Silut's station. That information was still secret to all the villagers and the dwarves that they didn't know, which was why she hadn't told Silut the real story about the scar. But when she turned, Silut was no longer there. She looked back at her father. "Did you see Silut step out?"

Her father shook his head. "No, I've been too busy designin' this. I thought he was under ya guidance."

"He is. I thought he had enough to do with makin' and shapin' the different bars, but he's gone."

Her father shrugged and smiled cheekily. "Maybe nature called, an' he had to obey its order."

Emelyne screwed up her nose. "I guess that's fair. Hopefully he won't be too long, because we have a lot more to do."

"Even though we have a lot to do, we still all need breaks." Her father eyed her seriously. "Otherwise, we would collapse from exhaustion."

"I understand. That is so true. I just get worried we'll never get it done, an' we'll never start the palace to help these people have a safe village again."

"One step at a time," her father said.

Emelyne continued to help her father with different parts of the dragon, watching his artistic craftsman side come out. Every little bit that he weaved was more and more like Monut made of metal. She'd never seen anything like it—not that Emelyne had traveled far.

"This will be stronger than any gate I've seen in my lifetime," her father said proudly.

They worked together for the rest of the afternoon, weaving and designing it. The dragon's spread wings made it seem larger, and a nice long tail would also secure part of the gate on the outside.

"Perhaps we should get Monut to baptize this with dragon breath when it's done. That should make it even stronger. After all, it has been our secret ingredient for our metal products and weapons," Emelyne said.

"That was my intention all along. If we have a dragon as magnificent as Monut, why not use his skills?" Lozzeak asked.

By the time the afternoon was on its last rays of sun, the tail had been woven and designed with the spikes on the end. Silut's area was still vacant.

"I wonder what happened to him." Emelyne picked up the hammer he had used, tossing it before catching it in her fingers.

"Maybe you wore him out. He has been working hard all week," her father said.

Emelyne laughed. "Oh, the poor thing! I'll have to work him extra hard tomorrow."

# CHAPTER THIRTY-THREE

A welcome lightness washed over Samara's heart, knowing that Paxton's family was safe and well. At least that was one positive for their family. Not only that, but she had also found a couple of farmers for Paddosha Palace Village. Finally, something was going right. All they had to do was set up the village and restore it. It was the only way that the people could grow strong and secure in their own means.

First, she and Ulrieg had to make sure the dragons were safe. The sun had set, and the sky grew dark enough to cover the dragons, giving them the opportunity to take off again under the pale moon.

She climbed onto Monut's back and hugged his neck, grasping his scales and hooking her legs tightly over the front of his wings. They covered much ground in the darkness, with the dragons following Ulrieg. The black dragon had a better understanding of their bearings than Samara. The dragons took advantage of their night vision, studying the land below them for any sign of the coterie.

They passed over many villages with their lights burning below. Every time she glanced over Monut's side, her stomach lurched and her body rocked, and she felt the surge of vertigo kicking in. She swayed and quickly clasped Monut's scales, digging her fingers into any crevice she could find.

*I will not let you fall, little one.* Monut's deep voice echoed through her mind. *You may not be my bonded, but after what I've learned from being with you, I will care for you over this trip, for I feel you will help my bonded grow her future and her kingdom. So if you fall, I will catch you. Do not be afraid.*

Warmth radiated through Samara's heart. "Thank you, Monut. I appreciate that. As much as I appreciate you taking me for a ride, I am actually glad that my dragon cannot carry a human. I think I am meant to stay on the ground rather than a dragon's back." It was an experience she would never forget, and she was honored that the princess's dragon chose to carry her, but the thought of being so high wasn't for her.

A deep rumble issued from Monut's throat as he chuckled. *You do not have the daring spirit of my bonded, but you are a brave heart. I know this because only a brave heart would go against the coterie after what you have seen and experienced. Ulrieg has informed me of what you have been through, and I admire you for that. But it takes a special kind of person to ride a dragon so high above what is natural for their beings.* His throat rumbled again. *If it's the height that you are afraid of, focus your sights on the horizon. It won't seem so high then.*

Monut's words settled Samara's heart, and she found it easier to remain still and keep her eyes focused on the lights flickering on the horizon, instead of the ones directly beneath her.

*But I must say, Ulrieg flies slowly compared to the likes of me and the larger dragons,* Monut grumbled.

"He is a much smaller dragon, so of course he flies slowly." Samara brushed a strand of hair from her face.

*Way to go, picking on the small guy.* Ulrieg suddenly appeared next to Monut.

*You should know it is rude to sneak up on a dragon. You risk your life by doing so,* Monut warned in a friendly manner.

Ulrieg snorted a plume of steam and flew faster, disappearing for a moment until he gained distance from Monut. They flew for a while longer, until the moon was well into the sky, and

Ulrieg slowed again to be in line with Monut and Samara. *I think I can see the barrier we opened,* Ulrieg said.

Samara strained her eyes, trying to see ahead, but she couldn't find what Ulrieg was talking about. "I can't see it with my eyes, but you would know much better than I do."

*I assure you, it's up ahead.* Ulrieg twisted his neck to see her. *What, don't you believe me?*

*I don't know what you're talking about.* Cyrra flew up beside them.

*As if you would. You don't know what it looks like,* Ulrieg snarked. *Just follow me.*

Not long after, Ulrieg started to descend, and the other dragons followed him. They spiraled down until they landed. Ulrieg was careful not to lead them to the barrier, ensuring that the larger dragons wouldn't run into it and cause damage to themselves with the speed at which they could fly. Several thumps sounded from the twenty dragons as they landed in front of the vine creeping over the opening.

Samara stood back, recognizing the spot she and Ulrieg had visited a while before. Slowly, she approached the barrier, feeling her way along it. Unable to get past it, she headed toward the tunnel that was covered with the vine, under the arch that Ulrieg couldn't fly over. She felt for her arrows in the darkness, the ones she had shot into the barrier last time. She found several under the arch, embedded into the barricade, barely able to see the shafts in the dull light.

She shifted her hand, and it passed through, but the hole was not big enough to let larger dragons enter. She had not accounted for dragons of Cyrra's or Monut's size.

She backed up, grabbing an arrow from her quiver, and called to Ulrieg. "I need you to breathe fire on the tip of the arrow again after I spell it. We need to open a bigger hole."

Samara glanced back at Monut, his scales beaming in the sunlight, and she realized that he couldn't even fit under the bridge. She would have to make a large hole in the barrier in the sky above the arch. "We have our work cut out for us. I hope you have a lot of that special fire because we're going to need it."

She pulled arrows out of a quiver, telling the dragons to stand back. She ignored their chatter as she spelled her arrows and had Ulrieg breathe his dragon fire on the tip. She loosed them into the opening beneath the arch, doing so several times before checking that the hole was big enough by first having Ulrieg pass through it, then sending the other dragons approximately his size through.

Each passed through without snagging on the edge of the hole. Samara then stood back and had Ulrieg return through. She aimed the spelled and dragon-blessed arrows exactly above the arch next, forming a large circle. Noticing the arrows sticking out even in the darkness, she saw the circle of shafts faintly glimmering in the moonlight. She turned around to the large dragons remaining. "Who would like to go through and try it?"

*I'll do it,* Cyrra offered. She rubbed her talons together. *How exciting. I can't wait to go and see Dragoria.*

*I can guarantee you there are many who want to see Dragoria, Cyrra. But you do the honor of being first for the larger dragons,* Monut encouraged.

Cyrra lunged into the air and flapped her wings before plowing through the invisible hole. She passed through without a problem and was able to return as well. *I got through fine. Everyone else, follow me. I can't wait. Come on, guys,* she said excitedly.

*I will not come with you, but I would like to come through and see what it looks like,* Monut said. *The curiosity is killing me.*

Samara walked under the tunnel, entering the land that they suspected was Dragoria. "Do any of you dragons know if this is definitely Dragoria? The barrier was harder to cut through than any of the others, and we could not see into the realm from the other side of the barrier."

*I have no idea,* Cyrra said, *but it looks exciting. I can't wait to have a closer look. Perhaps there'll be some guardian dragons. They might have some wisdom for you, Samara, so you know how to use your magic better,* she said encouragingly.

Samara smiled. "That would be nice if they did. I could certainly use the help. And if it is Dragoria, I need you all to find more dragons and start rounding them up, because I think we will need dragon help on this side of the realm. Do you think you can do that?"

*Of course we can,* Cyrra said.

"If you can do that and get the dragons on our side, the other realms will have a better chance of standing up against the coterie. Hopefully, we can work together to bring our kingdoms freedom from the Sacred Flame." Samara slung the bow over her chest. "We could also use any dragons willing and big enough to train with a rider, along with the dragon elves and guardian dragon combinations."

Monut did a quick circle of the area, studying the

realm, staying far away from the barrier so he didn't hit it. *It feels good to fly in this realm. It feels like home. It must be Dragoria. I can't wait to explore this realm, but first, I must assist my bonded to rebuild her village and her realm.*

# CHAPTER THIRTY-FOUR

Samara, Ulrieg, and Monut said goodbye to the dragons, leaving them at the border of Dragoria to explore farther within the exposed realm. Still under cover of the night, they headed back to the spot where they had found Paxton's father. The moon had fully crested in the sky and was lowering toward the other horizon by the time they returned. They landed in the area where they had met, and they split up to search the hidden landscape, thinking the men might have fallen asleep in a space less open. Owls hooted in the distance, and an opossum scurried in the nearby trees.

A few minutes had passed when Ulrieg called, *I found him. He's fallen asleep against the rock.*

With Monut following her, slowly stomping across the plain, they went back to the place where they had spotted Paxton's father earlier. He remained asleep against the rock, snoring softly with his head tilted to one side. Blade's father was not far from him.

Samara approached Paxton's father and gently rocked him, calling his name to help rouse him from his nap. Rubbing sleep from his eyes, he startled, and his eyes widened as he pressed up against the rock, preparing to take on the person in front of him.

"Relax. It's just us. You're safe. We've returned as we promised." Samara released his arm and straightened her back.

He climbed to his feet and shook Blade's father's shoulder, waking him. His reaction was much like Paxton's father's.

"I'm so sorry. I was meant to be on guard, and I fell asleep. I was so tired." Blade's father gazed guiltily at Paxton's father.

"Relax. We're actually in the middle of nowhere, so it's all right. I didn't expect to see anybody else. We'd have to be pretty unlucky, plus we were in a sheltered area," Paxton's father said. "They have returned to pick us up, as they promised."

The two men led the way, with the dragons and Samara following. Samara remained close to the dragons for their eyesight under the dim moonlight. They walked for several minutes toward a large copse of trees before they weaved through it. Trunks were scattered densely around the area, providing a good shelter from the sky or from anybody outside of the trees. Monut struggled to get through the small spaces, eventually giving in and staying put as the others progressed.

Finally, they come across a small area with a fire in the middle and several people sleeping around the outside. They had no shelter, and the possessions scattered around them were meager. Samara stepped up to the camp's center to have a closer look at the sleeping people and found Paxton's and Blade's mothers. Samara's eyes landed on the next lot of people—a man and woman asleep together and, not far from them, six children ranging from five years old to near Samara's age. The man's face looked familiar, causing her heart to speed up in anticipation as she stepped closer, taking in his appearance and the woman beside him. She blinked, trying to clear her eyes, unable to believe what she saw.

"Papa? Mama?" Samara knelt beside them, resting a comforting hand on their upper arms, squeezing them softly to bring them out of sleep in a relaxed state. She felt Ulrieg's eyes on her, watching her every move as he sat close by.

Paxton's father gave her a strange look. "You know these people?"

Samara nodded. "This is my family. These are my siblings. If I had known you had my family, I would have come before I took off to the borders. How did you meet them?"

"The same way I met Blade's father." He raked his fingers through his hair. "We stumbled across each other on our paths, all trying to escape and find a place to settle out of the coterie's reach. They looked lost when we ran into them, such a large family with so many mouths to feed. But we are all trying to catch enough food until we find a safe place to settle and build our farms so that we may live and eat again. Between all of us, we have a few coins, but we've been buying things along the way, trying to blend into the crowds. It's been difficult when we have elves and halflings."

Samara was horrified. "Surely things are not the same as they were in your area and your village?"

"No, it's not like that. It's just trying to blend in and hide from any members of the coterie. After knowing what they could do because of our children, we wanted to escape their apprenticeships. It's not our children's fault they can't support the evilness of the coterie. Despite it all, we're actually quite proud of them." He tugged at the hem of his tunic. "We have been keeping a low profile."

A body stirred beside her, and she turned to see

her papa's eyes open and staring at her. Gently nudging his wife with a hand, he tried to wake her. "Samara?" His gaze held disbelief.

Tears leaked from Samara's eyes. "Yes, Papa."

She opened her arms, and he sat upright, throwing his arms around her. "I'm so glad you got out of there. You could have been in so much danger if they caught you after what I've done to the coterie."

"From what I've heard, you did the right thing, and we couldn't be prouder." He squeezed her tighter.

Her mother opened her eyes and threw her arms around Samara at the same time, stroking her hair. "You still have the markings of the coterie," her mother said, concerned.

Samara petted her hair, embarrassed by the color. "Yes. I don't know how to get rid of it, but it is slowly fading. Hopefully, it'll soon be gone, and my hair will be back to my natural color. I stand out so much like this and cause so much distrust."

"Where have you been all this time?" Her father pulled back, concern filling his face. "We heard that you had escaped quite some time ago."

"I have been out looking for the princess of the realm. Hopefully, we can rebuild it and build up some sort of resistance against the Sacred Flame," Samara said.

Her mother squeezed her shoulders. "We are so proud."

Footsteps thumped beside her, and Ulrieg turned visible not far from her. Her parents flinched, pulling away.

Ulrieg snorted, adding sarcastically, *Ah, great! More people afraid of me. Fantastic! Way to start the relationship.*

Samara comforted her parents. "Don't be afraid of him. He looks far worse than he is, and he also has a grumpy temper, just like he looks, but he is my familiar and is more loyal to me than anyone. I'm sure he would do anything to protect to you, too, since you're my family." She gave him a scrutinizing gaze.

Ulrieg huffed. *Of course, I'd look after your family. They're not my bonded, but I will treat your extended family with just as much respect.* He bowed mockingly. *I'm here as your servant.*

The sarcastic tone wasn't lost on her family, and Samara's father pulled a strange face. "You're a snarky one, aren't you?"

Samara sighed. "Yes, he is, but he's the one who taught me to see the truth about the coterie and how they aren't as they seem, as much as they pretend to do right by the apprentice's families. After we joined, they held it over us constantly, threatening to take away that privilege—nearly every day that we were there. I bonded to the dragon by mistake, and it has been the best mistake of my life." She straightened.

*And mine too,* Ulrieg said. *It was as much of a surprise to me as it was to her. We bonded by pure accident, but this is turning out to be a good relationship, and it makes me so proud to see that she is willing to fight on our side to help stop the dragons from being culled and tortured.*

"Samara?" A small voice pulled her attention away from her parents.

Samara turned to see one of her younger siblings had woken up and was looking at her, eyes blinking, from a few feet away. "Rina!" she called excitedly as the other siblings stirred, all spotting her at once. Once the shock had worn off, they sprang to their feet and wrapped her in a warm embrace.

When they had finished, and all the tears had dried, with Paxton's and Blade's families looking on, Samara stood. "All right. You all need to get up. I know you're probably tired and need more sleep, but we have to travel under the cover of darkness, because I have two dragons with me and one cannot turn invisible."

"One of the dragons *can* turn invisible?" Zaos, one of her younger brothers, asked.

"Yes. Ulrieg, my bonded, can." She indicated the glaring red eyes and the spiky-spined dragon that was half her size.

He was barely visible at night, with only the glimmering fire illuminating his black form until he turned invisible, causing everyone around him to gasp.

"Yes, it's a very neat trick, but I also have a large dragon with me who cannot carry everyone or turn invisible, so we will have to walk."

"Where is it?" Tiarsus, her youngest brother, asked as the parents gathered their things, packing them into the bags.

"Follow me." Samara led them out of the thicket and to the outskirts of the thinning trees, where Monut sat on his haunches waiting for them to return. A small beam of moonlight shone down on his gray head, accentuating his spikes and considerable size.

The siblings around Samara gasped in awe, the parents not far behind, and the ones who had not seen him, especially Samara's family, were stunned at his majestic form.

"Together, with Monut, we will take you to the Paddosha Palace Village. They're in great need of farmers, and you're in dire need of a home. They distrust me at the moment because of the color of my hair, but I have some connections there who can help you blend in and join them. Monut's bonded to one of them." Samara smiled affectionately at the large dragon.

Samara's parents stood on either side of her.

"Lead the way," Samara's father said. "We are keen for somewhere to settle."

Before the light had hit the sky, Emelyne set off to work in the blacksmith shop, knowing her father would not be far behind her. They still had a long way to go before they finished the village's front gate. As for the positioning, they did not know where it would be at that point.

Monut hadn't yet returned from his trip with Samara, and her heart longed for her large dragon. She hadn't worked out where he could safely stay out of the villagers' sight until it was the right time to expose him. Perhaps they would have to make the fence encircle the far side of the forest, where the dragons had hidden when they'd arrived.

Igniting the furnace, she prepared for the day's work. The flames jumped to life from a slow trickle to fast burning as she added more coals.

In her days of being there, the villagers had slowly become accustomed to her one by one, warming to her as they realized how much work she and her parents were putting in to help them. Helping the community made Emelyne feel good, whether she was a princess or not. Making them safer filled her with such pride that she would be content with just doing that. As much as she loved her work and loved her dwarven village, Bhal-wahrum, she was more fulfilled because she and her parents were helping humankind build a strong, sturdy village.

All they needed was more farmers, enough for the village to become self-sufficient and not rely on trading with other villages so much. That way, if they were ever besieged, they could survive within their own walls. She stacked more coal in the furnace, and a satisfying flame ignited. Heat pressed against Emelyne's skin. She could even feel its warmth through her leather gloves and the overalls that she wore for blacksmithing.

Thinking of the village safety, she wondered if any of the villagers had been trained in weapons. If they hadn't, they should start to look at that as well. They would have to find out if anybody in the village knew how to use a sword or fight with an ax, or even use bows and arrows. She had seen the ex-sorceress, Samara, wear a quiver full of arrows and her bow. It was an indication that she must be an expert archer, with the ability to teach others and build their strength and hunting skills. She would have to ask Samara when she returned to see if she could help the villagers with that or if she knew others who could train them to fight. Though weapons were not much use against magic, at least it would help them protect themselves.

She set to work molding the different beams and spikes for the fence. They wanted to make it extremely strong. So even if they built a stone wall, they would still reinforce the outside with the metal fortified by a dragon. That alone could take them months.

Straightening from stoking the furnace, she glanced around the smithy in search of her apprentice. Silut still hadn't come to work. He was often there early, before dawn, even before her father arrived. Yet he still had not turned up, though he'd left work early the previous day. She would have to call on him to see if he was all right. Perhaps he felt unwell. Better to find out the reason he hadn't come to work. It would be disheartening if he'd had a change of heart and wanted to find a new profession. As much as she could understand if it was too hard for him, too much physical work, his leaving would put them behind in production. She hoped that wasn't the case, because they honestly needed as much help as possible.

"Mornin', love." Her pa entered the blacksmith shop, his tone more cheerful than usual, and Emelyne wondered if it was because he was proud to help people. They had something more meaningful to work toward than the usual jobs at the dwarven village.

"Mornin', Pa." Emelyne arranged her tools, ready to start work. "Have ya seen Silut?"

Her father wiped his bleary eyes, trying to clear them of sleep. He looked around the room as if looking for the dwarf then splashed cold water on his face. "No, I haven't seen him. Ain't he turned up yet?" Splashing more water on his face to ensure the clean water got into his eyes, he blinked a few times.

"No, he ain't here. I'm hoping he hasn't changed his mind 'bout workin' with us. Or he could be sick. I'll check on him later, because it ain't like him to just not turn up."

Once her pa had finished washing his face, he went to his work area, ready to finish the final touches on the first gate before starting on the other side. He welded the dragon figurine to the front of several spikes that had been lined up, giving the gate more strength. He and Emelyne flipped it over, and he welded the curves onto the other side.

The dragon had turned out beautifully. He had a much finer artistic talent than Emelyne and could make some wonderful figures at times. She couldn't think of anything better than having a dragon figure like Monut on their gate for the Paddosha Palace Village, because she had bonded with a dragon, and the palace village would have at least one dragon to protect it.

As she worked on all the different bars for the fence, she watched her father recheck all the connection points for the welded dragon, making it extra secure. They worked for most of the morning, until it was light, then she put down her tools. "I'm going to the bakery to get some bread for breakfast. Do ya want some?"

Normally, her mother would bring her breakfast. But she was currently at the village, volunteering in the bakery to help make more bread for the extra number of people. She volunteered in the mornings, starting her day before Emelyne, then often joined them in the smithy later when the bakery had quieted down. The hours her mother worked in a day were astounding, way more than Emelyne's.

"A couple of knotty rolls would be good. Thank

ya, love." Lozzeak paused his hammering. "An' say good mornin' to ya ma for me."

"Will do," Emelyne called cheerfully as she headed out the door, her stomach rumbling at the thought of the freshly baked, knotted rolls.

Emelyne passed through the village streets, waving to the different humans who passed her heading off to their work for the day. Some returned her wave, and others still avoided her gaze. But she hoped that they would have time to work on the ones that still held onto their suspicion. Soon they would see she wasn't there to steal, but rather to help.

Heading to the bakery on the corner of two streets, she passed the shop owners setting up their market stalls and the trade of whatever foods or crafts they had. When she arrived, the door and front windows were wide open. With a nice big counter and a small door at the front, the smell of freshly baked bread wafted out to the streets, causing Emelyne's stomach to growl more loudly with each step.

Her ma stood in the corner, kneading bread and molding it before setting it aside to rest. When she saw Emelyne walk through the door, a big smile lit up her face. "Mornin', love!"

"Mornin', Ma." Emelyne returned her smile. "Pa said to say mornin' too."

Another lady worked on the other end of the counter, kneading bread, and a third in the back added the baked loaves to the cooling racks before placing the cooled loaves in the display basket.

Emelyne said good morning to both, and each acknowledged her, returning her greetings politely. She knew the ladies were only happy to see her because her mother had worked so hard proving her worth to the village. She was slowly winning their trust one individual at a time.

"Is it a busy day for ya?" Emelyne knew it was, but she consistently tried a little conversation to break the ice and hopefully warm them to her more. Each day, her reception was a little friendlier.

The woman at the front nodded. "I heard a large group of visitors arrived this morning. A large group usually means lots of hungry people."

Her ma quickly finished the dough she was working on then climbed off the tall step that sat behind the counter, making it a better height for her to work. She grabbed a few knotty rolls, placing them in a leather bag, and handed them to Emelyne. "Here ya go, love. Say mornin' back to ya pa for me. I'll be over as soon as we finished here."

Emelyne accepted the bag before leaving the

store, calling goodbye to her mother and the other two, happy for their friendly acknowledgment as she left. She hadn't seen the farmer since the first day, but she hoped the word about how much her family was helping the village reached his ears.

She halted at the door as a small crowd of people Emelyne hadn't seen before stepped inside with the sorceress. Several more waited outside.

"Samara? You've returned, and who are all these people with you?"

An uneasiness grew between the two bakery staff as Samara entered, the arrows in her quiver clacking as she talked to Emelyne.

A rare genuine smile lit her face. She turned to the bakery staff. "These travelers are starving. Can you please arrange some loaves for them to share? I'll pay you."

Samara fiddled with the quiver strap slung across her body as she turned back to Emelyne. "You wouldn't believe it, but on our way back, we ran into my family. We had run into a couple of families on the way there as well. It turned out that I knew them, and I promised to come collect them and their companions on the way home. Then, lo and behold, there were my parents and my siblings." Samara proudly looked outside at the group of children in a range of ages that hovered near the door. "The good news is that they're all farmers, and they can help. They've been searching for a home after we told them to run from their original ones because the coterie would soon be after them."

Noticing that the bakery staff hadn't moved, Samara turned her attention back to them. "Do you have a problem with my request? These people are farming families."

The two women glared at the sorceress.

Emelyne tried her luck, thinking that the staff were probably put off by Samara being one of the people who came with Callista to destroy their village not so long ago. "I can vouch for Samara. She ain't here to destroy the village. She is also here to help."

The staff didn't move.

Emelyne's mother climbed down off her stool and grabbed some fresh knotted rolls and large cobs of bread for them. "I'll pay for this lot, love." Gibobo placed several loaves in a spare leather bag and handed it to Samara.

Samara nodded and thanked the dwarf before addressing the apprehensive bakery staff. "I promise you, my family are expert farmers and have managed many farms over the years. Paxton's parents manage sheep and spin wool. They make clothes and all kinds of other things." Samara indicated Paxton's parents and brother. "As for the others, I'm unsure, but I know they are also farmers. They lost their son to the coterie. He died while in training there. The sheep farmers—their son is in deep trouble with the coterie, if he's not already dead."

Samara continued to press her point. "They may need a little financial help until their farms are established and they can trade. We need them strong if we want to set them to work instantly. The sooner the crops are planted, the sooner the village can reap the reward of the produce. Can you imagine the type of support that would be to the Paddosha Palace Village?"

A glimmer of guilt crossed the bakery workers' faces, and Samara took that as a step in the right direction.

"Do you know where they could start setting up a farm? There must have been farms here before."

The two bakery workers nodded, and the one turning out loaves answered, "Besides the farmer who captured Emelyne to start off with, we used to have a lot more farms around the outskirts of the village, but the coterie destroyed them all. This devastated a lot of the food supply. There may be beds for them inside the village for now, but they would need to start working on the farms and the food before they start on the homes."

The other bakery worker wiped her hands on her apron. "We don't have an inn anymore. It was at the front of our village but got destroyed. Probably the only place available would be the ruins of the Paddosha Palace with Emelyne and her family."

Emelyne turned to Samara. "There should be more room in the Paddosha Palace."

Samara turned up her nose. "When I was there, it didn't provide much shelter. I stayed there before, the first time I came to this village, and it was definitely not comfortable."

"You'll find very few places available that will be. You would think destroying the kingdom and the palace would be enough damage to satisfy them, but no. The coterie kept focusing on us, making it worse as the years passed. They wanted us to struggle harder, and many people left, including the farmers." The loaf turner turned back to the oven and pulled out some more baked loaves.

Paxton's father had snuck into the bakery as they talked. "The ruined Paddosha Palace would be more secure than where we have been sleeping lately. We'd be more than happy with that until our farmhouses are rebuilt."

"Thank you so much for the information," Samara said.

The bakery workers' faces seemed to soften slightly toward her.

"I promise you, you will not regret adding these families along with ours to help you rebuild your village." Emelyne turned to leave.

"We have seen how much work you have done," the bakery worker said. "It'll be nice if others work just as hard and bring new skills like the farming back to the village."

# CHAPTER THIRTY-SIX

A couple of weeks passed, and each of the newcomers were slowly proving their worth. The village had become more content with each improvement. Samara had helped the farmers, and seedlings were already starting to grow in rows.

Emelyne and the sorceress had grown to know each other better, and she had opened up to Emelyne about wanting to rescue her beloved, but she reluctantly put it off until her family's farm was more established. Selfishly, Emelyne hoped she would stay longer. That way, the people would have more time to perfect their archery skills, and more fields would be planted. She knew how much her sword combat students had improved over the short time. Samara had also given Paxton's parents some of her hard-earned money to buy sheep, while she had helped her parents purchase seeds and other items they needed to build their farms.

Emelyne and her father had continued to work on the fences, building them to go around the outside of the farms and the forest as well. The farms must be protected just as much as, if not more than, the rest of the village.

Since he had returned to the village with Samara, Monut had been staying in the forest. It wasn't ideal, but she couldn't think of anywhere safer. He had grown restless hiding there, but she hadn't yet told the villagers about his presence. It would be a problem if he became too restless or if someone wandered into the forest and stumbled upon him. Not that Monut would harm them, but it would scare the person and probably turn into a dragon hunt—something she hoped to avoid for both parties.

The dragon figurines on the front gate were finished and looked impressive, and she couldn't wait for the villagers to see it. The dragons left little room for someone to climb the gate, which was finished with tall spikes above the figures, making it impossible to breach. There would only be one way past, and that was through the open gate, not over the top.

Each day, as they worked on the fence, there was no sign of Silut. Emelyne had been through all the village and the outskirts, searching for him anywhere she could think of and asking different people if they had seen him. It was so strange that he had suddenly disappeared, with no warning or indication of where he had gone. She hoped he was okay, and she missed his sly comments that kept her on her toes. She had often teased him over not being strong enough to do the work. Perhaps that was the real reason why he left.

As her apprentice had taken off, the workload became overbearing. Soon she would have to announce to the villagers that they needed a new apprentice. With the warmth of the community increasing, it gave her hope that people would be willing to join them.

A human apprentice would also help her learn how to speak like a human. As much as the villagers didn't seem to discriminate against the dwarves, she didn't think they would appreciate having a princess that talked like one. It seemed important to mold herself into the human image of a princess that they would have in their minds. It wasn't her end goal to become the princess, especially a girly one. But if that was what the people needed, that was what she would do, even though she would be happy to simply keep helping their village rebuild. She didn't need a title for that.

With the gates finished, the spikes for the fence came together much quicker. Once the metalwork was done, they would have the builders make a stone wall behind it for added protection. That was how they would make it extra hard for anybody to get into the village unless they went through the approved channels.

They would employ people to stand on top of the wood towers they intended to build on each side of the gate, so the guards could watch and decide who could come through. Later, she thought it would be a good idea if they built a second stone wall closer to the main village, which would add more protection for the people within. Seeing the progress, more and more of the villagers offered to help build the fence around the village as they recognized the benefit of having one.

Emelyne had gone to look at the new fields that the farmers had plowed. She could see the hard work that had gone into it, the bushes they'd had to uproot and destroy to plow the fields and plant crops. A variety of fruits, vegetables, and grains had been established, giving them more supplies for the near future.

Not only did the newcomers help the village grow, but they also brought more skills to train others in. It brought smiles to the villagers' faces. They had pride in their village once more, and a lot of the frowns caused by the worry about the coterie and the condition of their village were fading. They were being replaced by a lightheartedness and happiness and hope for the future, each step making Emelyne's heart soar.

Forgrac decided that he and his actors should perform a play at nightfall to help build the village culture. It was one that they had been performing before they decided to help rebuild the town—a story about the lost royal—and it seemed to hide a subliminal message. Emelyne's heart warmed as she watched the faces around them taking in the story, which she knew was about finding her and some of her history.

The history about her parents was a lovely addition, confirming the details she had heard before. It told the story of how the royals had once ruled their realm before they were destroyed, killed by the coterie members. Many of the villagers nodded throughout the play. On stage, as the lights ignited and went out, Emelyne knew that Ulrieg was invisible, working in the background and using his dragon fire. She wondered why the people didn't question how it worked. But then she thought they probably imagined Samara was responsible and using magic, since she had once been a coterie member.

It amused Emelyne that the sorceress played the part of Bianca. Her performance was captivating, dragging the audience into the story, and many faces seemed to soften over her efforts. Samara's hair color was slowly fading, with only traces of pink through the bottom half. That, too, seemed to help the villagers accept her presence.

The play had the villagers laughing and clapping in certain parts, and in others, they wiped tears away. When the story finished, the audience clapped, the approval crescendoing when the actors took their final bow. It made sense that they earned good coin as they traveled, and at the same time, they were smart enough to pass on the news about a royal who had gone missing but was still alive.

When the clapping continued for quite some time, Forgrac lifted his hands, pressing them repetitively toward the ground to quiet the crowd. Sensing that the players hadn't finished, Emelyne waited for the next part of their performance. She stood in the back, leaning against one of the broken buildings that needed repair as she watched.

Once the crowd was quiet, Forgrac addressed

them. "I will say this in a way you will understand, using the human language, for it is too important to miss. If you hadn't noticed, this play contained a message. Some of you will say they already know this and that it is true."

Several people in the crowd nodded.

"That means you know there is a royal out there hiding, their identity unknown to the coterie and to the people. Well, tonight, we have some news for you. It may come as a shock." Forgrac surveyed everyone in the audience. "The royal is much closer than you think. As we traveled around Slosiaran, we kept an eye out for her, following a trail after someone said a person they knew had met a person with the markings of the royal." He paused as the audience struggled to take in the information. "We traveled far to follow this lead, and as it turned out, we found the royal."

A soft murmur went through the crowd.

Once the murmuring faded, he continued, "Not only did we find the royal, but we found out that she had bonded to a dragon."

A new round of murmurs passed through the audience.

Forgrac read the crowd, taking in their responses and seeming to see which way to go with the conversation. "As you've seen, the blacksmiths have made a beautiful gate, strong and sturdy with a dragon emblem on it." He again surveyed their faces, seeming to revel in their response. "Would you find it hard to believe that a dragon is nearby?"

The murmurs rose through the villagers.

"We brought the royal with us, but we haven't told you because we wanted you to see what she was like and let her work with you before we introduced her." He spread his arms, milking the drama.

The people scanned the crowd, looking at the newcomers. It was a mixture of confusion and curiosity when they searched, as if they could spot the royal among them, ignoring the ones that had dwarven or elven heritage.

"I know you're struggling to believe this, but she is definitely here. Would you like to meet her?" Forgrac asked.

Emelyne's heart thumped wildly in her chest. She wasn't expecting him to introduce the royal after the play, and if her friends were telling the truth, it was definitely her, as much as she did not feel like a royal. The crowd nodded, each of them pressing closer, trying to listen harder, keen to see who Forgrac was talking about. Yet Emelyne's chest would not settle. Her heart thundered against her rib cage as she worried about how they would react when they found out.

"Emelyne, can you come to the front, please?" Forgrac gestured for Emelyne to walk to the stage.

Her arms were numb, and her legs refused to cooperate with her mind, causing her to stumble as she made her way through the crowd to the front.

# CHAPTER THIRTY-SEVEN

Heart thumping against her chest, Emelyne made it to the stage, the people parting to create a path for her to walk. She hadn't expected an introduction like that, though she didn't know what she had expected. If she was honest, she didn't mind staying the way she was, continuing to help the village and seeing the happiness grow on the villagers' faces. It was reward enough that they took pride again in their village and the work that was happening around them. She was tired from all the work they had done over the last couple of weeks, but her adrenaline kicked in. The blood raced through her body, making her unsteady on her feet.

When she stood next to Forgrac, he held her by the elbow, helping her stabilize. She cleared her throat. "This is a surprise. It's completely thrown me off bal—"

"What makes you say she's the royal?" A man interrupted at the back of the audience.

Emelyne remained patient and strong, thinking of her friend Thiznabo and how taking her rightful place would help avenge her death.

"Yeah, what makes you think she's the royal? I mean, it's great. She's been working and helping us rebuild our village, but you must have some proof!" a woman in the front row yelled.

Toward the far left, a man called, "She's just a human that's been raised in a dwarven village. She doesn't even sound like a human. How can she be our royal?"

Forgrac stood in front of Emelyne, holding up his hands, indicating for them to be quiet. "We have proof. There is a mark on her flesh." He turned to Emelyne. "If I may?" He held out his hands, requesting hers.

She slowly placed it in his palm. Forgrac pulled off the glove that she wore constantly to hide the mark of the royal, and showed it to the crowd. Resting between her forefinger and thumb was a crescent shape.

"This is the mark of the dragons, given by a water dragon to Bianca just before she escaped the palace on the day it was besieged. This is a dragon bite passed down with each generation of the royals. Every royal baby born after Bianca has had this mark."

"Then where are her parents to prove it?" the man in the back yelled again.

Gibobo and Lozzeak walked onto the stage, and Emelyne's ma stepped to the front. "Merely hours after Emelyne were born, her mother and father were killed by a coterie member. I had worked for her mother, helping her with the daily chores, as my family has done for generations. My ancestors used to work in this village and used to wait on the royals. When Emelyne's mother saw the coterie member come to her village, she quickly passed Emelyne to me and asked me to protect her. Little did I know that this would end up being a lifelong commitment. My husband and I have raised her with the dwarves, which has caused her to speak like one. We raised her this way so we could hide in the caves, somewhere she could be hidden every time a coterie member came to our village to buy something from us or demand something from our people." Gibobo dug around for something concealed in her clothing. "As additional proof, I have this bracelet handed down from generation to generation that her mother gave to me for safekeeping."

She held it aloft, allowing people to see it. It held a turquoise stone framed in a solid gold band. She turned to Emelyne and took her hand, smiling into her eyes before she slid the bracelet onto Emelyne's wrist. "This bracelet has a twin. The royal females would often wear one on each wrist. The other one was stolen or went missing, but this one I managed to keep hidden and safe, along with Emelyne. I am giving it back to her now."

The audience fell silent as they witnessed the different evidence proving that Emelyne was part of a royal family.

Samara saw the bracelet and moved forward. "Callista has the other bracelet, as she also has the original headdress. She obtained the bracelet sometime over the last year and uses the crystals on these jewelry pieces to power her magic. She is a crystal witch, and the crystals on them make her stronger."

A ripple of shock passed through the crowd.

"Another thing we have to reclaim from the Sacred Flame coterie," Forgrac said.

"You said that the princess bonded with a dragon!" a man from the middle of the audience yelled.

Forgrac smirked. "Yes, I did, and that is true. Would you like to see him?" He studied the audience. "Are you for dragons or against them?"

"We're for anything that goes against the coterie!"

a woman yelled from the front. "We are tired of their aggression and their dominance over us and the way they treat us."

"Now that is something I can understand. We thought you might want to meet him, and he has agreed to come." Forgrac looked pleased to unveil the first dragon the people would have seen in a long time.

Emelyne paled, and she gave Forgrac a strange look.

"Please step forward and confirm that you are bonded to the princess," Forgrac announced loudly and clearly.

Emelyne looked everywhere, searching for Monut. It didn't take long. The destroyed palace was the backdrop to the stage, and over the top, Monut climbed the broken pieces, his large form enormous even against the ruins. Emelyne spun and smiled, pride engulfing her. Destroyed pieces of the palace crumbled to the ground. Large stones clattered as they fell. Monut descended to the ground, stopping in the area behind the performers and Forgrac.

He stood protectively over Emelyne, his eyes scrutinizing the crowd before him, looking for anybody who would go against her. Emelyne turned and reached out a hand, touching his snout. He nuzzled it, his eyes still glaring threats over the top of her at anyone who might wish her harm.

Forgrac turned to address the gaping crowd. "Do not fear. He is not here to attack you unless you want to harm his bonded or anyone his bonded cares about. So in other words, if you protect Emelyne or treat her with respect, the dragon will also treat you with respect. Imagine a world with a princess who is not only bonded with a dragon but who also can sword fight and ride that dragon."

Monut leveled his gaze at the audience, his throat rumbling. *What he says is true. I will honor and protect anyone who treats my bonded well.*

Forgrac turned to the crowd. "What do you think?"

Silence echoed through the audience as they watched, some with mouths open, taking in Monut's massive form.

The man at the back yelled, "Everything I've seen so far has confirmed that she is who you claim! Lost royal, or not, if she is willing to rebuild this village, to bring it to its old glory, and fight against the coterie, I think I can speak for most of us when I say that we are happy to support her."

Nods of agreement rippled through the audience, and many people started to talk among themselves.

Samara stepped to the front of the stage beside

Monut. "I would also like to say something." She remained wary as she waited for the audience to settle. "I know I was here with Callista a little while ago, and she terrorized the village. I did not want to be a part of that—I was not a part of that. Though I did not do anything because I didn't know how to stand against her. I do not have the education or power to defy her on my own. I am deeply regretful that I could not help save some of your people. But I would like to prove to you that I am on your side."

"Why should we trust you?" an elderly woman called from the front row.

"I understand your frustration and the desire to distrust me because I have looked so much like a member of the coterie for so long and because of my past. But I ask you this, have you ever wondered what my familiar was? Because I have never revealed my familiar to you, and every member of the coterie has a familiar if they are a strong, powerful magic wielder."

"Who cares?" someone yelled from the audience. "You basically support the coterie anyway. You look exactly like one of them."

"Eventually my hair will fade to its natural color." Samara pushed her lips to one side. "My familiar turned out to be an enemy of the coterie." She turned and faced Monut. "This isn't the only dragon that you have in this village at this moment. My familiar is also a dragon."

Standing right next to her, the black form of Ulrieg appeared, his glowing red eyes set on the audience. The collective gasp was astounding, louder than the one expressed for Monut, because Ulrieg had appeared out of nowhere.

"It was an accident, but bonding with Ulrieg opened my eyes toward the coterie, which is why I am here now. I am working against them, and you can thank this dragon for that."

Ulrieg snorted a plume of smoke, and more gasps escaped the audience.

"Ulrieg has been within your village for quite some time now, and he was also here hiding and working against Callista when she was here, persecuting your people. We did our best to fight her and to prepare for the royal's return. We have been on a long journey, searching for Emelyne to bring her back here and offer protection while we rebuild your village."

Lozzeak shifted to the front. "While the two dragons are here, I would like to show ya our secret of how me family has made the strongest weapons in all of the land. As ya know, Emelyne an' I have been preparin' an' workin' on the village gates. We have a long way to go before the fence is complete, but we have completed the front gates. If ya come with us, the magic touch an' the secret ingredient to our work will be put on them tonight." Lozzeak walked down the street, leading Emelyne.

The crowds parted for them as Monut and Ulrieg walked side by side, each behind his bonded. They headed through the village and along the road, and ended up out front in the darkness. Many held sconces high, trying to spread the light. They stopped where the two gates rested flat on the side of the road, ready to be assembled and put to work.

Emelyne's pa gestured for the audience to step back. "Now, me dear Monut and Ulrieg, if ya wouldn't mind blessin' our work with your magic fire…"

The two dragons breathed plumes of fire over the metalwork, sealing it with their magic fire. They started on one side of the gate and finished on the other, making sure they also included the metal dragons. A cheer went through the crowd.

"This will make these gates much stronger than any gate ya have ever come across or heard of." Pride washed over Lozzeak's face.

That night, much celebration took place. The villagers knew they had a lot of work to do, but they had hope to live for. They pooled together their meager supplies and shared them, even happy to share with the newcomers. They would celebrate, and the next morning, the men would gather to help install the new gates at the village boundaries. During the night, people gazed upon the gates with awe and nervous laughter. The symbol of the dragon was a defiance against the coterie and what it stood for—a bold statement, and something that would undoubtedly bring them trouble in the future. On the other hand, it also seemed to bring with it courage to the villagers, especially after seeing two live dragons.

The villagers had agreed that the metal fence

would surround the entire village, including the farms. So it would be a long, drawn-out process to make the final fence. From then on, they would have to train people to be on guard and hone their fighting skills.

While the villagers celebrated, Samara had opted to keep watch around the front of the village. As she was heading to the outskirts of the village with Ulrieg walking beside her, Emelyne raced up to her.

"Samara!"

Samara waited for Emelyne to catch up as Monut's enormous form followed closely.

The princess jogged to her, barely panting. "I've been meanin' to ask ya if ya honestly think ya dropped the dragons off at Dragoria. Monut told me where ya took them."

Samara adjusted her quiver and bow. "I've only been to the border, but it looks different from the rest of the realms and has a different feel. The buildings look run-down. I haven't gone any farther. We've been on a mission to find you and to rebuild Slosiaran. But not long after I left the coterie, Ulrieg and I discovered the boundary that would not let us see into the realm. It's unlike the boundaries between the different kingdoms. And unlike the other borders, I could only open a small hole with Ulrieg's help. If it is Dragoria, I think it's best to keep it a secret until we have built up enough of a resistance and know what condition the dragons are in."

*We hope there are more dragons like me and especially like Monut. We need more fighter dragons.* Ulrieg walked between them. *And hopefully, we'll find some guardian dragons. They are the brains and the ones who can transform, unlike the rest of us. If there are guardian dragons, we need to find dragon elves.*

"Dragon elves?" Emelyne asked.

"Yes, elves who bond with dragons. Their magic is extremely strong when they do so."

"I don't know about all that." Emelyne shook her head. "I'm sure I have a lot to learn."

*As I said, you're as naive as Samara was when I first met her,* Ulrieg grumbled. *Hopefully, that's a basis for a good leader. But being naive isn't all bad. Sometimes, it makes you more open to learning.*

"Will the dragons come back once they're finished? I can't wait to hear back from them," Emelyne said.

"I'm not sure. I guess it depends on what happens in there. It's been a long time since the dragons of Dragoria have been exposed to the outside world. It all depends on if they've gone mad or not. But I do know that the dragons in these realms need protection against the coterie. Though the normal dragons don't have magic, the guardian dragons apparently do, especially if bonded with a dragon elf, and we need their kind of magic to go up against the coterie. In the meantime, we can do our best to try stopping the coterie from treating everyone the way they do." They reached the edge of the main village, and Samara scanned the horizon.

"Thank you for ya help in doin' all of this," Emelyne said.

"I would do anything to go against the coterie after what I've seen them do, and my family also needed a place. So thank you for taking them in, though I know you won't regret it," Samara said.

"What're ya plannin' on doin' in the future? We need to train more people in weaponry. Are ya able to help them?" Emelyne asked.

Samara paused. "I am trained in archery, and that is my favorite weapon. I can teach more people while I'm here, but I plan on leaving soon."

"Where are ya goin'?" Emelyne asked.

"My beloved is trapped in that terrible orb underneath the coterie building. He's there because of me. He only got involved in all of this because of me." Samara took a deep breath, trying to calm her emotions. "Every day I'm away from him, my heart yearns for him, and the guilt racks me from thinking that he could still be there. Others at the coterie are secretly working against the Sacred Flame, but I don't know if they've been able to get him out, and I have to set him free if it's the last thing I do. I've spent so long away now. The orb could be eating away his goodness and turning him to something evil, or it could be killing him. I won't know which until he comes out—if I can free him." Her shoulders sagged.

Emelyne placed a hand on her shoulder. "I understand ya leaving then. If ya ever get back here, ya always welcome. I'm sure we could use ya help."

Samara rested a hand on her upper arm. "I think you'll make a great leader. You know how to listen, and you have a heart. I can get behind that. You certainly have your work cut out for you. But at least the people seem to be on your side." Samara pulled an arrow out of her quiver and nocked it. She barely had to aim before hitting a rabbit quite a distance away.

Ulrieg flew out and fetched it, bringing it back to Samara. She pulled the arrow out and handed it to Emelyne. "Food for another day. I'll keep an eye out for more while I'm on watch."

Emelyne picked up a small stone from the road and threw it into the distance. "Have you seen Silut lately?"

Samara shook her head. "No. I thought he was working with you."

"He was, but then, the other day, he disappeared before the workday was over, and I haven't seen him since."

Samara frowned. "That's odd."

Emelyne nodded. "I've been to where he sleeps and checked every place I can think of but haven't seen any sign of him."

"I'll keep an eye out." Seeing the tiredness in Emelyne's eyes, Samara smiled. "You should go to bed, Princess. You have an early day tomorrow preparing more of this fence to protect the village. Hopefully, one day, you'll have a house to live in or a palace that's been rebuilt and will give you more comfort than living in a broken-down room with not much shelter. That shows just how humble you are."

Wearily, Emelyne shook her head. "Oh, I don't need a palace."

*But you should have one.* Monut walked beside her. *You are the princess.*

Emelyne squeezed her arm and kicked a rock off the road. "These people don't need a palace. They need food and supplies. They need to be able to look after an' defend themselves."

"And that is what you'll give them as well as train them and teach them how to do this. So you need your rest. Good night, Princess," Samara said.

"Ya right. I'm tired an' I have a lot to do, thankfully with help. Night." She turned to leave, taking the rabbit with her.

*I will guard with you both tonight.* Monut kept pace with Samara.

"Thanks, Monut. We could use your help. It's such a large area to watch over." Samara observed the princess as she walked away, many thoughts running through her mind. She honestly thought Emelyne would be a good princess and would rule the people with fairness. She had shown levelheadedness and had certainly not been brought up to be rude or think she was above any other class. Samara took in a deep breath of the night air, glad that, so far, things had turned out and the village had accepted Emelyne. They were all willing to pitch in to rebuild the village. She just hoped that the coterie would stay away.

Samara was happy for the village, but the pull to help Paxton was growing too strong, and she knew it would ruin her if she ignored the call. Being trapped in that evil orb underneath the coterie building would be horrible. No, she wouldn't stay long. She was determined to go help him, even if it meant her death.

As Monut and Ulrieg made their rounds of the village outskirts, a couple of owls flew over her, taking her back to her early days in the coterie. She wondered how Gray was, since she had left him behind and he no longer had to act as her familiar.

The night had been uneventful so far, exactly as she had thought, but it was best for someone to be on guard and prepare for the worst. If the coterie received word of what was going on, then she had no doubts they would come.

She saw another rabbit in the distance heading for the newest growth of seedlings, and she shot it, turning what would have been lost produce into added meat for the villagers. She didn't particularly like killing animals, but they needed to eat, and the sheep were too few to use as food yet. She grabbed the rabbit and added it to her small pile near the destroyed inn at the forefront of the road into the village. She would take them inside in the morning.

As she paused near the collection, something black flew over her, and she gazed up. She could have sworn in the dim moonlight that she saw a crow. Cringing, she remembered the senior apprentice Mist and her crow familiar, Okak. It was strange to see a crow flying at night. They weren't nocturnal.

She straightened and watched it pass again, determining for sure that it was a crow. Her stomach whirled. Many bad memories flooded her of dealing with Mist in her final days at the coterie. Dread trampled down her spine as worry swamped her that Mist was close. She would cause nothing but trouble, with no mercy along with being an excellent fighter. Being on the opposite side of Mist gave them very little chance of success.

# CHAPTER THIRTY-NINE

The crow landed on one of the destroyed walls, watching her for quite some time, each moment setting Samara more on edge. She attempted unsuccessfully to shoo it away. Instead, it stubbornly stayed and watched her for a little longer before deciding to take off into the night, expelling several caws as it flew away.

Unease swamped Samara. Nothing about that crow was normal, making her think again that it was Okak. She paced the road before the destroyed building of what used to be the inn. Her eyes wide, taking in her surroundings, she considered what to do if the crow was Mist's familiar. If it was, that was a sure sign that trouble loomed just around the corner.

*Ulrieg,* Samara called through their bond.

*What is it?* her bonded replied.

Ulrieg was still on duty, the two dragons circulating the area above the village, Monut remaining more to the back. That way he could keep out of sight of anybody who might see him in the darkness.

*A crow just stayed here watching me for quite some time. It's really unusual behavior for a crow at night. I have a bad feeling. I think you should warn Emelyne to hide.*

*Wingless flight! How did Mist find us so quickly, if that's her familiar?* Ulrieg groaned. *We haven't been here that long. Not one part of the village has been rebuilt.*

*I don't know. I'm not quite sure that it was Okak, but it could very well be, and I don't want to take that risk. Monut should hide as well.*

*Something tells me they won't cooperate so easily,* Ulrieg said.

*I understand, but I think it's best we take precautions. They could be near to undertake a visit ordered by Callista because she's still looking for the crystal.* Samara tugged at a strand of hair.

Ulrieg grumbled, *It's almost like we should have built the village in a different spot and made it a new village. That way we wouldn't have been discovered this soon.*

*You would think that would be better, but there is a certain pride in taking back your original land and rebuilding this village after everything they've been through just because they've been associated with the royals.* Samara worried her lip. *If it's Mist, I hope that nobody has given away the fact that the princess is here.*

*All right. I've already told Monut, and he's on his way back. I shall go and find Emelyne and instruct them where to go.*

That put Samara slightly at ease, knowing the princess would be hidden somewhere secret and safe that only Ulrieg knew about. It was too soon to lose the princess when they were only starting to rebuild the village. The village needed the princess to survive more than anything, if they wanted to raise the whole human kingdom.

The sun peeked over the horizon in the far distance, slowly bringing light to the area.

Samara hoped that it would bring a positive feeling for the village that day. She waited, her unease itching at her soul with each additional ray of light that spread across the land. Normally, she would have packed up and headed back home by then, ready for some rest before helping her family with building more of the farm. But she felt as though she should stay awhile longer, at least to give people warning if someone like Mist did turn up. She would wait until it was full daylight, and others could keep an eye on the horizon to check for any person who might be coming.

Samara paced, longing for Ulrieg to return, and when he finally did, the sun had almost risen.

He turned visible on the ground next to her, his shining red eyes intense. *It took a lot of effort to get them to hide. They were determined to stand and fight for the village. I admire their tenacity, but the last thing we need is for them to be captured by the coterie, or worse, killed.* He marched next to Samara as she paced. *I'm going to fly out there and look around. I'll be back as soon as I can.*

*That's a fantastic idea, Ulrieg. I've had a very uneasy feeling since seeing that crow, and I'm worried that Mist is just around the corner.*

Nodding, Ulrieg pushed off into the air, turning invisible halfway through his first flap of wings. She worried her bottom lip. She didn't know what she would do if it was Mist. Her powers were likely far superior to Samara's. Her recent education in magic was far from admirable.

She didn't wait long before she heard Ulrieg. *I hate to break this to you, but Mist is just over the distant grassy knoll. You'll see her shortly, even with your weak human eyes.*

A deep chill ran through Samara's spine. She didn't know what to do. She was the only one in the village who had a chance of fighting the coterie member, and she knew that chance was pitiful.

She started working on her best skill—pulling out her arrows and charming each one with a spell, ready for when Mist, or Okak, came into range. Her suspicions were confirmed. It had been Mist's familiar sussing her out. Sure enough, like Ulrieg said, only a few moments passed before she saw horses in the distance with riders on top.

*Ulrieg, what are we going to do?*

*We have to warn the villagers and tell them that we've hidden Emelyne. At least that should keep their hopes up, enabling them to face what may happen.*

*Shouldn't I stay here to defend the village when she comes?* Samara's lack of confidence was clear in her shaky words, but she wouldn't let Mist hurt the princess without a fight.

*You could do that. I'll leave briefly and tell Forgrac. He can spread the word through the village.*

Emelyne couldn't believe it when Ulrieg woke her and told her to hide. Annoyance roiled through her that they would think she couldn't stand and fight for her village after all the effort she had gone through to rebuild it. If it was the powerful sorceress, as Samara feared, they hadn't even had a chance to put up their first gate to stop enemies from entering the village from the main road. She wondered how they'd found out so quickly.

They hadn't been there long enough for the word to spread about her presence, especially since they'd only announced last night that she was the lost royal. But Ulrieg didn't give her a choice and said that Monut would be hiding with her. They both wanted to argue, until the black dragon said that the village needed her and her bonded dragon alive to have hope to continue rebuilding. If they didn't have her, if their last living royal was taken away from them, then the people could fall apart and give up completely.

Ulrieg led them down some tunnels under the Paddosha Palace. The dank, musty smell was strong as they wove through them. She hadn't been down there before, but she knew that there must be underground areas because of Bianca's story. They wound through the massive underground tunnels barely large enough to fit Monut yet much bigger than the dwarven cave entries. They seemed to be built as though they had once had dragons wandering the streets and needed to accommodate them as well. Excitement ran through her as she pondered the possibility that the royals were bonded to dragons before the coterie's reign.

The little black dragon led them down deep, through many tunnels and for quite some time, until finally he settled on a spot he was certain the coterie member wouldn't find. As Emelyne looked around the dank area, she realized that probably nobody in the village knew it existed either.

*Stay in this area,* Ulrieg commanded. *It's quite some distance from where Bianca escaped in the earlier times. Just over that way not too far is the exit to the forest, in case you hear them coming.*

Though it was for their safety, Emelyne thought it was gutsy of the little dragon to boss them around when it was her village that needed protection, until Monut nodded, leading Emelyne to apprehensively agree. She still didn't understand why she couldn't go out and fight. If not for the thought of making the villagers lose hope if they lost her, she would be out trying to help Samara. Instead, she hid underground with her large and powerful dragon while Ulrieg disappeared, undoubtedly to assist Samara in whatever way he could.

It seemed like Ulrieg had discovered the tunnels and knew exactly where to go. She wondered if the coterie members had heard the stories about Bianca. If they had, they, too, might know about the tunnels.

The more she pondered the idea and thought about her villagers being exposed to danger as she hid, the less she agreed with it. She would be out there in a flash if not for Ulrieg's insistence that if she got caught or injured, the village would no longer exist, and that would be the end of the royal line. Yet it still didn't sit right. It made her angry that she couldn't be up there defending her people. "I don't know 'bout all this hidin' while everyone else is above. It doesn't sit right with me."

Monut growled, the sound echoing through the tunnels. *I understand what you mean. Though my first duty is to keep you safe, I had hoped our days of hiding were done.*

"If only I had magic to prove to them that I shouldn't hide. I'd love to give a coterie member a taste of their own medicine." She paced the floor, her boots clopping noisily on the stone. The temptation gnawed at her as worry for everyone she loved grew. "I don't think I've ever seen Samara use magic. I wonder if she's strong enough to go against a member of the coterie."

A deep rumble vibrated through Monut's throat. *I must agree with you there as well. The young sorceress may not be powerful enough, though her heart seems to be in the right place.*

"That doesn't sound good for the people we love." Her footsteps grew louder as her pacing morphed into stomping the underground room, before she met Monut's gaze. "This is ridiculous. I can't stay down here an' hide. Are ya comin' with me?"

Monut exposed his large array of teeth in what was supposed to be a smile. *Absolutely!*

Emelyne nodded, feeling a surge of relief, despite knowing she would face danger. "Jus' a quick stop along the way to grab me sword."

# CHAPTER FORTY-ONE

Samara was still wondering what to do when she faced the crumbling building beside her. Partial walls stood with bits of roof covering only a small portion of the inside. It looked stable enough to hold her weight on some parts, and she needed to get a higher perspective for a better look to know when Mist was coming. Carefully, she climbed the walls, avoiding any stones that looked like they would fall. She went to a higher part of the roof that had not collapsed. Satisfied she had found a secure spot, she sat on the edge and peered into the distance, watching Mist slowly approach. Okak circled her. Samara grabbed an arrow out of her quiver and spelled it, ready to fire at the sorceress if she came too close.

She thought about whether to let Mist get close enough to hold a conversation or if she should just shoot her with an arrow before the sorceress got anywhere near her. Perhaps at a distance would be the best place to defeat her. She was certain that Mist would have kept up with her training, and she had already been a passionate fighter before Samara left the coterie. The memory of how Mist often lacked empathy chilled her body. She doubted that talking would be a good choice.

When the clip-clop of the horse's shoes on the dirt road became audible, she nocked the arrow that she had spelled and waited for Mist's white hair to grow clearer. Samara balked. Killing was still hard for her. Even hurting people was difficult. Mist was in her sights, drawing closer, the scowl on her face growing visible.

Taking a deep breath, Samara perched precariously on the roof, with just enough balance to do what she needed to do. Pulling the string, she braced herself. It seemed like such a waste of life to do something so final.

Seconds passed, and Mist approached, one hundred yards away from the building where Samara perched. If she hadn't already, soon the sorceress would see Samara. Perched with Mist in her sights, she closed her eyes and released the string. The arrow whistled through the air, her aim true. A slight thud reached her as she imagined the arrow embedding into Mist's side, exactly where Samara had calculated. She waited for the spell to activate.

When she didn't hear the change, she opened her eyes to find that Mist had knocked the arrow aside. Okak cawed loudly as he circled his bonded's head.

Cursing, Samara loaded another arrow and fired again, that time watching as Mist swatted the arrow aside with magic. The arrow clacked as it hit the ground.

Instantly, Mist's eyes landed on Samara, filling with malice. "Hello, Samara!" Nothing in Mist's voice was kind.

Samara cringed. Not knowing what else to do, she nocked another arrow, only to have it flicked aside again as the sorceress moved closer. Ducking behind part of the roof, she spent a little time taking in Mist's companion. They were surprisingly short, causing Samara to wonder if Mist had taken on a dwarven servant. Whoever it was, they didn't seem to carry any weapons, so she continued to focus on the sorceress. With difficulty, she shifted on the corner of the house, trying to find spots that wouldn't crumble beneath her. When she finally settled enough to shoot another arrow, Mist reached up and caught it before it could reach her. The sorceress threw it to the ground.

Samara cursed. *Ulrieg, are you seeing this?* She hadn't heard from him since he'd turned invisible.

*Yes, I see. I'm on my way to intervene.* Samara had no idea where Ulrieg was. What she could see was the distance between Mist and herself closing rapidly. Soon, Mist would be at the edge of her building, and at that point, she didn't know if she would have long to live. It would depend on if Mist intended to kill her or take her back to be persecuted by Callista at the coterie building. As much as it scared her, she would rather Mist take her, instead of destroying the village before it had a chance to grow. She still couldn't see who was with Mist, as the person seemed to fall into her shadow, blocked by the sorceress's body. The one positive was that the companion didn't look big enough to be another sorcerer.

Suddenly, Mist's back arched, and she cried out in pain. Ulrieg must have scraped her flesh with his talons. It seemed to be his favorite thing to do when he was invisible and could freely attack. Okak protested, screeching as loudly as possible. But as soon as Mist pulled herself together, a blast of power shot at Samara. It knocked her from her perch and onto the ground. She landed on her back, her head throbbing, and the wind had been knocked out of her. She groaned, feeling the quiver digging into her back. Her bow had been knocked aside.

Ulrieg screeched through their bond. *Samara!*

Dizziness engulfed her as she dealt with the pain roaring through her back and side. She mustn't lie there. It would be the end of her. She scrambled to her feet, her head spinning as she tried to stand, grabbing the destroyed building's wall for support. Blinking, she attempted to clear her vision, looking for her bow that had flown out of her hand. The rock wall beside her exploded, shattering into pieces, and she jumped to the side, losing her balance and landing on all fours.

Mist screamed. Ulrieg must have attacked her again, trying to stop her from going after Samara, but his attempts didn't last for long. The sorceress aimed spells into the air around her, trying to ward off Ulrieg. Okak cawed his protest, attempting to attack the invisible dragon.

A plume of fire shot through the air, aiming directly for Okak. It singed the crow's feathers, causing the bird to drop to the road, cawing his displeasure. Though it deterred the crow, it also gave away Ulrieg's location to Mist, and she shot him with a stunning spell.

Ulrieg fell to the ground, his still body morphing into visibility.

Samara cursed. The coterie knew about her dragon and had quickly become good at aiming for the invisible familiar. She spotted the tip of her bow several feet away. It would be difficult to grab it without Mist attacking her again. She chastised herself for not remembering better spells that didn't involve her arrows. Having to use the arrows took too much time. It was too difficult to react quickly.

Mist climbed off her horse, drawing her sword and exposing the person behind her. Samara's eyes widened. It was Silut. She couldn't see any restraints on him. He must have betrayed them to Mist.

The last thing they needed was for coterie members to know about the princess. But she wasn't sure Silut knew Emelyne was the princess, because he had taken off before the announcement the previous night.

"Well, Samara, we finally meet again." Mist's taunting voice reached her around the corner of the building, where she had pressed her back the against the last section of the tallest wall. "Isn't this nice? It's been a while since we've attacked each other. Those combat lessons with Zofia were so much fun. It's just a shame we couldn't use our powers back then.

Though, using our weapons on each other was fun too."

Samara scurried to the side, trying to distance herself from Mist.

"Are you going to face me like a true member of the coterie? Or will you prove yourself a traitor again and hide, attacking from the dark?" Her footsteps sounded closer to the corner of the building, her pace slow and purposeful.

"We know the princess is in the village. I'll destroy her right after I've finished with you."

"I don't know what you're talking about." Samara clung to the hope that Silut didn't know Emelyne was the lost princess, though something told her it was futile.

"Oh, I have it on good authority that she's here. I have a certain informant sitting on the horse behind me, insisting he saw the mark on this person's hand that you have so happily been spreading the word about in your play. You know, I saw your play not so long ago, but instead of capturing you there, I recruited this dwarf to follow you and report back to me when you were successful. And like a good little threatened dwarf, he came running to me when he saw the scar marking her as the lost royal. As to how the coterie members have missed her for this long, I don't know, some sly human trick to keep her hidden or, from what I've heard, the dwarven village."

"He must be mistaken," Samara called. "This is just a village trying to rebuild itself and its dignity, nothing else."

"Ah, so they are rebuilding the village, just as this imbecile said. That proves to me even more that a royal is here. These villagers had no backbone before, then suddenly they have enough courage to rebuild their village. You have got to be kidding me. There are definitely signs of a royal in there, even though I have heard firsthand that one exists," Mist taunted.

A spell from Devi's class suddenly entered Samara's head, and she spun around the corner of the building, aiming it at Mist. Mist spotted her and darted to the side after her hand sprang up, the spell narrowly missing her. Scrambling to her feet, Samara cursed and ran to the other side of the building. Her eyes connected briefly with Silut's.

He didn't look happy. "I'm sorry, Samara. I didn't want to, but she threatened me family. They've been holding them captive ever since I was left on the side of the road and you picked me up. This is the sorceress that put me there."

"Oh, minor details." Mist sounded nonchalant.

Samara pondered his words. It made sense.

Forgrac had been adamant that the dwarves never betrayed one another or worked with the coterie. It was the perfect ploy.

His face was distraught, begging Samara to believe him. "I couldn't let them die. I'm so sorry."

Samara nodded. It made too much sense not to believe him. He had seemed genuine in wanting to join them, though something had always felt off. This explained everything. She could understand wanting to protect his family, especially when he had children.

Samara snuck to the side of the building, ready to shoot a spell at Mist. Okak cawed, alerting Mist, and she spun, shooting a spell at Samara instead. Samara flew backward, her quiver rattling, and landed on her back again. She could have sworn she heard the arrow shafts break. She groaned, her back aching.

It did not look good for her or Ulrieg. She had to think fast, or not only could it be the end of her, but also the end of Paddosha Palace Village and the princess. She hoped Emelyne stayed hidden. That was the only way the royal would live.

Mist shot her with spells again and again, and Samara tried to crawl to a stand to defend herself. Yet again, she was shot with a spell, and her body flew back as it was lifted and bounced like a rock skimming on water—without the soft landing. Mist was playing with her like a cat played with its food. Again, Mist hit her with some more spells. Pain coursed through Samara's body, and her head thumped against a rock. It was a struggle to remain conscious. Something caught her attention in the distance, and though her vision was blurry, she could've sworn she saw Emelyne heading her way.

# CHAPTER FORTY-TWO

S tressing, Samara struggled to get to her feet, but it was a mission just to lift her head. She didn't know how she would protect the princess. She couldn't even protect herself. Emelyne should've stayed hidden.

The princess looked to be on the outskirts of the main village, still some distance away, yet not far enough. The glint of a sword caught Samara's eye. As if the sword would protect the princess from the sorceress. It didn't matter how good of a swordsman Emelyne was.

Samara couldn't let her be killed. She pulled together all her strength, trying to get up and failing. It was too difficult.

"Lie still." The whispered voice sounded familiar.

Turning, Samara searched for the owner,

wrestling with dizziness, only to come up empty. She had hoped the person was there. It would mean she wasn't alone.

"I'm going to inject you with healing power."

Samara blinked, thinking her sight must be too clouded.

"You can't see me, silly. I've turned my cloak invisible. I'm going to inject you with healing power, then I'll try and protect the village and the princess."

Samara couldn't believe her ears. "Henriette?" she whispered, her shock making the word come out louder than she meant. How she missed that voice.

Henriette was the only one who could turn her cloak invisible and sneak around like Ulrieg—a magic that had fit her mischief right from the start.

Henriette shushed her. "Yes, but don't say it so loudly. Mist doesn't know I'm here. I'm supposed to be in another village, pursuing something else."

Samara felt hands touching her, and a healing power seeped from them into her body, much like when Paxton used to heal.

"How did you know we were here, though?" Samara lowered her voice.

"I was forced to travel with Mist to learn from a senior sorceress. The lot of senior apprentices from your year have been promoted to be some of the main coterie members, and their magic has increased. So I was told to go along with her, to investigate what was going on in the villages. Rumors are that certain people have started to rebel. Mist was determined to put a stop to that."

"I'm sure she was."

Henriette nodded. "But while we were there, I saw her capture the dwarf that's with her now and threaten his family, taking them as hostages."

"So, what he said was true? They are honestly in danger?" Samara asked.

"Yes. The poor dwarf didn't have much of a chance going against her. Then, when he returned, he was desperate and reported that he knew where the princess was. I didn't know you were here, but I came with my invisible cloak and Pixie."

Samara couldn't see the ferret, but she heard his quiet chatters from about the same distance as Henriette.

"We had to come investigate and see if we could help the princess in any way. I've learned a lot more from Devi lately. She has taken a personal interest in training me and Peadar in defense." Henriette pulled her hand away from Samara. "I must go now. I'm going to try stopping Mist from getting into the village."

Samara reached for Henriette, managing to grab her cloak. "I think the princess is coming down the road. She and her dragon need your protection." When the healing power took hold, Samara released her. "Thank you." She wanted to ask her so much more, but it wasn't the time.

Mist's footsteps sounded on the dirt not far from Samara, and she sprang up quickly, shooting her with a spell. The wrong one came out of her mouth, and all it did was make Mist itchy. Samara cursed her stupidity. She had to make more time to practice if she got out of their fight alive.

Mist scratched momentarily, until she stopped it with a counterspell. She hit Samara with a similar spell then stood over her as Samara thrashed in pain. "Let's see you get out of that one, seeing as you probably haven't learned anything in quite a while. You left as a traitor before you had the chance to learn much." She gazed up into the distance. "What do we have here? Is that the princess? Oh, goodie. I don't have to go looking for her."

Samara watched helplessly as Mist traveled past her, heading straight toward Emelyne. "Oh, I see a dragon too. That's even better. Not only do I get to find the princess. I also get to torture another dragon, and he's a good size too. Look at that."

Samara cringed, dreading what Mist was about to do. *Where did Henriette go?* She was the only hope Samara held that Emelyne would be all right.

Mist's crunching footsteps on the dry ground grew softer as she headed toward the princess. A glint of silver flashed through the air in front of Emelyne as the princess twirled her sword, ready to fight Mist. That was it—the end of the princess.

The retreating footsteps halted. Frustrated and in pain, Samara managed to roll to the side to get a better view. It took a while to realize Mist was banging against an invisible wall.

A barrier had been put between the sorceress and the princess. Mist glowered, thumping the barricade, banging and testing the boundary as she moved along the edge of the blockade. The sorceress called over her shoulder. "Since when did you work out how to do barrier spells?"

Samara didn't answer, watching as Mist attempted to pursue her prey, silently banging against the invisible wall. When that didn't work, she kicked the barrier. Unsuccessful in her attempts, she kicked harder, groaning with the effort.

Samara marveled. Henriette had learned a lot since she'd left. She wasn't exaggerating. If Samara survived, she would have to get Henriette to teach her. A hand landed on Samara again, and she jumped.

"Is that you, Henriette?" she whispered, knowing Mist was still close.

"Yes, I'm injecting a little more healing magic into you. Then I've got to put up more barriers before Mist finds the edge of them. I can't make huge barriers like the ones Callista placed around the borders. I put a few small ones up for now, but she'll find the edge if she keeps going the way she is. So I've got to continue making them."

Samara glanced up to see Okak having a go at the barrier as well, way above Mist's head, but he was unable to pass through. The minutes ticked by, and Mist had bounced her way along the barrier, not having any success, until finally she stood still.

"All right then. If I can't get through your barrier, which I am surprised that you managed to build in the first place, I shall try another tactic."

Okak landed on her shoulder as if summoned, and Mist threw back her head, her arms out to the sides, palms facing up, as if calling to a more powerful force. In the distance, dark, ominous clouds circled, covering the outskirts of the village. Minutes ticked by, and the clouds seemed to darken and grow until eventually they were an enormous black cloud with a hole in the middle. The clouds twisted around the sides of the hole as it grew unnaturally tighter over the village. Samara didn't know what was happening, but she knew it wasn't good. Lightning cracked in the sky, shooting over one side of the clouds and down into the village, hitting the outskirts.

Head still foggy from the earlier injury, she witnessed the circle grow tighter with lightning striking around the clouds, until eventually it hit the ground. Trees ignited, and other materials crackled as flames sparked. The lightning strikes grew more frequent. Head held back, Mist spread her arms, palms facing the sky, and she cackled with pleasure.

"If I cannot get through to your village, I will kill it with fire and lightning. That will be just as satisfying as ripping apart the villagers one by one." More lightning strikes hit the earth around the village, some just missing the buildings on the edge. Grass fires sparked to life, and Samara hoped Mist wouldn't hit the farms. The villagers needed those crops. They were their hope of future food. Either way, Samara didn't want to see the village burn down before they had even had a chance to rebuild it. Lightning hit again, and screams radiated through the air. She must be hitting the people with the strikes as well. With each bolt of lightning, it looked worse for the villagers and their living quarters.

# CHAPTER FORTY-THREE

Emelyne spun. Samara didn't have to see her face to know that the princess was upset. Her village was being destroyed further, and the people she had grown to love were being injured and possibly killed. To make matters worse, she could do nothing about it. She wouldn't know how to fight that.

Mist continued her rampage, frying the edges of the village, tightening the wild storm's circle. Occasionally, she checked the barrier to see if she could find the edge. So far, she'd had no success as Henriette continued to work under her invisible cloak.

Samara didn't know if that was good or bad. Though Mist couldn't go into the village, she was still wreaking havoc from a distance, tightening her circle of devastation. She released several bolts of lightning at the center of the village. The resulting flames were visible from where Samara lay.

Screams of pain and terror motivated her to get to her feet, just in time to see Emelyne run back to the village, Monut keeping pace. Thankfully, she wasn't facing Mist, but at the same time, she could be hit by one of the lightning strikes, unless Monut was lightning proof.

Still, if Henriette didn't put up enough barriers to stop Mist, Emelyne could still be facing the true danger. Eventually, Mist would find the edge and work her way into the village. Her determination proved that.

Reaching into her quiver, Samara pulled out several arrows, each split in half, until finally she found one that was whole. Spelling it, she searched for her bow. She wobbled over to her bow, though she felt better after Henriette's healing magic. A spell hit her from behind, thrusting her face-first onto her bow. Several more lightning strikes hit the village, and more buildings burst into flames. The flames grew higher and more visible from where Samara had fallen.

She could not go down like that, nor could she let the village where her parents had taken refuge be destroyed. Not only would she let them down, but she would also let all the kingdom of Slosiaran down. They would lose their leader, their village, but also the one hope that people clung to, that someone would lead them against the Sacred Flame coterie's rule.

Samara reached for her bow, hoping Mist was preoccupied. The amount of power she held was ridiculous for one person. It wasn't natural and certainly wasn't acceptable if the person had evil intentions in mind. Samara nocked the arrow and didn't have time to spell it. She fired, the arrow landing in the sorceress's leg. Mist yowled, distracting her from attacking the village. Even in the short amount of time that she had the arrow sticking out of her leg, Samara could see her bracing herself, ready to execute another attack. Samara quickly nocked another arrow and shot as she lay on the ground, lacking the strength to get up.

Mist bellowed, "I would kill you if I could. But for some reason, Callista wants you returned alive." Her teeth clenched. "I think you have annoyed her so much that she wants to deal with you personally."

Samara cringed at the thought. It was bad enough having to deal with Mist, let alone having to deal with Callista again. Pulling all of her strength together, she climbed to her hands and knees, wobbling on all fours. In her peripheral vision, she could see Mist bracing herself, readying to attack her. Suddenly, Miss went flying backward away from the village, her head hitting a rock on the destroyed building. She looked like she was out cold.

*Ha. That'll teach you!* Ulrieg roared, his frustration evident as he turned visible. He stood on top of Mist's unmoving body. *I'm so over being stunned from the sky. That's completely embarrassing, and I feel so helpless!*

Beside him, a panda-colored ferret scrambled out of nowhere moments before Henriette pulled off her invisibly spelled cloak. Her skin was still as pale as Samara remembered, contrasting greatly with her turquoise waist-length hair. After she tied Mist's hands to stop her from casting spells, she offered Samara a hand. Samara took it, needing help to stand straight.

She looked up at Henriette's pale face. She had never been so happy to see those extremely pale blue eyes.

Henriette grinned at Samara before wrapping her in a hug. "I missed you, big sis."

Pride swamped Samara. Henriette did feel like a little sister to her. "I am so glad to see you. How did you learn so much magic in such a short time?"

"After what happened to you, Devi decided to take me and Peadar under her wing, and she has been teaching us more defensive arts, letting us excel above our level." Henriette left her arm draped over Samara's shoulders.

Samara squeezed her around the waist. "You know there's room for you here if you want to join us. We could certainly use your help, as you can see. And I need to expand my training."

Sadness passed over Henriette's face. "I wish I could, but right now, I need to make sure my parents get out safe. The last thing I want is for them to be attacked or killed. It would destroy me if they went through that because of me."

"Tell them to come here. We need help rebuilding this village, especially now that it's been destroyed more. Not only that, but my family is here, along with Paxton's and Blade's parents." A glimmer flashed through her eyes. "At least that's something good that has happened out of all of this."

Samara knew Henriette had been fond of Blade.

With Mist out of action, the clouds slowly dissipated from the sky. Okak cawed aggressively, and Henriette shot him with a spell, stunning him and letting him fall to the ground.

Ulrieg scooped the crow up and threw him on Mist's back.

Her brows knitted together. "Joining you may be something to consider in the future. I'll see what I can do because Peader's parents need help too. And I can't leave Peader there on his own, so I'd have to discuss things with him. It wouldn't seem fair if I left him there and took off."

Pixie scrambled up to Henriette's shoulders as the two sorceresses approached Silut.

The dwarf climbed off the horse and held up his hands. "I'm honestly so sorry, Samara. I'm so scared for me family. I didn't have a choice. I didn't want to. Ya were all so nice to me, but once I found the princess, it was the one way to know for sure that I would get me family back."

Samara leaned on one leg with her arms crossed. "You can never trust anything the coterie say. There was no way to guarantee that you'd get your family back."

The dwarf's gaze fell to the ground. "I'm sorry. I didn't know what else to do. Please. I hope one day, ya find it in ya heart to forgive me, but I completely understand if ya don't."

"Why don't you come back to the village and rebuild what you have destroyed?" Samara suggested. "Perhaps then we can forgive you."

"I would love more than anythin' to do that, but I cannot. Me family is still in danger. The sorceress, Mist, has them tied up and ready to be executed, an' I don't know where they are."

"I know where they are," Henriette said. "I'll help

you release them, then you can do what Samara said, as long as it comes from your heart that you are deeply sorry."

Pixie chirped in annoyance on her shoulder.

"Come back as soon as you can. Emelyne was most upset that she didn't have your help anymore. And now, as you can see, we definitely need that fence to stop people like Mist from getting into the village."

"I will keep this barrier up for now," Henriette said. "It's designed to keep out Mist, but you may need to build something better, or that fence better be magical to stop the members of the coterie." Her eyes scanned the village and the plumes of black smoke that rose from different parts. "I'll put Mist aside for a bit and keep her tied up. I'll have to sort something out with her so my cover doesn't get blown. But I'll do my best to buy you time before we go back to the coterie building." A deep frown creased her forehead. "Don't waste any time rebuilding the village and putting a barrier around it. You'll need it, because if this gets back to Callista about the village and the princess, as well as you being here, she'll probably come herself or send her best people to bring you down and return you to her dungeon." She put her hands on her hips. "At this point, I don't think anyone has upset her as much as you." She shook her head and laughed. "And they think I'm mischief."

"I'm not surprised, but thank you for buying us time. Be careful, Henriette, and if you get to a point where you feel safe enough to leave, we will always welcome you into this village." Samara hugged her. "That also goes for Peadar and Devi, for all the help you three have given me."

Seeing Mist's still form, Henriette nodded toward the unconscious sorceress. "Do you have enough strength to lift her?"

Samara nodded, and together they put Mist onto the back of her horse. Henriette hugged Samara. "It's so good to see you again. The place hasn't been the same since you left, but we're doing our best to survive."

Samara had been putting it off, but she had to know before Henriette left. "What about Paxton?"

Henriette's eyes filled with sadness. "He's still stuck in the orb. We haven't been able to get to him. They've put up extra security measures. Devi can go in there, but she can't do anything on her own. It would be too obvious. I'm sorry, Samara. We haven't found a way to get him out."

Tears ran down Samara's cheeks. Knowing tore her apart. It was the worst she had feared. She had hoped deep down that Henriette, Devi, and Paedar had been able to release him, but she knew she would have to go. "I'll say goodbye to everyone here, then I have to go to the coterie building. I can't leave him in there any longer. It has to be done, whichever state he exits in."

Henriette squeezed her arm. "I'll see you soon. I hope, together, we can get him out."

# CHAPTER FORTY-FOUR

Black ash and burned-out buildings littered the village. The outskirts had suffered more blows from the lightning strikes than the middle. They needed builders, badly. It was too much work for the villagers and the few handymen. It seemed to be a constant occurrence for the village. They were always in need of more tradespeople. Emelyne didn't blame them for leaving. It would be dangerous living in a village often targeted by the coterie.

Emelyne wiped the soot off her hands onto her blacksmith's clothes. She had been helping some of the villagers gut their home after the lightning strike. Hopefully, they could gather more people and rebuild the village, but if the coterie kept attacking them like that, it would make things difficult.

She knew that they had been taking in people who were enemies of the Sacred Flame, making it a coterie-aggressive zone, so they expected a lot more attacks. But that didn't matter, because the coterie knew that she existed, or at least one member knew that she existed, and wherever she was, the coterie would attack.

It had been a close one a couple of weeks ago. The sorceress that had heard about her was strong. Samara said had they were lucky that one of her friends from the coterie had been traveling with her and managed to help fight the sorceress Mist. Knowing that she could conjure lightning was daunting. It made Emelyne wonder what other powers the magic wielders held. No wonder her adoptive parents had hidden her every time a coterie member came near. She was very grateful for Samara's friend. She hoped that the young sorceress had more friends like that. Samara's friend had even taken the sorceress Mist to a place away from the rest of the coterie, so the Paddosha Palace Village would have more time to prepare for the next attack.

Emelyne had forgiven Silut. Family was everything, and if they were under threat, she knew she would do almost anything to keep them safe. The dwarf had been putting in extra hours in the smithy, helping rebuild the Paddosha Palace Village. Emelyne had accepted his family also, which was another reason for the coterie to visit.

The dragon gates that had been blessed by the dragons had been installed at the front of the village, past the inn where Samara had been attacked. They hoped that the farther away they kept the danger, the harder it would be for other sorcerers to attack them. Many of the men in the village helped them raise the gates, securing them with their posts, and slowly, the metal fence around the village was being constructed.

As for rebuilding the village, it was hard to know where to start because so much work had been created by Mist's visit. They decided to focus mostly on the outside fence. The villagers with houses let the ones whose homes had burned down stay in their living rooms until they recuperated each of the houses.

Samara had checked on the farms to make sure that the produce was still all right and that the seedlings were still growing before she left. Emelyne understood why she had taken off a little over a week ago.

Now, a few weeks after the attack, Emelyne still wished her the best and hoped that she could save her beloved from being trapped within the orb she had told Emelyne about. The thing sounded pure evil. She also said that she would possibly be sending more people their way to help rebuild the village. Some of them sounded like they were the sorceress Henriette's family. On top of that, they were builders, so their help would be more than welcome.

*What is it, my bonded?* Monut had been following her along the streets of Paddosha Palace Village.

"I was just thinking about all the work that we have to do and how one sorceress has made it so much harder," Emelyne said.

*That is understandable. I also miss the dragons. It would be nice to have more of my kind around.*

"Yeah, I actually miss that grumpy black dragon, Ulrieg, too. He does have a good heart despite his personality. Both he and Samara are more than welcome back here anytime. But hopefully, Cyrra is working on bringing us more dragons. Maybe she can lead them back here. But I guess we'll have to wait and see." Emelyne placed a hand on Monut's leg as they stopped in the center of the village and gazed around at the destruction. "Maybe we should look at somewhere for the dragons to stay and build something for them as well."

*It would be nice to sleep somewhere when the weather*

*is bad. That can be the last priority because dragons can quite happily sleep outside in the open.*

Emelyne glanced around at the different stores, seeing the bakery on the corner and knowing her ma was in there baking. The villagers had started to accept them completely after seeing how much they had put in to rebuild the village, and they could sense that Emelyne honestly cared for them.

They had lost a few lives on the day Mist attacked. Thankfully, none of them were her parents or any of Samara's family. Though each life counted, their loss didn't affect Emelyne quite so personally because she didn't know the people who had passed. She wanted to do so much to honor those people, and she was just starting to scrape the surface.

"Who knows? Samara may even bring back some more magic wielders who can stand against the coterie. We can only live in hope. Because I have a feeling that the Sacred Flame is far from finished with us. I'm also far from finished with them." Emelyne scowled. "After all these years, good should triumph over evil, and it's got to start somewhere. So it might as well start here."

~~~~~

.   .   .
~~~~~

THANK you for reading Dragon's Royal. If you have a few minutes, I'd love for you to leave a review or rating on Amazon. Your feedback helps to spread the word about my books.

YOU CAN FIND the next book here: Royal Alliance

# ACKNOWLEDGMENTS

I would like to thank all of my loyal readers for their support.

The last couple of years have been a big roller-coaster ride. My hereditary kidney disease has thrown me into the end stages. Thankfully, modern medicine has progressed over the last two generations, and kidney disease is no longer terminal. However, it is a lifetime of treatments, including dialysis and hopefully a transplant for a fuller life.

I'm currently undergoing regular dialysis treatments that suck the creative energy away, although they make me feel better than before I started them. I do my best to write when my head is clear and my days aren't filled with medical appointments and operations.

Because of this, my story production has been slower. But thankfully, the editors can help me produce quality stories when my brain lacks the alertness that comes with health.

Hopefully, I'll receive a transplant soon, along

with the health benefits and energy that come with it.

As always, my husband and sons have been tremendous supporters. My husband has been a helpful first reader and, at times, been an excellent motivator.

A huge thank you to my editor, Amanda K., for her editing and writing tips and my proofreader, Caroline P., for picking up the things we missed.

Thank you to all my readers who have loved my work and continue reading my stories. I'm looking forward to writing many more.

BOOKS BY KATRINA COPE

Pre-Teen Books

**<u>The Sanctum Series</u>**

JAYDEN'S CYBERMOUNTAIN

SCARLET'S ESCAPE

TAYLOR'S PLIGHT

ERIC & THE BLACK AXES

ADRIANNA'S SURGE

~~~~~

Young Adult Urban Fantasy

**<u>Afterlife Series</u>**

FLEDGLING

THE TAKING

ANGELIC RETRIBUTION

DIVIDED PATHS

TRUTH HUNTER

**<u>Afterlife Novelette</u>**

THE GATEKEEPER

~~~~~

Young Adult Urban Paranormal Fantasy

**<u>Supernatural Evolvement Series</u>**

(Associated with the Afterlife Series)

WITCH'S LEGACY (Prequel)

AALIYAH

~~~~~

Young Adult Norse Mythology Fantasy

**<u>Valkyrie Academy Dragon Alliance</u>**

MARKED (Prequel)

CHOSEN

VANISHED

SCORNED

INFLICTED

EMPOWERED

AMBUSHED

WARNED

ABDUCTED

BESIEGED

DECEIVED

**<u>Thor's Dragon Rider</u>**

SAFEGUARD

PURSUIT

ENTRAPMENT

HOODWINKED
~~~~~

RELINQUISHED

SHROUDED

ASSIGNED

ACCOSTED

DESTRUCTION

~~~~~

Young Adult Epic Fantasy

**<u>Dragoria: the Lost Dragon Realm</u>**

Part 1:

DRAGON MOON

DRAGON HEART

DRAGON BREEZE

Part 2:

DRAGON'S ROYAL

ROYAL ALLIANCE

ROYAL RESISTANCE
~~~~~

# ABOUT THE AUTHOR

Katrina is an author of several books in epic fantasy, young-adult fantasy, and a middle-grade sci-fi thriller series.

Her series include:

Dragoria: The Lost Dragon Realm - Coming of Age Epic fantasy

Valkyrie Academy Dragon Alliance - YA High fantasy

Thor's Dragon Rider - YA High fantasy (Spin-off of Valkyrie Academy Dragon Alliance but can be read separately)

The Afterlife - YA fantasy (contemporary)

The Sanctum Series - Middle-grade Sci-fi thriller

She often talks to creatures of all kinds and has a passion for animals, nature, and travel. She lives in Queensland, Australia, with her husband and has survived teaching her three children how to drive.

Katrina's online home is at www.katrinacopebooks.com

You can connect with Katrina on:

tiktok.com/@katrinacopebooks

facebook.com/Author.Katrina.Cope

instagram.com/katrina_cope_author

bookbub.com/profile/katrina-cope

x.com/Katrina_R_Cope

pinterest.com/katrinacope56